Dr Dan, Married Man?

Laurie Graham

Dedicated to Dr Dan's fans, who asked for more

Chapter 1

We woke up to snow. My thirtieth birthday. They say it takes five years of training to become a doctor, but that isn't the half of it. Yes, you spend five years in medical school but it's only after that you really start learning. They set you loose on patients and all you can think is, please let a grownup be checking on what I'm doing, please don't let me be so tired I miss something or confuse a dosage and kill some poor soul. Then gradually you find your feet and stop feeling so unsure of yourself. 'Hello,' you say. 'I'm Dr Talbot.' And you enjoy the sound of that. You might slip up occasionally, when you're under pressure, but nothing major, you hope.

In General Practice, the more patients you see the more you realise, every consultation is unique, even if you've seen them before and think you have a pretty good idea what you're dealing with. When the consulting room door opens, you never know what you're going to be called upon to be. Agony uncle, stern adviser, Sherlock Holmes. Sometimes all three.

That was where I was at as I turned thirty. Over the worst of my rookie nerves and fairly happy in my trainee post but anxious about one last hurdle I needed to clear: the final tests before I could register with the Royal College of General Practitioners. Not only that, but my girlfriend, Chloe, needed me to be Mr Calm and Steady. She was starting a new job, at a cardiology clinic in Solihull. She'd suffered a bit of a setback when she didn't get the registrar position she'd been so sure of, robbed of it by a friend, a former friend, in spite of passing her MRCP. I think it was the first time in Chloe's life that things didn't go her way. But, predictably, her father stepped in and pulled a few strings.

Laurence Swift knows a lot of useful people. Medics, lawyers, someone who can get you a cheaper deal. So, a cardiologist acquaintance was prevailed upon and a job was found for Chloe at the Arden Private Clinic. The money was good and the commute wasn't bad, but she was understandably nervous about being the new girl. Also, she'd come down with a serious case of wedding fever.

As soon as she'd passed her exams we'd fixed the date - July 6th - and booked the church. I was under the impression that there was stacks of time to arrange everything else but that goes to show how little I knew about weddings. Apparently wedding gown shops class five months as a rush job. Mam told me to tell Chloe that Tesco's had some very nice, reasonably priced wedding dresses but I didn't. When Mam gets to know Chloe better, she'll understand why.

The tradition at The Lindens is that you bring cake on your birthday. I stopped off at a supermarket and bought a Mega Chocolate Tray Bake. The snow was turning to rain and slush by the time I got to the surgery. There were three cars already parked. Helen Vincent's, Nurse Linda's and the Mazda belonging to our new Practice Manager, Kasper Kowalski.

In the six months since I'd joined the practice as a trainee, there had been some major changes. Trevor Buxton, Senior Partner, had handed the reins to Helen Vincent and was supposed to be taking life easier. He was suffering from what he called 'emphysema' but what everyone else now calls COPD, chronic obstructive pulmonary disease. A lot of people look forward to retirement. Not Trevor. Much as he loved his wife, he loved his work more. He was The Lindens. The practice had been his father's before him. We had patients Trevor had known all their lives. So, when a staffing crisis hit the practice, he jumped at the opportunity to delay his departure. He had Bruce Macdonald to thank for that.

Mac had been accused of unethical behaviour. He was the Lindens' geriatrics man and the accusation concerned one of his nursing home patients, Hilda Ruck. He, or his sister, depending on which version of the story you heard, had bought Miss Ruck's house without it ever going on the open market. Her heirs, who had never shown much interest in the old lady until she died, only found out about the house sale after the event, and they were on to the GMC in a flash. Mac had been sent on leave, without the option, pending a tribunal and though he hadn't been the most industrious of the Lindens' doctors, he still left a hole that had to be filled.

Trevor was happy to take up some of the slack, particularly the nursing home visits. He wanted to repair any damage to the practice's good name. Antony Vaz, the junior, took on more patients, Pam Parker, the part-timer, offered to do an extra weekly surgery, and I shuttled between them all, learning on the job. Officially my training supervisor was Helen Vincent, but she was a busy woman. With the Health Service in a perpetual state of reorganization, committees and panels spawned more committees and panels and Helen seemed to spend as much time at meetings as she did with her patients. There could be a three week wait for an appointment with Dr Helen and I spent very little time with her. It suited me.

With Helen I was never quite sure where I stood. One minute I was just the trainee, expected to observe in silence, the next, as though she'd suddenly remembered I was there, she'd put me to the test. She'd been known to criticize me, publicly, but then the next day she'd turn around and be super friendly. Actually, on a couple of occasions she'd been a lot more than friendly and only a chance interruption had saved me from a dilemma: to enjoy the moment and risk the consequences, or to reject her advances and live with a different set of consequences. But all that was now over. There were signs that Helen had transferred her interest to Kasper Kowalski.

Kasper had joined us as practice manager in January. He replaced Stephanie, who'd left in a long-threatened huff, and he couldn't have been more different. Stephanie had always on the lookout for trouble, quick to identify a grievance. Kasper didn't have time for any of that because he was only with us two and a half days a week. We shared him with a similar sized practice in Wednesbury. He was pleasant and efficient and Helen, who'd interviewed the candidates herself, was very pleased with her choice. The fact that he was tall and single with cheek bones and pale blue eyes and a sexy Polish accent may have had nothing at all to do with her selection.

Mary was on Reception. She took custody of my cake.

'You've got fifteen booked for this morning and another fifteen for the afternoon,' she said. 'Happy Birthday.'

You never get to see all fifteen. I could generally reckon on at least two no-shows per session, precious time for a cup of coffee.

Nurse Linda came out and gave me a birthday card and a kiss. I can cope with Linda. She has phenomenal appetite for men but it's all very open and light-hearted. And, unlike Helen Vincent, she doesn't have any influence on my career.

At the start of the year Trevor had vacated his office and given me permission to tidy up his mess. He said it was so I could have a proper base instead of hanging around other people's rooms like an afterthought but there was more to it than that. He knew I'd been called Mr Learner Doctor. He'd heard patients say, 'so you're not a proper doctor yet.' He understood that little things like a designated office and my name on the door gave me more authority or at least the illusion of it. He even unscrewed his old name plate himself and that

5

must have caused him a pang. He may appear shambolic but Trevor has hidden depths.

Dr Daniel Talbot. I loved seeing that on the door. I took a photo of it and sent it to Mam. The carpet and curtains had been steam-cleaned but there was still a faint smell of ashtray. His bookshelf was still there, laden with ancient textbooks, but the bureau had to go. It had woodworm. I didn't make a lot of changes. I took down the skin disorders chart and replaced it with a painting of the Brecon Beacons, but I left the photograph of Desert Orchid winning the 1989 Gold Cup because that was very Trevor.

I did move the desk though, turned it 90 degrees so I was squarely facing the door. When you can only give a patient ten minutes, every second counts and that includes watching them as they walk in. One of Trevor's pearls of wisdom is, 'The first two minutes with a patient tell you almost everything you need to know. Except when they don't. Sometimes they're too scared or too embarrassed to spit it out, so always watch for the lingering exit as well.' He was dead right.

Vaz had come in behind me. Could he have a word before surgery started? He was beaming. Vaz had met a girl while he was volunteering at a church soup kitchen on Christmas Day and since Teresa came into his life you could run the National Grid off his smile.

'Dan,' he said, 'I would like to invite you to my wedding. It will be on 20th of April.'

I said, 'Vaz, you fast mover! You only met her in December.'

'You think I'm making mistake?'

'No. I don't know. It just seems very quick. But yeah, if you're sure, why not? Congratulations.'

'Definitely, I am sure,' he said. 'We are very well suited and we would like to have sexual relations.'

No pre-marital nookie for Vaz.

'There is something else. We will have marriage at registry office in Birmingham. I would like you to be witness.'

'I'd be honoured. I'll put it in the diary. But I'd have expected you to have a church wedding.'

'We will, but in Kerala, in December. My parents are too olderly to come to England. They will find it too cold, even in summertime. Dan, I am very happy.'

I'd have given him a hug only Vaz isn't really a hugger. All those failed Internet dates, and my pathetic attempt to fix him up with one of Chloe's mates, and suddenly he was overtaking me. He'd met the right girl and was getting on with it. It couldn't have happened to a nicer guy.

As Vaz was leaving Trevor arrived. I heard his distinctive wheeze outside my open door. His most recent spirometry results put him at 60 per cent normal lung function, which was a deterioration from his previous test. It was as you'd expect. He was still smoking a couple of cigarettes a day and anyway, you don't make a comeback from emphysema. You might slow it down, if you're careful, but it's a one-way street. He swears his condition is worse if he's sitting at home and not working. I don't know if that's true. I've seen him need oxygen a couple of times, usually when something has caught him on his funny bone.

He always knocks, even when the door's ajar.

'What's with Vaz, grinning like a loon? Has he won the Lottery?'

'Kind of. He's getting married.'

'Is he indeed? To that Mary Poppins he met at Christmas?'

'Teresa. She's a teacher, not a nanny. And she's a very nice girl.'

'Good for him. Good for her. I hope she's going to take charge of his wardrobe.'

Vaz does the rounds of the charity shops once a week and, being of slight build and sartorial cluelessness, he has been known to buy women's jackets.

Trevor said he'd appreciate my opinion regarding the 3 o'clock at Wetherby. Rebel Rebel or Coromine Bill? I tossed a coin. My method of choosing horses seems no less successful than his.

Chapter 2

It was a pretty normal surgery. Crystal Hussein with sinusitis. A couple of tickly coughs. Pauline Swinney who has TATT on the front of her file. Trevor's shorthand for 'tired all the time'. There's a lot of that around. Sandra Kerridge came in with a whitlow on her finger. Sandra has a Buxtonism scrawled on her file too: WO. It stands for Witters On. I'll say. She was pondering whether to resign from the Patient Participation Panel because the meetings sometimes clashed with her book group, but then, on the other hand, she didn't want to shirk her civic duty. We agreed to leave the whitlow alone. She's had them before and as they're viral, they come and they go.

My last patient of the morning was Legend Busby, brought in by his Mum, Karen Checkitts. Family trees are so much more complicated than they used to be. It's quite rare for me to see children who have the same surname as their mother.

Legend was fifteen. A round-shouldered boy with bad skin and the shadow of a moustache. So far he hadn't lived up to the promise of the stupid name he'd been given. He was feeling under the weather with a sore throat.

Karen said, 'He's been off school and that's not like Ledge.'

The lymph glands in his neck were enlarged. I was checking the rest of his glands when I heard a police siren. Armpits clear, groins clear. Any reason to do bloods, any reason to check for CMV or toxoplasmosis? Not really. Legend had a classic presentation of infectious mono.

I said, 'You've got a viral infection. It'll run its course. You need to drink plenty of water and rest.'

His Mum said, 'What about tablets?'

'Just ibuprofen if he's in pain. But he's going to need a few duvet days.'

'What's them?'

'Lots of rest, at home, for two or three weeks, and even after that he'll need to take things steady for a while. I'll give you a letter for the school. He shouldn't do anything too strenuous until he's back to normal.'

'What about his footie? You love your footie, don't you Ledge?'

He nodded. Legend was a boy of few words. I suggested they come back to see me in a month. In the meanwhile, no footie. Outside, another siren. An ambulance went past, at speed.

We were all in the kitchen cutting up my birthday tray bake - me, Helen, Vaz, Nurse Linda and Kasper. I noticed Helen now calls him Kaz. Linda said we should save some cake for Pam Parker.

Helen said, 'Don't. The last thing she needs is cake. What's the point of us telling people to lose weight when we've got someone like Pam waddling around? What must patients think?'

Linda said, 'They like her though.'

And Helen said, 'We're not here to be liked.'

10

'Just as well,' whispers Linda, but only because Helen had left the room.

Trevor looked in again after lunch.

'Are we having a whip round for Vaz? For a wedding present?'

'I suppose we will. Plenty of time. It's not till the end of April.'

'Right. I thought it was imminent, that silly smile on his face.

'He's in love.'

'Yes, yes. Well, marriage'll soon fettle that.'

'That's a very depressing attitude.'

'No, don't get me wrong. I'm not saying marriage kills love. It just disperses the pink fluffy cloud. After that, clear blue skies with occasional thunderheads. If you're lucky. Big excitement on Cherry Tree this morning. Police and an ambulance. Any idea what happened?'

Nurse Linda knows everyone. She made some phone calls. The first information was that there had been a fatality. An adult male. The second instalment was that a row had erupted between a member of the Bibby clan and one of the Dearloves, there had been a chase along a walkway and a man had fallen to his death. All afternoon I found myself hoping the casualty wasn't Kyle Bibby. He's one of our most infuriating patients, a chancer, a cheeky sod, unemployed and unemployable, but I really didn't want the deceased to be Kyle.

It was closing time before we heard anything more. Chad Dearlove had been chased by Wayne Bibby, recently released from Long Lartin prison. The issue was Chad's usurpation of Wayne's conjugal rights or, as Linda put it, 'Shagging Wayne's baby-mother while Wayne was doing time.'

11

Chad, perhaps still half-asleep at 11.30 in the morning, had run, wearing nothing but his trackie bottoms, misjudged a leap to safety and landed, head-first, on concrete. He was killed instantly. Wayne had been questioned by the police but had been released without charge, having no weapons on him. He'd claimed all he'd wanted was a quiet word with Chad.

Trevor said, 'A quiet word. As in, "Dearlove, you're dead." Which is now indeed the case.'

'Are either of them on our books?'

'No. The Dearloves and Bibbys all defected to a practice on Darleston Road years ago. The word was, they prescribed more generously. Only dear Kyle stayed loyal to us, so how lucky are we? Well I hope Chad doesn't go to waste. I hope they've harvested his corneas if nothing else. Anyone for a swift half? I'm buying.'

I'd have liked to take him up on it. I enjoy Trevor's view of the world from that corner seat in the lounge bar of the Black Bear, but I had a prior commitment. Chloe said there were a million wedding decisions to be made and we had to set aside a whole evening. First item on the agenda: colours.

We seemed to be spending an undue amount of time choosing a colour scheme for our wedding but it's apparently a huge decision and one not to be made lightly or unadvisedly. I'd assumed it wasn't anything I needed to worry about but then I'd discovered that the colours, once chosen, would apply even to me and any men in my party. For the best part of a month I'd been under orders to source emerald waistcoats and cream and gold ties for myself and Rob. Fortunately, I hadn't done anything about it because suddenly all bets were off and we

12

were considering teaberry, sage and ivory. Teaberry is a kind of pink. I wouldn't have minded. I can wear pink. But Dee who, against all my wishes, is to be Chloe's chief bridesmaid, jibbed at wearing teaberry.

I said, 'If it's the colour you want, stick to your guns. Change the bridesmaid, not the colour.'

I'd have been happier if Dee didn't even attend the wedding, least of all in an official capacity. She could be gobby enough when she's sober. After a skinful of champagne I dreaded to think. But Chloe said you can't un-ask someone. It's just not done.

In my opinion Chloe's sister, Flo, would have been a much steadier choice. Easier to satisfy fashion-wise too. She seems to throw on the first thing that comes to hand, usually topped by a quilted bodywarmer. I'm sure she wouldn't have cared whether she had to wear teaberry or khaki. Also, as mother of the flower girls, she would be usefully on-site to herd them up the aisle and keep them penned during the ceremony. But Chloe said it would be uphill work to get Flo to have her hair done or even wear a bit of lippy.

'It'd be like having Worzel Gummidge in the photos. Dee's very photogenic.'

'So you're giving up the colour you want, to satisfy Dee?'

'It's okay. I've gone off teaberry anyway. We're having indigo, sage and ivory. And I wish you'd reconsider who you're having as your best man. What if his flight's cancelled?'

I'd asked Rob because he's my best mate, even if he does live on the other side of the world these days. He was flying in from Sydney.

13

'If it's cancelled, they'll put him on another flight. We've got two days' wiggle room.

'Your brother would be a better choice.'

Chloe hadn't yet met Adam. If she had, she'd have known this was not the case. With Adam there was always the likelihood that he'd call the night before and say he couldn't make it. He hates social commitments. And as for getting him to wear teaberry pink or sage, not a chance.

I said, 'He wouldn't. He'd be a terrible choice.'

'Then why don't you ask Slow? I'm sure he'd do it.'

'Because I've asked Rob and to quote you, you can't un-ask a person, plus, a best man needs to be reliable, personable and witty. None of which apply to your brother or mine.'

I didn't add that by July, Charlie 'Slow' Swift might well be behind bars. He'd been caught driving under the influence of cocaine, and in possession, and was waiting to go to court. Chloe was quite convinced that her father's useful lawyer friends could keep Slow out of prison. I wasn't sure that was within even their powers.

I'd had very little to do with wedding plans so far. Chloe knew what she wanted and if she was happy, I was happy. Mainly. There was to be a rehearsal dinner with Mam and Da at the Swifts' house on the Thursday evening. Mam was all a-flutter about that already ever since I told her Chloe's folks have a big old house. She'd got it into her head that the Chummery is like Downton or Brideshead.

The wedding was booked for 12 noon on the Saturday at St Botolph's. The church is almost next door to the Chummery.

14

Then there'd be drinks and a hog roast for seventy in the garden, followed by dancing to an all-girl band called The Catfish Queens. They do Fifties retro stuff. The Swifts were springing for a marquee with a proper dance floor and Chloe's brother-in-law, Henry, was donating a porker he'd earmarked for us.

I'm told seventy is quite a modest number for wedding guests. All I know is that Chloe's list was twice as long as mine, mainly because of a bunch of aunts and uncles and cousins we were obliged to invite. I had no idea why. I'd met very few of them. From my family there'd just be Mam, Da, Gran Talbot, Aunty June and my brother, if he could be arsed to drive up from Cardiff. Da's an only, so there are no extras on his side and Mam has one sister but they're not on speaking terms. Aunty June's a family friend, not a blood relation.

'Better than your official aunty,' Mam always says. 'June'd give you the coat off her back.'

My guest list was modest, but Chloe still queried some of the names. Helen and Clifford Vincent for instance.

She said, 'Why are we inviting Bitch Face?'

'Because she's my boss. You're inviting people from the clinic.'

'But her husband's that creep who was hitting on me at your Christmas party.'

'Well I can't invite Helen without her husband. It'd look odd. Anyway, he might not come. Maybe neither of them will.'

'And Pam Parker? Why is she invited? Make sure you keep her out of the photographs. She looks like a Weeble. And you've duplicated. You've got two Bob Parkers.'

15

'Yes, Junior and Senior. The old chap lives with them and he's got a touch of dementia. If Pam can't get someone to mind him, I don't want her to feel she can't come.'

'Great. So now we're inviting dements.'

'Granny Orde-Sykes is just as demented as Bob Parker Senior.'

'But she's my grandmother. That's nothing like the same as inviting the gaga father-in-law of that blimp you work with.'

I stood firm. Both Bob Parkers stayed on my list. The final item on the evening's agenda was our honeymoon. My thoughts were, we'd rent a nice, secluded cottage, maybe on the Pembrokeshire coast. Chloe had in mind Zanzibar. She had a pile of brochures.

I said, 'That seems like a very long way to go.'

'But look at the beaches.'

'Barafundle Bay is really beautiful.'

'Where's that?'

'South Wales.'

'I want to wear a bikini on my honeymoon, Dan, not a bloody raincoat.'

'We could get a cottage with a nice log fire.'

'That's what old people do.'

'We'd probably need a shit load of vaccinations for Zanzibar.'

'So? It's not like we don't know any doctors.'

'Where did Flo and Henry go for their honeymoon?'

'No idea. Somewhere boring, no doubt. Oh yes, I remember. They went to Malvern. Henry was showing some of his pigs at the Royal Three Counties.'

'With his new wife cheering him on.'

'Flo's never aspired to much. You know, I don't think she's actually been abroad since Vieux Glion finished finishing her.'

'But she seems very contented.'

'Anyway, she'd have hated somewhere like Zanzibar. She gets pink and blotchy and bad-tempered in the sun whereas I'll get a gorgeous all-over tan.'

'All-over?'

'Well I'll certainly go topless.'

'Isn't Zanzibar Muslim?'

'Not at this resort. Look, it's a kind of walled compound.'

'Sounds like prison.'

'It looks fabulous. Honeymooners inside, ayatollahs outside minding their own business. And you can get a six-day extension, going on safari in the Serengeti. We could do that first, then the beach.'

'How much holiday can you take?'

'Don't know. To be negotiated. As much as possible. Tell Bitch Face you'll need two weeks at least.'

'I won't get two weeks. You know how we're stretched. I had a case of glandular fever today, by the way. Classic presentation.'

'Snoggers' disease.'

'I don't think Legend had been doing much snogging.'

'Legend? What kind of name is that?'

'A cruel and regrettable one. I can't see him living up to it, unless he's a very late developer. We get a lot of kids with odd names. We've got a Bronte and a Wolf. Same family. We've got a Conan. And a Nivea. Are we done, wedding-wise?'

'You are kidding? There's loads to be done.'

'I meant for the time being. Stuff that involves me.'

'I suppose. You'll have to buy presents for the attendants.'

'I'm already paying Rob's air fare.'

'You'll still need to give him something, as a memento. And then something for the she-brats.'

Chloe's nieces Daisy, Poppy and Lily are going to be flower girls.

'How about muzzles and ankle shackles, personalized with their name and the date?'

'And something for Dee.'

'So that'll be three junior size muzzles and one extra large.'

'What do you think about white scabiosa in a bouquet?'

'Sounds like a skin disease.'

'Let's have sex.'

'Did I tell you Vaz and Teresa aren't sleeping together till after their wedding?'

'They are weird.'

'I think it's rather sweet. Old-fashioned. Couples never used to have sex before marriage.'

'Yes they did. Granny Orde-Sykes was up the duff with Mummy when she got married. Have you stopped fancying me?'

'No, why?'

'I said, "let's have sex" and you haven't moved a muscle.'

'That's what you think.'

So that evening I believe we established that:

1.   I'll be wearing an indigo waistcoat and sage green tie.

2.   One of my remaining duties is to buy gifts for our attendants.

3.   Granny and Grandpa Orde-Sykes had pre-marital sex in the Chummery gazebo.

4.   We are almost certainly going to Zanzibar for our honeymoon.

Chapter 3

A final year student was coming to spend time at The Lindens, to get a taste of General Practice. Chandra Mukerjee. Helen had agreed to have her, but it seemed there was no plan what to do with her.

Trevor said, 'Who's the nervous Nellie hanging around in Reception?'

'Student. Her name's Chandra. We've got her for the week.'

'Is Helen minding her?'

'Supposed to be. Unless she's forgotten about her. I'm not even sure if Helen's coming in this morning.'

'We can stick her in with Vaz, if all else fails. By the way, it's nice to see our sign vandals are honouring the big occasion.'

I hadn't noticed anything when I drove in.

'What big occasion?'

'According to Mary, it's Chad Dearlove's funeral today.'

Our receptionists seem to know everything that's going on. They're not gossips. They just know. Like mothers.

I went out with Trevor to look at the sign. It now said SHIT END.

'Which indeed it was,' says Trevor, 'even for a Dearlove. Chased from his love nest to a violent death under Walkway D. I might drive over there later. Station myself somewhere along the processional route.'

'You think it'll be a big affair?'

'I guarantee it. They may live knee deep in old pizza boxes but when it comes to funerals, they spare no effort. Weren't you here when the Bibby lad carked it?'

'Kyle's brother? No, it was before my time. Did he get a big send-off?'

'Black horses with black plumes. Glass hearse. You'd have thought it was Queen Victoria not Scott Bibby. And of course, this time we've got the added ingredient of internecine how's-your-father. A Dearlove death caused, allegedly, by a Bibby. It'll be like the Capulets and the Montagues.'

I don't always catch Trevor's literary references, but I got that one. We did Romeo and Juliet for GCSE.

'Do you think there'll be trouble?'

'I wouldn't be surprised to see a tinnie or two thrown. Let's hope the horses don't get spooked.'

'How do they afford horses and glass carriages?'

'How indeed?'

There was a name on my morning list I wasn't thrilled to see: Ron Jarrold. Ron's wife Freda is a regular at the surgery. BOG, to quote Trevor. Been on Google. Freda's always confident she's diagnosed what's wrong with her and what tests she needs but it's usually possible to distract her with some alternative ideas. As long as she feels you're taking her symptoms seriously, Freda's okay. Ron's a different matter.

My dealings with him had so far been through the Patient Participation Panel where he's a consistent pain in the arse. He loves meetings. The longer they drag on the better he likes them, and he writes notes on what's said, copies them, sends them to everyone before the next meeting. You get nothing past Ron.

He was already in the waiting room at 9.30 although he was booked in for my 10.10 slot and that made me feel under pressure. Ten minutes can easily drift to fifteen. Some patients need a bit more time. Before you know it, you're running half an hour behind. I had Elsie Turney in, just to check her blood pressure. She's a sweet old lady with lots of stories about the neighbourhood and the practice. She's known Trevor since he was fresh out of medical school. I was determined not to rush her but all the while she was reminiscing, I kept picturing Ron Jarrold sitting in the waiting room, fuming and checking his watch. By the time his turn came I was feeling hassled and not inclined to take any shit.

Ron, though, was not his usual bumptious self. His face had that drawn look that spells chronic pain. His was in his lower back and hips.
I said, 'You do know Dr Vincent's our expert on back pain?'
Ron said he preferred to consult a male doctor.

We see a lot of bad backs. Spasms brought on by careless lifting, aches caused by age or a sagging mattress, sciatica, the occasional prolapsed disc. Most of them get better without us doing anything. I have a checklist I work through. How long had Ron had the pain? Since Boxing Day. Very precise. That was too long for it to be a pulled muscle. Had there been any incident immediately before its onset? A fall? Unaccustomed activity? Shovelling snow, for instance? No fall, and they paid a man to clear their snow. Unaccountable weight loss? No. Episodes of fever? No.

I got him up onto the exam table and did the straight leg raise test. That will usually tell you if there's a disc problem. No red flags there. Neither was there was any neurological deficit that I could detect. Tenderness over both hip joints, though. Ron had already had his ten minutes.

He said, 'It's obviously nothing major. I won't keep you. Just give me a prescription for something stronger than ibuprofen.'

I don't generally take advantage of a person's misfortunes, but it was a good opportunity to teach Mr Jarrold a lesson. He's always going on about punctuality and unacceptable waiting times.

I said, 'Ron, I'm not done with you yet. Come and sit down. If you need more than ten minutes, you'll get more than ten minutes. This isn't a ketchup production line.'

Back of the net! Ron's a manager at Sau-Cee Foods.

So, persistent sacro-iliac pain in a 62-year-old male with no sign of trauma or infection. I asked him if he had any bladder problems.

'Such as?'

'Needing to pee frequently? Difficulty getting started?'

'No.'

'Any problems with erectile function?'

'Absolutely not.'

That answer was a tad too emphatic, so he probably wasn't quite the man he used to be but, as Trevor would say, at his age, who is?

I said, 'I think I'm going to check your urine for an infection anyway, and I'll refer you for an X-ray.'

'Fair enough. What about a CT scan?'

'An X-ray's the first step. You can learn a lot from that. Come back to me in a couple of weeks and we'll take it from there. Depending on what the X-ray shows, we might take a blood sample, check your PSA levels.'

'I've heard of that. For the prostate.'

'Yes.'

'Do it now if you like.'

'No. One thing at a time.'

'You see, in my line of business we aim for optimal efficiency. If you have to stop a machine to check one nozzle, might as well use the opportunity to check them all.'

'The problem is, Ron, I can't bring my surgery to a halt to do a full MOT test on all your nozzles.'

He laughed.

'Point taken,' he said.

We parted on quite friendly terms.

I felt cross with myself for the rest of the day though. For one thing I needn't even have mentioned PSA testing. Now Freda would Google it, Ron would come back to me with pages of print-out, and I'd have to remind him to abstain from ejaculating for 48 hours before I take his blood. I was also annoyed with myself for avoiding the simplest and most obvious way to eliminate his prostate from my investigations: a DRE. I hate doing them and because I hate doing them, I do them hurriedly and don't necessarily learn anything useful. I just didn't want to put my finger up the rectum of a man who'll be sitting opposite me at the next Patient Participation Panel meeting. Cowardice comes in many forms.

Tegan Strange was my last patient of the morning. She wanted a tattoo removed. It was on her right arm, a sort of curved ribbon with the words GERG AND TEEG 4 EVAH. I told her there was zero chance of getting it removed on the NHS. She'd have to pay to have it done privately.

She said, 'Where am I going to get that kind of money?'

'Are you working?'

'Can't afford to.'

A lot of them say that. They're better off claiming benefit.

'How much did the tattoo cost?'

'Two hundred.'

'You'll have to save up again, then. There are a couple of laser clinics in Birmingham.'

'They'll want a thousand, two thousand if it takes a lot of sessions.'

'Why do you want to get rid of it?'

'Because he's fucked off.'

'Gerg?'

'Greg, not Gerg.'

'The tattoo says Gerg.'

'Whatever. So, you're not going to get it done for me?'

'No.'

'What about self-harm?'

'What about it?'

'If I self-harm you'll have to help me.'

'That's true. But then I'd send you to a psychiatrist, not a laser clinic.'

'Fucking Nora,' were Tegan's final words to me.

Trevor looked in on me again after lunch. He had a letter in his hand.

'Did you see anything of the funeral?'

24

'Oh yes. It was a spectacle to behold.'

'Plumed horses?'

'No, stretch limos. One white, one pink. And don't try buying any flowers this week because the Dearloves must have cleaned out every florist between here and Birmingham.'

'Big wreaths?'

'Very big. Including a pair of shoes made from dyed blue chrysanthemums. I'd forgotten about Chad's occasional sideline. He used to do Elvis impersonations, around the social clubs, when there was a lull in his day job.'

'What was his day job?'

'Breaking and entering. Did you see the letter about Glenys Allsop?'

He passed it to me. Glenys had had a liver transplant. There had been no complications during surgery, she'd been transferred from the ICU after 48 hours and was likely to be home by the beginning of April.

I said, 'Well that's a good outcome. How much of the aftercare will we be responsible for?'

'Depends. She'll be on immuno-suppressants for the rest of her life, but if everything settles down, she'll be fine. She's a nice woman, Glenys. I'm really glad they found her a donor.'

He lingered. I got the feeling he was about to say something else, but Chandra Mukerjee appeared with her raincoat on. I was taking her to a couple of house calls.

'Ah,' he said. 'Venturing out onto the front line? Good. I won't keep you then, Dan. I'll catch you some other time for a quick word. Nothing urgent. Maybe a pint, after close of play one of the evenings?'

'Friday's good. Chloe's going to London for the weekend with her Mum. Wedding shopping.'

'Ouch. Friday it is then. Unless. Are you spoken for on Saturday night?'

I wasn't. All I had lined up was a microwaved Thai and a boxed set. His face lit up.

'Wolverhampton,' he said. 'First race is at half past five. I'll pick you up from here at five. That'll give us time to get a sandwich and a beer before the second race. My treat, mind. Just bring a few quid for your bets.'

'Won't it be getting dark?'

'It will. But don't worry. They fit the horses with headlamps.'

He went off whistling.

Chapter 4

I only had two visits to make but I thought I'd take Chandra to meet a couple of shut-ins as well, if time allowed. John Adkins was our first call. He's an elderly gentleman who lives with his daughter, Susan. He had a history of urinary infections that generally announced themselves by his behaviour becoming crankier than usual. Trevor was very good at coaxing him to give a urine sample, but we have to find ways of managing without Trevor. He won't be available forever.

Chandra asked if she should stay in the car. Trevor was right, she was a nervous Nellie. I was probably the same at her age.

John's greeting was, 'You can fuck off. Where's Buxton?'

I said, 'Dr Buxton's a part-timer now. He'll be retiring soon. Do you feel unwell, John? Can I take your temperature?'

'No. Who's the Paki?'

I said, 'This is Miss Mukerjee. She's a student. And as a matter of fact, she's British. Halesowen, born and bred.'

'She don't look it.'

Susan mouthed, 'sorry.'

The secret to dealing with John is to get him talking about his time in the air force.

'Remind me, where was it you got that snake bite?'

'Foot. It swole up like a football.'

'And where were you based?'

'Cyprus. Akrotiri.'

'Would you pee in a bottle for me?'

'No.'

'Are you drinking plenty?'

'Are you buying?'

It was the first time I'd ever seen him smile.

'Can I examine you? Take a quick look at your belly?'

'Not with the Paki in the room.'

It was the excuse Chandra had been looking for. She bolted for the car.

John's bladder was very distended. His daughter said he hadn't peed properly since the previous afternoon.

He said, 'You don't know that. I don't tell you every time I go to the jakes.'

I said, 'Well you certainly need to empty your bladder now. Will you do that for me?'

'Don't want to.'

I phoned for an ambulance. He needed to be catheterized ASAP.

Susan said, 'You always see him at his worst. He only gets so nasty when he's not well. I feel terrible about the little Indian doctor.'

I told her not to give it another thought. Seeing people at their worst goes with the job and Chandra surely knew that. Sometimes, amazingly, we see people at their best, or at least at their bravest.

She was in the car writing up her John Adkins experience on a notepad. Delirium associated with urinary retention in a 77-year-old male.

I said, 'Not really delirium. He's not hallucinating, and he's not confused. But a sudden onset of personality change? Yes. He's verbally challenging, let's say. Mr Adkins has a history of recurring UTIs and before he moved in with his daughter, they'd go untreated for far too long, so he's probably got scarring, and given his age the muscle tone in his bladder won't be A1. I'm sending him to Sandwell. They'll put a catheter in, not for the first time and probably not for the last.'

Our next stop was Ruby Stackhouse, a 69-year-old with unstable angina. Ruby and her husband are both smokers. Chandra, I discovered, had a zero-tolerance attitude to smoking.

She said, 'Why are we visiting this lady if she won't help herself?'

Ruby had been advised to quit, of course, but how could she with her husband sitting beside her, lighting up all day long?

'We're visiting to give her reassurance. Her angina comes on at night. She wakes up in a panic, her husband calls the out-of-hours. They say to give her nitro-glycerine and if that doesn't help, to call an ambulance. Otherwise to refer to us in the morning. Which is what always happens.'

The Stackhouses live in a maisonette on Brook Glen. We parked outside. Three boys cycled by, nine, maybe ten year olds. They gave us the finger. Why weren't they in school?

Chandra brought out her notepad again.

'The lady's angina occurs only at rest?'

'Yes. Although as she's almost always at rest I'm not sure how significant that is. I imagine going down the street to buy her cigs is the only exercise she gets. This isn't a neighbourhood where people go to the gym or run. Unless they're running from the police, and that doesn't happen much. A visible police presence, I mean.'

I was starting to sound like Trevor.

'She experiences crushing chest pain?'

'Some, but mainly radiating to her left shoulder. You know women with cardiac episodes often present differently to men.'

I told her the story of Margaret Spooner who'd only dragged herself through the surgery doors when her jaw pain became unbearable.

'Acute angina?'

'It was an MI, and a fatal one.'

We went in to see Ruby. She's a tiny woman, very lined. My Nan could give Ruby fifteen years and she has much better skin. Dave Stackhouse is small and wrinkled too. They're like a pair of kippered garden gnomes. Ruby said Dave shouldn't have called us out. She said she was right as rain.

He said, 'You wasn't right as rain at three o'clock this morning. You thought you was a goner.'

Flog It! was on the telly. When Trevor goes to patients and the television's blaring, he asks them to turn it off. I haven't quite got the nerve up yet.

Ruby's pulse was normal. I asked Chandra if she'd like to take some blood. It'd be good practice. She shook her head.

Ruby said, 'What do you want blood for?'

I looked at Chandra.

'Would you like to answer that?'

'To test for cardiac biomarkers?'

30

'Such as?'

'Serum levels of troponin?'

'Yes. Anything else?'

'Creatine-kinase?'

'Correct.'

Ruby said, 'What's she saying?'

'We'll take blood to see if there's been any damage to your heart muscle. And you know what else I'm going to say to you, don't you?'

'Yes.'

'Even cutting down a bit would help. We have a support group now, you know, for people who are quitting smoking. You and Dave could come together.'

'How much?'

'It's free. Mondays, from 7 till 8. Give it a try. We've had a lot of success stories.'

'Yeah?'

'Yes. People who've been smokers as long as you have and managed to give up. And do you know what they say? They don't just feel better, they're better off as well. All that money they were spending on cigarettes. How many packs a day do you and Dave get through?'

He said three. She said he smoked more than half of them.

I said, 'And they're what, seven quid a pop? So say twenty pounds a day. How's your maths? What's twenty pounds a day, for a year?'

Chandra said it was £7,500.

I said, 'You could do a lot with that money.'

'Yes,' says Dave. 'We could sit here reading us bank books and feeling crap.'

When we got back to Shit End, Moira was on Reception. She and Mary used to work alternate days but now their mother is on her way out they don't get much sleep so they sometimes split half days. They both look exhausted, but they don't want to stop working. They love their job and their Mum can't last much longer. She's in her nineties and slowly fading away.

Moira said, 'Dr Dan, I've got a treat for you this afternoon.'

'If it's Amber Evans, I'm not seeing her. She'll have to wait for an appointment with Helen or Pam.'

Chandra said, 'Are you allowed to choose who you see?'

I explained about Amber. She's one of our more rampant nymphos so she's only allowed to see female doctors.

Moira said, 'It's not Amber Evans. Allow me to know my job. It's Kyle Bibby. He begged and pleaded for an appointment, so I've squeezed him in at 5.15. More than likely the Willetts woman won't turn up anyway.'

I hadn't seen Kyle for a few weeks. He wasn't his usual chirpy self. He smelled of booze.

'Hello, Doc,' he said. 'You'll have heard.'

'Heard what?'

'We've had a tragedy in the family. Accidental death. I've been at the funeral. I won't lie to you, I've had a few.'

'Do you mean Mr Dearlove? I didn't know you were related.'

'Cousin. We was really close.'

'Then I'm very sorry for your loss.'

'It's doing my head in, Doc. I need something stronger than me usual tammies.'

We prescribe temazepam 20 mg for Kyle but he's always angling for a higher dose.

I said, 'Kyle, grief is a natural process and we all have to go through it some time. Pills aren't the answer.'

'It's not just that. It's the flashbacks.'

'Did you witness the accident?'

'I seen the body. I've got that PMT.'

'PMT? Are you sure? I've never come across that in a man.'

'How d'you mean?'

'Pre-menstrual tension.'

'No. PMT, like squaddies get. Afghanistan. Iraq.'

'That'd be PTSD. Post-traumatic stress disorder.'

'That's the one. I reckon I'm going to need a lot of help getting over this. I reckon I'm going to need to up me tammies to 30s.'

'We could look into getting you some counselling.'

'Could do. Probably a long waiting list though.'

'So Chad Dearlove was your cousin?'

'Yeah. My Mum and his Mum are sisters.'

'And where does Wayne Bibby fit in?'

'Half-brother. Might be. He says he is, when it suits him, but we don't really know. His Mum says my Dad was Wayne's Dad. He don't look like a Bibby though. He looks more like a Dearlove. Mum tried to get on Jeremy Kyle one time, to sort it all out, get him tested. She wrote in, only nothing come of it.'

'And from what I understand, it was an argument between Wayne and Chad that led to Chad's death?'

'Fair play to Chad. Wayne had been away. Kayla didn't know he was due for release. She says she wasn't even sure if he'd be coming back to her so you couldn't really blame Chad for getting in there. Leave your bike unattended somebody's bound to take it for a spin, right?'

'Kayla being the bike, so to speak?'

'Yeah. She's a lying minger, any road.'

'Is she related to anyone in this story?'

33

'Fuck no. She's from Walsall. Only she's got a kid she says is Wayne's. Can't trust them though, can you? Women? They tell you a kid's yours but unless you get on Jeremy Kyle and have it all tested, how can you be sure? Unless it's a half-bake, of course, then she can't fool nobody.'

'A what?'

'Half-bake. Like Jade Shotton done. She got a kid with a black yardie, tried to pass it off as mine but there was no way. I'm not daft. So can you give me some 30s, for my flashbacks?'

I thought for a minute.

I said, 'Okay Kyle, here's the plan. Flashbacks can be a sign of serious post-traumatic stress, so I'd want an expert opinion before I raise your temazepam dose. I wouldn't want to make things worse.'

'You won't, don't worry.'

'All very well for you to say. If things escalated and you ended up sectioned under the Mental Health Act, heaven forbid but such things can happen, your family would want my hide.'

'No they wouldn't. They couldn't give a toss.'

'But I do give a toss and I'm not prepared to dice with your mental health, Kyle. I'm going to refer you to the Psychological Therapies Service for an urgent and thorough assessment. If they recommend 30mg of temazepam, that's what you'll get. In the meanwhile, we'll keep you on 20s. Better safe than sorry.'

Checkmate. His face was a picture. He soon recovered though.

'Very clever, Doc,' he said. 'Very clever.'

'I'm only doing what any conscientious doctor would do.'

'Right. Still, don't bother with the shrink appointment. All the cutbacks and that, I don't want to be a burden. I'll soldier on.'

'Are you sure, Kyle? PTSD is no joke and there's no stigma in getting proper help.'

'I know. Mental health. It's a big thing now. On the telly all the time. Like Liz McDonald.'

'Who?'

'Off of Corrie. She's had depression. Stephen Fry. He's had something.'

'There you are then.'

'Thing is though, Doc, I have my reputation to consider. Word gets around. Kyle's gone a bit loopy. Bibby's turned into a window-licker. That'd be a very hard thing to come back from on Cherry Tree. I'd be like a wounded lion. The youngsters'd be circling, like on the nature programmes, ready to finish me off.'

I told him I completely understood. To see how things went for the next week or two and come back to me if the flashbacks persisted.

I said, 'But any worsening of the flashbacks, I'll get you an emergency appointment with a psychologist.'

'Right,' he said. 'Cheers.'

And off he went, the Lion King of Cherry Tree, with a prescription for 20mg temazepam in his hand.

Chapter 5

Chloe was on the phone when I got home. I heard her say, 'He's just walked in.'

'It's Eirwen,' she whispered. 'Do you want a word?'

Chloe calls my Mam by her first name now, same as I do hers.

I said, 'Let me guess. Wedding talk.'

Mam said, 'What it is, I was asking Chloe about accessibility. About a ramp at the church, in case we need a wheelchair.'

'Is Nan in a wheelchair? When did that happen?'

'Not your Nan. It's your Aunty June. She's waiting on a knee replacement so I'm just thinking ahead. She might not be so good on her feet for hours on end. Chloe's going to look into it. She's a lovely girl, Dan.'

'You've changed your tune.'

'No, I haven't. I just needed to get to know her better.'

'How's Da?'

'He's alright. Touch of rheumatics in his feet but that's what you get when you stand around in wet socks.'

'Holes in his wellies?'

'He tried to mend them with puncture patches. Anything to put off buying a new pair. He can be as tight as a duck's

36

derriere, your Da. He's round at your Nan's tonight, doing her light bulbs.'

Da replaces Nan's most crucial light bulbs once a year without fail, so she won't be plunged into sudden darkness.

'How's business?'

'His or mine?'

'Both.'

'Well I can't speak to your father's work because all I hear from him is a mumble. You know what he's like. "Llandovery. Gimmer hoggs. Pass the salt. Mumble, mumble." You have to join up the dots. I'm pretty busy. We've got the sangria bulge coming through just now.'

'The sangria bulge?'

'Holiday babies. They go to Spain for a week, overdo it with the sangria and bang, they're pregnant.'

'You bought your big hat yet?'

'Who says it's big?'

'Isn't it traditional?'

'People don't do traditional much now, Dan. Anyway, I can't wear anything too big, with being on the short side. I don't want to look like a table lamp. I might get a fascinator.'

'How's Nan?'

'A bit fanciful but not bad otherwise. She'll make a hundred, that one.'

Chloe was working on her wedding lists. She has a ring-binder full of spreadsheets.

'You're going to London this weekend, right?'

'Friday afternoon. Mummy's driving up here and we're getting the train.'

'Are you staying at Charlie's?'

My future brother-in-law has a flat in the Docklands.

'God no. Slow doesn't have any beds for guests. Just a super king for his shagathons. We're staying at a hotel in Knightsbridge. Boutique. What will you do while I'm gone?'

'Eat red meat. Watch porn. Scratch myself.'

'You could buy your wedding shoes. Break them in a bit. You could fix that towel rail.'

'I'll try. Actually, I've got a date for Saturday night.'

'Very funny.'

'I have. I'm going to the races with Trevor.'

'Why?'

'Why not? I've never been. Trevor's lonely. I'll be at a loose end. It might be fun.'

'Which course are you going to?'

'Wolverhampton.'

'Wolverhampton! Dan, it'll be packed with mouth-breathers.'

'You don't know that. What about all those prosperous Midlands business types? Anyway, don't they call it the Sport of Kings?'

'Wolverhampton isn't Ascot. Well I hope he's taking you to the Members' Enclosure. Is he giving you dinner?'

'Just a burger and a beer, I think.'

'Is she going?'

'She? You mean Mrs Buxton? I imagine not, else why would he have asked me.'

'How much money do you plan on taking with you?'

'Haven't thought about it. Don't worry, I won't raid the Zanzibar honeymoon account.'

'Seriously, Dan, set yourself a limit, and don't go down among the bookmakers. Go to the Tote. I think they let you have a £2 win bet. And watch out for pickpockets.'

'You seem to know a lot about it.'

'We used to go to the Warwick course sometimes, when the Swift grands were alive. What are you going to wear?'

'No idea. What do you think? Mouth-breather casual? Stained trackie bottoms and a beanie?

'Wear your waxed jacket. And take a tie, in case. Wolverhampton though. You probably won't need it.'

I'd been looking forward to a bit of action in the sack but there was nothing doing. Not in the mood, she said, and she turned her back to me and punched her pillow in a 'preparing for sleep' kind of way, just so I didn't cling to any hopes about persuasive foreplay.

It's a weird thing but Chloe used to be very keen on sex. Even when she was working long hours and revising for exams she couldn't get enough. Lately though she's gone right off the boil. It makes you wonder if Vaz and Teresa have the right idea. Nothing more than a fully-clothed fumble until that ring is on her finger.

Friday evening, we were late getting to the racecourse. Trevor had to stop for petrol, then there was traffic. He said he never bothered with the first race anyway. He liked to take his time, wander down to the parade ring and wait for the runners in the second race to appear. The Bateman Heavy Plant Maiden Fillies' Stakes. Eight girls who had never won a race but one of them was about to change that.

I decided I was going to bet on Ribtickle Tess. She seemed to turn her head to look at me every time the lad led her past me. It felt like an omen, but Trevor said not to rush to judgment. He took me along the row of bookies.

I said, 'I'm under strict orders to bet on the Tote. No more than £2 a bet.'

'The Tote's for the ladies,' he said. 'Who are not here to police us. Live free or die, lad.'

Not wishing to appear a wuss, I parted with a tenner. £10 to win on Ribtickle Tess.

Trevor looked at the odds board and murmured, 'Into the valley of death.'

We stationed ourselves on the rail at the finishing line. The race was run over seven furlongs, which meant nothing to me. There are eight furlongs in a mile, apparently. So much for going metric.

'Just once round the track,' says Trevor. 'That's the thing with racing on the flat. Blink and you've missed it. With the jumps you can nip to the bog and still be back in your armchair in time for the finish.'

It was very exciting. I was trying to listen to the commentary, but it was too fast for me to follow. The only thing I could make out was that Trevor's horse, Melita Velita was the back marker. Then they came thundering past us in a bunch and they announced that it was a photo finish.

Trevor looked at me.

He said, 'Bloody hell, Dan. Do you need to put your head between your knees?'

'No, why?'

'Because you're in the frame. I'm not saying you had the winner, but she was definitely in the frame. You should have had an each-way bet. I should have suggested it. Well I need to sit down even if you don't.'

We went to a bar and he bought me a half of Guinness, to calm me, he said. But I was perfectly calm. If my tenner was gone, it was gone.

40

I said, 'How could you tell where my horse was? I couldn't even remember what colour cap her jockey was wearing.'

'Years of practice. We'll give the next race a miss, get a bite to eat. It's a Selling race and there are only four runners.'

'What's a Selling race?'

'The winner gets auctioned.'

'Poor horse. He's won his race and then he has to go home with strangers?'

'Better that than the glue factory. Anyway, the owner can bid, buy him back, if he wants to keep him. That often happens. I wish they'd hurry up with your photo-finish. Our supper's riding on it. Will it be a hotdog or a big fat sirloin sarnie?'

'How long does it take them to decide?'

The PA crackled. Trevor held up a nicotine-stained finger.

Ribtickle Tess won by a nose.

He grinned. 'Beginner's luck,' he said. 'Do you want me to get Securicor to pick up your winnings?'

'How much do you think it'll be?'

'I can tell you exactly how much. You've won £170. Didn't you look at the odds before you put your bet on?'

Maths isn't my strong point. That's why I could never work in places like re-sus, where you need to be super-fast. I always check and double check dosages when I'm writing prescriptions. A slip of a decimal point and you could kill someone.

Trevor came with me. He had to. I couldn't even remember which bookie I'd placed my bet with.

'Right,' he said. 'How do you want your steak sambo? Onions? Mustard? Horseradish? Rabbit food garnish?'

He insisted on paying.

'Put your ill-gotten gains in that honeymoon jar. Where is it you're going?'

41

'Zanzibar.'

'Sooner you than me. Mrs Buxton and I had a week in Torquay.'

'So,' he said, when he'd finished eating. 'I wanted a quiet word, away from Shit End. It's about Mac.'

Mac had become a no-go topic between me and Trevor. Months before there had been a request from Woodleigh Grange to visit one of their residents, Hilda Ruck. The nursing homes were Mac's territory, but he was on holiday so Vaz and I attended. Hilda had been agitated about something involving Mac and a solicitor, but it was hard to tell whether it was a case of senile confusion. Old people often think they're being cheated or robbed. Sometimes they are, though, so I'd raised it with Trevor, but he'd sent me away with a flea in my ear.

He said, 'I know I shut you down that time you came to me about Mac. I admit it. The thing is, I think we might have even more of a situation than we'd realised.'

'More allegations?'

'There's a lot of talk. Could be tittle-tattle. People jumping on the bandwagon.'

'What does Mac say?'

'I haven't talked to him yet. I've known him for so long, I'm not sure if I see him clearly. You've got distance. What's your impression of him?'

I hardly knew Bruce Macdonald. I'd gone out with a few times, on his nursing home calls and found him pleasant enough. A bit slick, a bit of a glamour boy, but the old ladies loved him. All I could say was, 'I liked him. I just wondered what he was doing in a practice like ours. He seemed out of place.'

Trevor said, 'You mean the three-piece suits and the Merc while the rest of us are shovelling shit on Brook Glen?'

'Sort of. Mac seemed more Harley Street than Tipton.'

He nodded.

'Of course, he's single, no kids. More disposable income. We can allow a man some style without him being a wrong 'un. Buggered if I know what to think anymore.'

'You haven't discussed the latest gossip with Helen?'

'No. I've been putting it off. She definitely doesn't see him straight. They had a little thing, you know? Years ago. On and off.'

'An affair?'

'Nothing major. Helen has these occasional adventures.'

'Yes, I know.'

'Ah. You don't speak from personal experience?'

'It was nothing really.'

'It's always nothing, lad. But Lord Almighty, she's old enough to be your mother.'

'Anyway, we didn't. She made a pass, but it was the night that poor old grandad got dumped on our doorstep.'

'Saved by the doorbell. Is she attractive, then?'

'There's something about her.'

'If you say so. Can't see it, myself. And I'm no great fan of Clifford Vincent but I imagine living with Helen must be like knowing you've got a piece of unexploded Jerry ordnance under your patio. Can it be defused or are we talking 'controlled' detonation? And you, Dan Talbot, have got that beautiful girlfriend.'

'Yes. And nothing happened with Helen. What are you going to do about Mac?'

'I'm going to wait and see. If nothing else crawls out of the woodwork before his tribunal, he'll probably get a reprimand

and we can go back to business as usual. Have you thought about your future plans?'

'Got to get registered first.'

'You'll walk it. And if Mac goes, Helen might offer you a job. You'd be an asset to the practice. She'd be a fool to let you go.'

'On the other hand…'

'Yes, I see what you mean. Anyway, thanks for your input. Now the next two races are handicaps.'

'What does that mean?'

'The horses carry different weights, to even out their chances. The better the horse seems to be, the heavier the weight it carries. If the handicappers have done their homework the runners should all cross the finish together. That's the theory. And then there's the Wolverhampton factor.'

'Which is?'

'This isn't Goodwood, or Ascot. It's a perfectly nice little course but it's not, what's the word? Prestigious. The handicapping tends to be a bit more generous. So one thing to look for is a clever trainer slipping a potential swan in among the ducks. That'll put your unsuspected horse sense to the test.'

I didn't tell him about the three secret tools I was going to employ: 1. Did I like the horse's name? 2. Did I like the owner's racing colours? 3. Did the horse look at me in the paddock. On this basis I backed Arctic Pearl in the 19.40. Quartered orange and maroon with a hooped cap. She sauntered home sixth in a field of eight. But I stuck to my method and picked Bibbetybobbity in the Highcrest Life Assurance Handicap. He definitely winked at me in the parade and he was carrying the chocolate and green silks of the Bullingdon Syndicate.

Trevor said, 'Bibbetybobbity? What kind of name is that to give a horse?'

I told him it reminded me of the Bibbys.

'Did I tell you Kyle came to see me after the funeral?'

'Looking for mood-altering drugs, of course.'

'Guess what he thought he was suffering from?'

'This'll be a good one. I can feel it in my bones.'

'PMT.'

'PMT.'

'He said he'd seen Chad Dearlove's body before they scraped him off the concrete and he was getting flashbacks, like squaddies who've been in a battle zone.'

'PMT. He's very good value, isn't he? Our Kyle. I shall have to sit down.'

I always worry about making Trevor laugh. He's breathless at the best of times and sometimes he gets quite purple in the face. He needed a whiff of oxygen the time we told him where Amber Evans had tucked her mobile phone.

I went and put his bets on for him. Ten quid each way on Tomintoul and a fiver each way on Goosefeather.

'A no-hoper, if ever I saw one,' he puffed, 'but it's for Mrs Buxton. If there's a grey running, I generally have a little wager for her. The ladies always seem to like greys.'

'How is Mrs Buxton?'

'She's very well. We're having a birthday party for her, in May. I don't suppose you'd want to come.'

'I'll come if I'm invited.'

'Then you will be. She took a shine to you when she met you. I can't get her to stop calling you Don, but she often asks after you.'

Goosefeather, Mrs Buxton's grey no-hoper, won by three lengths and Bibbetybobbity came second. Trevor's Tomintoul was pulled up.

There was going to be live music after the final race.

He said, 'Unless you have a craving to hear a Bee Gees tribute band, I suggest we have a swift half and then make an early getaway. You'll be wanting to get home to count your winnings.'

'In the future, if ever the conversation turns to this evening and Chloe happens to be present, can we just say I only bet on the Tote and I broke even?'

'Dan,' he said. 'You're talking to a veteran, 42 happy years strapped to the marriage mast. Your gambling history will never make it into my long-term memory.'

Chloe called me from London, very late, to tell me that her mother was getting on her nerves.

'I hope she's not within earshot.'

'No, she's in the bath, hogging the very nice freebies.'

'Was your shopping successful?'

'Yes. We bought loads. But all she talks about is golf. Even to the woman in the hat shop. It's so embarrassing.'

'All my Da talks about is livestock. It's good they have a passion. Imagine if they didn't have anything. Kids grown up and gone. Life could be pretty empty. I wonder what we'll talk about when we're your mother's age.'

'What do you mean?'

'Well I presume we're not entering into a temporary arrangement with this wedding. I'd like to think we'll still have things to talk about after years of marriage. Cardiac anomalies. Trends in general practice. Shower heads.'

'Shower heads?'

'I just thought of that. I think we need a new one.'

'No, we don't. It just needs de-clogging. Anyway, Mummy's life isn't empty. She has my wedding to think about.'

'So really you're cross because she's not talking about you all the time. Maybe a daughter getting married isn't such a big deal for her. She's already done it once, don't forget.'

'Flo's was a completely vanilla wedding.'

'What does that mean?'

'It means zero imagination. Typical Flo. Up the aisle to Lohengrin, reverse trip to Mendelssohn, a three-tier fruitcake and me plus two of her Vieux Glion friends, including the dreaded Annabel, dressed as absolute frights in persimmon satin.'

'The Annabel who did the food for your Dad's birthday lunch?'

'The very same. Are you missing me?'

'Of course.'

'Say it. In Welsh.'

Chloe doesn't understand, I wasn't much of a Welsh scholar. Mam and Da remember a bit from school but we never spoke it at home. I could tell her anything, I suppose. She wouldn't know.

 'Dwy'n colli ti.'

'And that means?'

'I'm dying for you to come home and get your kit off.'

'What have you been doing without me?'

'Fixed the towel rail. Didn't buy wedding shoes. Went to the races with Trevor.'

'I'd forgotten about that. Did you bet?'

'You bet.'

'Very funny. I hope you didn't lose loads.'

'I didn't lose anything.'

'Good boy. When I get home tomorrow let's order from that new Vietnamese takeaway and have really hot sex.'

It seemed like a plan.

When the taxi dropped them off Vinnie was laden with shopping bags and a hat box. I helped her load them into her car. She said she wouldn't come in. She needed to get home. Laurence had people coming over for drinks and she had a 10 am tee-off for some charity tournament she was playing in. I got an air-peck on each cheek.

She said, 'I imagine the next time I see you will be at the church.'

I said, 'I think we're having dinner with you before that. After the rehearsal? You and Laurence, me and my parents.'

'Oh yes,' she said, 'so you are. I'd completely forgotten. I must write it down.'

I suggested to Chloe that we have a plan B for the rehearsal dinner. Somewhere like the Horn and Trumpet. It wouldn't go down well with Mam if we turn up at the Chummery and all that's on offer is cream crackers and Annabel's cat-puke paté.

Chapter 6

Some days all you seem to get are piffling minors. Constipation, mouth ulcers, harmless twinges, worries brought on by reading health articles. It's not that you want people to have anything seriously wrong with them but sometimes you'd welcome something to get your teeth into. Monday and Tuesday had been like watching grass grow, then on the Wednesday I had Ron Jarrold and Keith Sideaway, consecutive appointments.

Ron had been for his hip and spine X-ray. He expected me to have received a letter from the hospital. I hadn't. I went and checked with Mary. There was nothing in the morning's post.

'Sheer inefficiency,' he fumed.

'How's the pain?'

'Terrible.'

'What did they say at the hospital?'

'They didn't. I've got an appointment to see a Dr Green, end of April. But they were supposed to write to you.'

'Is Dr Green an orthopaedist?'

'I don't know. They don't tell you anything. They shove you around from pillar to post. Go there, wait here.'

Pain can make you short-tempered.

I searched for Dr Green in the hospital directory. There were three. One was a gynaecologist, one was an orthopaedist, one was a urologist.

I said, 'Ron, let me make some phone calls after surgery. I'll see what I can find out and let you know.'

He didn't move. His face looked very drawn.

'Compared to when you first came to see me, would you say you're feeling worse? Or about the same?'

He picked at his fingernails. I could see he was deciding what to say. I played for time. Wrote down the extension numbers for two of the Dr Greens.

Then he said, 'That blood test you mentioned last time, for the prostate. You can do it today. Freda read up on it, so I know what's involved. I haven't... you know.... Not recently.'

'Ejaculated?'

'Yes.'

'Okay. We'll get your bloods sent off today.'

'Not that we don't. We have a normal married life, me and Freda. But with the pain, it's been....'

'Of course.'

I sent him through to Nurse Chris and ushered Keith Sideaway into my office.

Keith's one of those patients I don't think I'll ever forget. He'd come in last November, to Helen Vincent, and I'd been sitting in with her. Keith had presented with a drooping eyelid and a stiff shoulder. Nothing much, you'd think. One of those odd things that'll resolve itself. But Helen's instinct had been that there might be something sinister behind it and how right she'd been. There was a lung tumour quietly growing and pressing on a nerve trunk. I would never have diagnosed it.

50

What with the smell of Helen's Ô de Lancôme and her barking at me to remember my basic neurology, I hadn't been thinking too clearly.

Keith had had a very rough time since then. The tumour was at the very top of his lung, hidden behind his collarbone. A Stage III adenoma. He'd had chemo and radiation, to shrink the tumour. Now they were going to try to remove what was left of it surgically.

He wasn't looking great. A man of two halves. Right side normal, left side very depleted. Eyelid still drooping, eyeball sunken, hand weak.

'Good thing I'm right-handed,' he said. 'The reason I'm here is, I'm not sleeping great. I wake up around two and start thinking about everything. You know?'

'What about the daytime? Would you say you're feeling anxious?'

'No. I don't have time. I drop the kids to school. Do a few jobs around the house. I'd like to do a bit of gardening once the weather gets warmer but I'm not much use with this gammy hand. I'll just have to give the wife her orders and I'll make the tea.'

The ever cheerful, Keith. I wrote him up for Ativan.

'When are they doing the surgery?'

'Quite soon, but I have to go for another scan first.'

'Be sure to tell them you're taking a pill at night. It's very mild but the anaesthetist still needs to know about it.'

'Will do,' he said. 'It's going to be quite a production, this operation. I'll have three surgeons working on me. People complain about the National Health, but I think it's ruddy marvellous.'

51

The admirably chipper Mr Sideaway. I wished I could share his rosy view of the NHS but after an hour of being given the run-around about Ron Jarrold, I just couldn't. Radiology said a letter would have been sent out.

I said, 'But I haven't received a letter.'

'Well it'll have been sent out.'

Could they tell me which Dr Green my patient had been referred to? No, they couldn't. I tried Orthopaedics. The appointments secretary needed Ron's patient number.

'I don't have his patient number. He has an appointment with Dr Green on April 26th. Presumably you don't get that many Jarrolds.'

Heavy sigh. They had no-one called Jarrold booked for out-patients on April 26th. There had been some IT problems recently. There might be a backlog putting it into the system. The system. What did people blame before there was such a thing, when there were just handwritten notes and a typist sending out letters?

She said, 'Why don't you speak to Radiology again? Ask them to send you a new letter?'

I suddenly thought of Matt. I asked her to put me through to Dr Carey's number.

'Which Dr Carey?'

'Matthew Carey. Surgical registrar.'

Matt's phone rang and rang.

'Probably at Fracture Clinic,' she said. 'Or he could be in theatre. Try again later.'

I got him, eventually, on his mobile.

'Married bloke!' he said. 'How's it going? Long time, no drink.'

'I'm not married yet. July. You'll be getting an invitation. Matt, I need a favour.'

'Best man?'

'Sorry, Rob's doing that. He's flying over.'

'Want me to organize your stag? He'll be pushed to do that from Sydney.'

'I'm not having a stag.'

'Dan,' he said. 'Are you under the thumb already?'

'No. I'm starting a new trend. No stag.'

I told him my Ron Jarrold story, asked him if he could find out anything from this Dr Green.

He said, 'I'll ask, but it doesn't make much sense. Green's a shoulder surgeon. Anyway, she's about to go on maternity leave.'

We said we should meet for a drink sometime soon. I said I'd ring him when I had my diary in front of me. I wanted to have prepared an iron-clad reason why I didn't need him to organize a blokey piss-up in Bratislava.

I was looking forward to a nice relaxed evening. A quiet chill on the sofa with Chloe's head on my shoulder. It was not to be. There was an envelope on the mat, addressed to both of us, handwritten. Almost certainly another invitation to another wedding of some distant cousin of hers, which would cost us a hundred quid for a state-of-the-art juicer from their gift list, even if we didn't attend, plus a lost weekend if we did.

I left it for Chloe to open when she got in. She wasn't in the happiest of moods. She was having training sessions in cardiac catheterization and I had the feeling they weren't going too well. My supreme sausage and mash seemed to smooth the rough edges a bit. Then she opened the letter.

I heard her say, 'What the actual fuck?'

53

The vicar of St Botolph's had written to say that he looked forward to seeing us in church on a few Sundays before our wedding and also to getting to know us at one of his Saturday afternoon Preparing for Marriage courses which all couples were expected to attend. Seemed pretty reasonable to me.

Chloe said, 'Preparing for Marriage course? Who does he think he is?'

'I suppose he sees himself as our pastoral adviser.'

'Damned cheek. Well I'm not going to any course.'

I said, 'I think he's telling us we have to. Reading between the lines. No course, no wedding.'

'What does he think he's going to teach us? Birth control?'

'Probably not that. Probably more like, for better or worse, richer or poorer, that side of things.'

She was chewing the inside of her lip and glaring at the wall. Always a sign we're about to have a Chloe meltdown.

I said, 'You know, if you feel that strongly, we don't have to get married at St Botolph's. I'd like to, but it's negotiable.'

'It's not negotiable. Everything else has been arranged around that.'

'Then we'll do as the vicar asks.'

'Doesn't he realise I'm a doctor? I work on Saturdays.'

'Not since you started at the Arden, you don't. Hardly ever. I have a few weekend Out of Hours shifts but they can be rearranged.

'Whose side are you on?'

'Nobody's. But it is his church.'

She leapt up and grabbed her phone.

'Daddy'll sort him out.'

Laurence's phone was engaged.

'I don't think your father should get involved.'

'The money my family have given to that church.'

54

'Really? I didn't know that. How much?'

'Loads. Letting them have their Summer Fete in our garden. Bunging a tenner in the collection plate at Easter.'

Laurence's phone was still engaged and so was Vinnie's. I suggested sleeping on it, but Chloe doesn't tick that way. She's more a dog with juicy bone kind of person. Eventually her phone rang. It was Vinnie.

Chloe said, 'I've been trying to get you for hours. You'll never guess what your bloody vicar is demanding.'

There was a brief silence followed by a series of rising, howly 'whats?'

Then she said, 'But Daddy said he'd fixed everything' and threw her phone across the room.

I rescued it. Vinnie was still on the line.

She said, 'I'm afraid Chlo's terribly upset.'

'You mean about the vicar?'

'What? No. Why is everyone talking about the vicar? She's upset about Charlie. He's been told his case is likely to be heard in June.'

'Well we knew that was coming.'

She said, 'As a matter of fact, Dan, we rather thought it wasn't coming. Laurence went to a great deal of expense to see that it didn't. We'll get him a good brief, of course. Such a pity he never went ahead with that VSO thing when he left school. A history of voluntary work always goes in one's favour.'

'Do you know if he's likely to get sentenced the same day?'

Another howl from Chloe.

Vinnie said, 'I absolutely refuse to think about that. A whack across the knuckles, hopefully. I mean, he's never been in any trouble before, apart from speeding points, but we've all got those.'

I haven't. I thought best not to say so, though.

55

Vinnie said, 'Well I mustn't keep you when you need to go and comfort darling Chlo. It's a perfectly horrid thing for us to have hanging over us but do assure her it shouldn't affect the wedding.'

The world according to Chloe and her parents. Only other people go to prison for possession of cocaine and driving under the influence. Charlie 'Slow' Swift should get just a ticking off. Chloe was inconsolable. What if Slow couldn't come to the wedding? My future brother-in-law was hardly the cornerstone of our plans, but it clearly wasn't the moment to point that out. She said her day would be ruined.

'Why?'

'People will talk.'

'Only behind our backs.'

'He's my brother. He should be there.'

'So should my brother but I'm prepared for him not to be.'

'That's because your brother's weird.'

'And yours has been a plonker. What's the most important thing about July 6th?'

'What do you mean?'

'What's the most important thing about our wedding day?'

She blew her nose.

'My dress?'

'Also?'

'That it doesn't rain.'

'And arguably most important of all? You and me? Till death do us part etc?'

She said that went without saying. I said I thought attending the vicar's seminar might not be a bad idea.

Chapter 7

Pam Parker used to do just two afternoon surgeries a week but when Mac was laid off, pending his hearing, she offered to double her hours.

'Glad to,' she'd said. 'I've got two borderline bulimics and an Alzie father-in-law at home so either give me more work or book me into Halesowen Meadows for a full-blown nervous breakdown.'

Chandra, the student, was hanging around looking lost. Pam said she'd take her for the morning.

'Our Senior Partner not in again?'

Moira said, 'She's at a meeting. Should be in by 11.00.'

'And Trevor?'

'Hospital appointment. Spirometry.'

Pam said, 'This practice is held together with string and sticky tape. What's Helen doing agreeing to have students when there's nobody here to teach them? How's your training plan going, Dan?'

'I don't seem to have one. I'm getting a bit worried about it. I'm doing my AKT in May.'

'You don't need Helen for that. What about your Clinical Skills Assessment?'

There are three elements to registering with the Royal College of GPs. Workplace-based assessment, which was Helen's responsibility, an Applied Knowledge Test, which is a three-hour exam, and then the Clinical Skills Assessment. You get thirteen consultations, ten minutes per role-play patient. Sometimes you're face to face, sometimes it's a telephone consultation, sometimes there's clinical information available and sometimes not. And it's all being scrutinized by the examiners. They watch you via a video feed. I'd booked my CSA for September and I was nervous about it already. As I told Pam, I felt like I had a lot of gaps.

'Such as?'

'Paediatrics. Dermatology. We seem to get a lot of skin queries.'

Pam said, 'We do. But Dan, it's up to you to fill your gaps. Don't sit around waiting for Helen to arrange things for you. Be pro-active. Get yourself down to a few out-patient clinics at Sandwell.'

'I don't like to ask for time off while we're so understaffed.'

'Don't ask. Just set it up and then tell her. It's not your job to keep this place functioning. Your job is to get your registration.'

Pam was right. She so often is.

I saw ten patients at morning surgery, had two Jaffa cakes for lunch, made three home visits, attended a case of pressure sores at the Sorrento nursing home and made a small dent in my pile of paperwork before afternoon surgery. I was only able to pursue the Ron Jarrold mystery because mid-afternoon I had two consecutive no-shows.

I tried a new tack. Was it possible Ron had been given an out-patient appointment with the wrong Dr Green? Well, yes and no. Urology had him on their list for April 26th and it wasn't a mistake. I spoke to the registrar. Hadn't I seen the radiology report? No, I hadn't.

The X-ray showed a mass on Ron's prostate, also some areas of increased bone density in the pelvis and significant bone loss in both hip joints.

'So he's at risk of hip fractures?'

'Yes.'

'But he's not seeing an orthopaedist?'

'All in good time. There might be something to be done to stabilize his pelvis, but the priority is his prostate. We'll look at his PSAs and do an ultrasound biopsy first, to get his Gleason score.'

The Gleason score pulls together all the test results and grades the seriousness of a prostate tumour. I suppose there was once a Dr Gleason who invented it.

'The biopsy, do you do it per rectum?'

'Yes. It's a five-minute job. You didn't feel a mass when you examined him?'

'Actually, I didn't do a DRE. He can be a tricky character and he wasn't in the best of moods when I saw him, and in pain, so I thought I'd wait and see what the X-ray showed.'

Waited in the hope a gloved finger didn't become necessary, if you're honest, Dan Talbot.

'Well, now you know,' says the reg.

I said, 'I don't think my patient has any idea. And the letter to me still hasn't materialized. Lost in the system.'

'Yes,' he said. 'Shite, isn't it?'

An unexplained mass on his prostate and bone changes in the pelvis. It seemed Ron Jarrold was in trouble. What to do? Pick up the phone, ask him to come in? But if I got Freda she

59

wouldn't just take a message. She'd demand to know chapter and verse and to hell with patient confidentiality. Solution: do a Buxton. Mull it over for an hour or two, make no hasty decisions, call in my next patient. Who happened to be Bill Mutch, another prostate case but not a life-threatening one.

He said, 'Has Buxton gone finally?'

'He still does a few surgeries. Would you rather see him?'

'No, you'll do. It's my toe.'

It took Bill a while to undo his shoelaces and haul off his thick grey sock. The big toe on his right foot was hot and red. He said his other foot was fine and his fingers were okay.

'Is it worse at night?'

'I'll say. Can't even stand the sheet touching it.'

'You know what this is? Gout.'

'Is it? I thought that was a rich man's disease.'

'It used to be, in the days when only rich men could afford beef and a nice bottle of red.'

'Don't tell me I've got to stop drinking.'

'Nothing so drastic. Just take more water with it. Do you eat a lot of meat?'

'Normal.'

'Every day?'

'Yes. What else am I supposed to eat?'

'Try to cut down on red meat. It might help.'

'The wife won't be very pleased. She makes a very good steak and kidney pie. Everything from scratch. Puff pastry, the works.'

'Does she? Then you're a lucky man. Maybe once a fortnight, for a treat? I'll give you a prescription for Colchicine but if it makes you feel nauseous or gives you the runs, stop taking it and we'll try something else.'

'Right you are. What's Buxton doing with himself now he's a part-timer? He must feel lost to death. This place has been his life.'

'He drops by for a natter, even when he's not seeing patients. And he's usually to be found in the Black Bear between the hours of six and seven.'

'I'd go and buy him a drink only it sounds as if I'll be on the lemonade.'

'I'll tell him I saw you. How are your dogs?'

'Trouble on eight legs. How do you know about my dogs?'

'Because you told me about them when I saw you last year.'

'Did I? Well top marks for remembering. I like that in a doctor. Buxton always remembered things. Not like some of them, bundling you out the door with a prescription. They hardly look you in the eye. You'll go far, young man.'

I was signing letters when my phone rang. Moira had Ron Jarrold on the line. My dithering time had expired.

I said, 'I was about to call you.'

First fib.

'I've finally got some answers.'

'Good. Did the letter arrive?'

'No, but I spoke to someone on Dr Green's firm and he filled me in.'

Ron blustered a bit about the state of the health service.

I said, 'So here's the thing. Dr Green is a urologist.'

'Bloody neurologist? Why has he got my letter? I've got back-ache not brain-ache.'

'No, a urologist. Waterworks. Because the X-ray showed you might have a problem with your prostate…'

Second fiblet.

'Good thing we did that blood test, then.'

'Yes. So when you go to the clinic next month, they'll arrange for you to have a biopsy.'

Silence.

'It's a very quick procedure. You should be in and out in under an hour.'

'How do you mean? Biopsy? Is it cancer?'

'We don't know. That's what the biopsy will determine.'

'They'll cut me open?'

'No, no. They give you a local anaesthetic and then take samples from your prostate gland.'

'How? How do they reach it?'

'Via the back passage.'

'Whoah!'

'You might be asked to have an enema the night before. As I say, it only takes a few minutes and you shouldn't feel a thing.'

'I will feel a thing. I'll feel mortified. There'll be nurses in there, looking at my bottom.'

I was about to say women endure far worse giving birth but then I remembered that the Jarrolds hadn't been blessed with children.

He said, 'I don't know as I want to go through with this. I only came to you about my back.'

'Yes, that's the other thing. The X-ray did show some abnormalities in the bones of your pelvis, possibly connected with the prostate problem. They'll talk to you about that when they see you.'

'And then they'll send me to see a back man?'

'More than likely.'

A sigh.

'And between them they'll be able to sort it all out.'

'That's the idea. A multi-disciplinary approach.'

If you're lucky. Whopper number three.

'So let me jot this down because Freda will want to look into it. I'll have a biopsy. Any special name?'

'Trans-rectal.'

'I don't care for the sound of that. And what did you say about my back?'

'It's more your hips than your back. There are some changes in the bone that need to be investigated.'

'Got it. Well thank you very much. You've been very helpful. I must say I haven't always had the best impression of you from the Patient Panel. You come across as a bit bored, not very dynamic, but I can't fault you on the way you've dealt with this. I shall give you a special mention next time I complete a Patient Satisfaction Survey.'

I bet he won't. Not after Freda's been on Google, joined up the dots and told him he's probably got metastatic cancer. But we don't know yet. The jury hasn't even retired. Those biopsies can give false negatives too. Should I have mentioned that? No. I'm just his GP. His trainee GP. It wasn't my job to set alarm bells ringing unnecessarily.

Pam was in the kitchen, raiding the biscuit tin. She knows Ron Jarrold from the Patient Panel. I told her Ron's story.

'He seemed more worried about the indignity of the biopsy procedure that he did about what it might show.'

'Funny the things that bother people,' she said. 'To me, Jarrold's the kind of chap who looks like he's sitting on a rectal probe, even when he's not.'

'How's the student?'

'Nice enough girl. I'm not sure she's cut out for General Practice though. No conversation. Anaesthetics might be more her line. Something where she doesn't need to engage. Does the name Dawn Beamish mean anything to you?'

63

'It does. She came back from Nigeria with malaria.'

'Yes. And guess what?

'Has she had a recurrence?'

'Not so far. No, Dawn's been to see me to find out about artificial insemination.'

'Would this be to do with getting her boyfriend a visa?'

'Correct. Bear his child and oil the immigration wheels.'

'How old is she?'

'She's 43. She might still have a few lay-able eggs.

'But why AI? Why doesn't she go back to Nigeria and try to get pregnant the usual way?'

'She didn't like it out there. I can't imagine why. So, she wanted to know, if the boyfriend spunks off into a jam jar and puts it in the post, would it still have signs of life by the time it got here?'

'And you said?'

'Not if your post deliveries are anything like mine. Five days for a letter to get from Nottingham to Himley Green.'

'It'd have to be frozen. Special refrigerated delivery by courier.'

'Yeah, right. Dan, we mustn't encourage these people. They come up with enough barmy ideas without our help. I told her the lifespan of sperm outside the body is variable and the only thing to do was give it a try. A pickle jar of none too fresh Nigerian semen and a turkey baster? Not a prayer.'

'Did she tell you her boyfriend's name?'

'I don't think she did.'

'It's God.'

'No.'

'Short for Godwin.'

'Nice. I like that. So if it works, it will truly be an Act of God.'

Helen appeared. She looked tired.

64

Pam said, 'Go home, woman. Glass of wine and a long hot soak. Tell Clifford to microwave his own bloody dinner. Have you done anything about getting a locum?'

'I'm thinking about it.'

'What is there to think about? Do it. At least until we know Mac's fate. If one of us gets sick, you'll be up you know where without a paddle.'

Helen said, 'I know. And Vaz just told me he's looking for a new job.'

'No!'

'He wants a practice nearer his girlfriend's work. I suppose you knew, Dan? You two are great friends.'

'I didn't know. Only that he's getting married in April.'

'It's so inconsiderate, the timing.'

'Well,' says Pam, 'in that case I definitely hear the sound of shit creek lapping at our door. Trevor'll be happy though. He'll have to do more hours. Anything to delay sinking into his dotage.'

Helen said she'd discuss the situation with Kasper in the morning.

She said, 'Dan, did you go to the Sorrento?'

'I did. Clarence Bliss. He's got bed sores that don't say much for the standard of care he's getting.'

'How often do they turn him?'

'They say every two hours, but I don't believe them. When I got there the staff were all in the day room watching Countdown and Clarence's pad was soaking wet, hadn't been changed for hours. I prescribed hydrocolloid dressings and told them he has to be moved every half hour.'

And in unison Pam and Helen said, 'Good luck with that.'

I found Trevor in the Black Bear.

'Ah,' he said, 'let me press you to a half of bitter.'

I didn't really want to drink.

'How did the spirometry appointment go?'

'Not bad. I only waited an hour. Today's advice was "stay active". Last time it was "ease up". What excitement have I missed today?'

'Vaz is leaving.'

'Yes.'

'You knew?'

'He was nervous about telling Helen, so he came to me. I told him, she's the boss now. Don't fanny around, don't let her smell fear. Just go in and tell her.'

'Pretty much what Pam Parker said about me getting time off to prepare for my CSA. Don't ask, just tell Helen it has to happen.'

'She's right. And if Helen gives you any grief, I'll back you up. I suspect I owe you anyway. I've not done much to bring you on.'

The fact is, I've learned a lot from Trevor, although it might not be the kind of stuff they test you on.

He said if he were running the practice he wouldn't waste time with locums. He'd be advertising for a replacement for Vaz and probably one for Mac too.

'About Mac? He's a partner, right? There are legal implications, if he has to leave?'

'Yes, there's a deed of partnership. As I recall, Clifford Vincent drew it up.'

'That was what I thought. And are you still a partner?'

'Good question,' he said. 'Complicated things partnerships. How about a shandy or a Britvic?'

Sometimes Trevor changes the subject or acts vague because he doesn't want to give you an answer, sometimes it's because he can't.

'Nothing to entertain me this evening? You're a disappointment, Dan. I might as well go home and watch the telly.'

'Okay. Dawn Beamish?'

'Remind me?'

'Middle-aged woman with a Nigerian toy boy.'

'Dawn. Of course. How could I forget. Now what?'

'She went to see Pam Parker. She wants to have a baby.'

'Good grief, she must be older than Eve.'

'Pam says she's only 43.'

'A lot of clicks on her odometer, though. So is the boyfriend over here now?'

'No, that's the thing. She wants to try inseminating herself. She went to see Pam to find out if semen would be viable if he posted her a sample.'

He braced himself against the edge of the table, trying to talk and laugh at the same time.

'Help us and save us,' he said. 'Will he be sending it airmail, I wonder? Or FedEx?'

He wiped his eyes.

He said, 'I sometimes think Pam gets more than her fair share of fun. Anything else?'

'Only depressing news.'

'Go on. I can take it.'

I told him about Ron Jarrold.

'That doesn't sound too good. They're an annoying pair, him and Freda, but still.'

'And we've got a patient in the Sorrento with pressure sores. Clarence Bliss. There was nothing recent in his file so I don't even know when Mac last saw him.'

'Another black mark against Mac?'

'He might have forgotten to update the file.'

'Definitely a black mark against the Sorrento. Bloody nursing homes. I swear I'd sooner top myself.'

'That's very much what Mac once said to me. One last question.'

'As long as it's not about Mac or lawyers.'

'Calcaneal spurs.'

'Very painful, can be.'

'I had Mark Povey in this morning, asking for a steroid injection. What do you think?'

'Not worth the grief. I did do a couple, years ago and they were absolute belters. They must have heard the screams in West Bromwich. Not my scene at all. If I'd wanted to inflict pain, I'd have become a dentist. What did you tell him?'

'Ice pack, rest, Neurofen, calf stretches.'

'Quite right. Send him to a sports' injury clinic if he goes on about an injection.'

Chapter 8

The plan had been to drive down to Chloe's parents, put in an appearance at church to mollify the vicar and have lunch at The Chummery. Then Chloe announced she had to work on Sunday. She said she had no choice, but I think she'd volunteered. Chloe can wriggle out of anything she really doesn't want to do. I said I'd go anyway.

She said, 'What, without me? Why?'

'Because we need to keep the vicar onside. Besides, if you're working I'll be stuck here on my own all day.'

She said, 'Okay, but don't sign us up for any stupid marriage courses. And don't go upsetting Mummy and Daddy.'

That annoyed me. Not only am I a well-mannered, sensitive bloke, I also get on pretty well with Vinnie and Laurence.

'Why would I upset them?'

'By doom-mongering about Slow's court case.'

'Do you think he'll be there?'

'I doubt it. He doesn't really do Sundays.'

'Still under the Saturday night influence?'

'See, that's what I mean. You talk as though this cocaine incident defines him. But he's a hugely successful businessman.'

To me Charlie Swift is a high-rolling twerp stuck in permanent adolescence. He just happened to have found a way of making pots of money. But I let it go. Her brother may exasperate her sometimes, but she loves him.

St Botolph's is a pretty church. Lych-gate, old gravestones, the works. You can see its tower from the upstairs windows at The Chummery. There had been talk of Laurence and Chloe processing there on foot but that idea was kiboshed because of potential mud issues and Chloe's very expensive wedding shoes. The last I'd heard, Charlie was supposed to be sourcing a vintage Cadillac.

I introduced myself to the vicar.

'Rector,' he said. 'Not vicar. Different species altogether.'

As instructed, I explained that Chloe often worked weekends. He said he quite understood and not to worry, there was still plenty of time, and if we couldn't manage any of his scheduled Preparing for Marriage sessions, he was more than willing to see us privately, at our convenience.

When I got to The Chummery the dining room table was laid but there was no smell of roasting meat. Flo and Henry and the children were expected. Vinnie offered me a coffee and then spotted a cup she'd made for Laurence and he'd allowed to go cold, so she bunged that in the microwave for me.

'It was jolly pi of you to go to church. How was it?'

'Lovely. The rector was disappointed not to see Chloe.'

'Was he? Why?'

'Well we are getting married in his church.'

'He's not been there long and he's a bit of a stickler, apparently. Laurence, you should have him over for a drink, put him straight about a few things. Nicely, but firmly.'

70

I said I thought the best thing, in terms of the wedding, was to go along with whatever the rector wished.

'Really?' says Vinnie. 'Is that how they do things in Wales?'

The Packwoods arrived. Chloe's sister Flora is married to Henry Packwood. They have three daughters. Poppy, Daisy and Lily.

Flo's first words were, 'How long till lunch? The girls are starving and you know how cranky they get.'

Her children's blood sugar levels have nothing to do with their behaviour. Full stomach, empty stomach, they do as they please.

Vinnie said, 'We can eat as soon as you like. I thought we'd have a salad. Roasts are such a faff.'

Lily announced that she hated salad and Poppy mimed throwing up.

Vinnie said, 'Then Granny will see if she can find you some chicken dippers.'

Daisy said, 'Why do you call yourself 'granny'? Why don't you just say 'I'?'

Which was ignored although I thought it was a good question. I said I'd take a few chicken dippers too, if there were any. That was ignored as well.

Henry is a man of even fewer words than my Da. It must be to do with working with animals. With Da, conversation has to be about livestock, preferably sheep. With Henry it's pigs.

I said, 'Last time I saw you, when we were here for Laurence's birthday, you had two sows about to farrow.'

'Gilts, actually,' he said. 'Not sows.'

'Everything go according to plan?'

'Oh yes.'

'Thank you for your offer of a hog roast, by the way. Very generous. It's very much appreciated.'

'Pleasure,' he said, and stood and looked rather glumly at the lettuce and tomatoes Vinnie had just fetched from the fridge.

Flo said, 'Granny and Grandpa not coming?'

'No,' says Vinnie. 'Since this new manager took over, they get Yorkshire pudding and all the trimmings on Sundays, so they prefer not to miss lunch.'

'And why isn't Chlo here?'

'She's working.'

'A likely tale. I thought she got some jammy private job.'

I said, 'She still works very hard, let me tell you.'

'Ha!' says Flo. 'She should try being a farmer's wife. That's hard work. I was rather expecting to see her and sort out the girls' dresses for the wedding.'

Henry uttered a gentle groan. He knew what was coming.

Poppy said, 'I'm not wearing a dress. I'm wearing dungarees. Aunt Chlo said I could.'

Vinnie said, 'Darling, I don't think she did. She merely didn't argue with you when you said that's what you wanted to wear. It's not the same thing at all.'

Flo said she hadn't even been told what the colour scheme was.

I said, 'I can help you there. It's sage, ivory and indigo.'

Vinnie said, 'Gosh, are you sure? That sounds like something one might stuff into a turkey. And Dan, who is this Dee person? If Chloe must have an older attendant, she has plenty of attractive cousins to choose from, or even Flo.'

Flo said she wouldn't do it at any price. Vinnie said she didn't see why not. After all, Chloe had been one of her attendants.

'Chlo enjoys getting guyed up in silly, impractical frocks. I don't.'

72

I said, 'Dee is an Australian doctor she knows from the Queen Elizabeth. Obs and Gynae.'

'If she's a doctor,' says Vinnie, 'then I suppose at least she'll be a sensible, reliable sort of person.'

I didn't disabuse her of this idea. The mother of the bride has enough to worry about without anyone seeding doubts about the steadiness of the chief bridesmaid. Besides, I hadn't actually seen Dee since the night she got roaring drunk and offended just about everyone at our kitchen table. She might have calmed down. Stopped drinking, even. Who was I kidding?

'Does she have a husband?'

'She's single.'

'A boyfriend? A plus one?'

'Not that I know of.'

Vinnie looked at me.

She said, 'What's wrong with her? Is she fearfully plain?'

'No.'

'Oh God, she's not gay is she?'

Lily wanted to know what gay meant.

Poppy said it meant boys who snog boys. Daisy said, 'No it doesn't. It means pretty and sparkly.'

Flo said, 'What I want to know is what the girls are meant to wear if the colours are sage and onion?'

We sat down to lunch and Henry resumed his pig talk. Prices for stores and weaners had been sharp at the Rugby market. I reminded him that my Da's an auctioneer.

'Ah, yes,' he said. 'Sheep.'

Well, come the wedding, perhaps they can just sit in companionable silence.

Poppy said, 'Uncle Dan, what kind of doctor are you?'

'I'm a GP.'

'Like Dr Redding?'

'Is that who you go to?'

'Grandpoppa says he's a country bumpkin. Grandpoppa's a London doctor.'

Daisy said, 'We don't like Dr Redding. He's a grump. You have to sit still and not touch anything.'

'Quite right. I'm just the same. I growl at children who don't sit quietly.'

She thought that was very funny.

Lily said she was still hungry. So was I, and Laurence had very deftly nabbed the last slice of ham. No rhubarb crumble or apple pie for afters at The Chummery. It's no wonder Vinnie is so lean. She and Flo and the girls went off in search of biscuits, Laurence had to take a phone call and Henry and I ended up in alone at the table, awaiting coffee that was promised but never arrived. I asked if there was any news on Charlie.

'No idea,' says Henry.

'Vinnie does realise he'll go to prison?'

'She believes Laurence has things in hand.'

'Even Laurence has his limits.'

'Yes. Prison. That may be a first for the Swifts. They say one of my Packwood ancestors was hanged. Nineteenth century, though, so not terribly remarkable.'

'Chloe's anxious about it spoiling the wedding.'

'Really? I imagine one can get hitched without any help from Charlie. By the by, it comes with all the trimmings.'

'Sorry?'

'The hog roast. Crackling, stuffing, apple sauce, potato salad, coleslaw.'

'You're making my mouth water.'

He laughed, helped himself to a couple of sugar lumps and pushed the bowl across to me.

He said, 'If you hurry you might catch last lunch orders at the Horn and Trumpet.'

Chapter 9

I love my work. No two days are ever the same, but sometimes it can feel as if they are. That week I had a case of athlete's foot at every surgery. Well, with Karl Guest it was jock-itch, but it amounts to the same thing. Every day I heard myself saying that they could buy an anti-fungal powder over the counter for less than the cost of a prescription and every time I got the same reply: they were on the Social and got their prescriptions free.

Maisie Hastilow was my last patient of the morning. She had tonsillitis. Usually it's viral so they just need to ride it out, but Maisie was only six, the lymph glands in her neck were slightly swollen and she had a bit of ooze on her tonsils. I decided to check for strep throat. When I went to fetch a Strep Test from the nurses' fridge I bumped into Helen.

'Bloody ridiculous,' she said. 'And I have you to thank for this.'

And she stormed out of the front door.

Mary and Kasper were in Reception.

I said, 'What did I do?'

Mary smiled.

She said, 'It's His Nibs. Miles. He's frit to come inside in case he sees you. Best day's work you ever did.'

I'd wondered why I hadn't seen Helen's son recently. He used to be a regular, demanding money from his Mum, effing and blinding and treating everyone like shit.

Kasper said, 'What did you do, Dan?'

I couldn't really take full credit. Pam Parker was the instigator and I was just an accessory to the act.

'It was at the Christmas party. Miles was being his usual charming self to Pam's father-in-law. Nice old chap with a touch of Alzheimer's. So Pam grabbed Miles in a bear hug and I palpated his testicles, at her suggestion. Discreetly but firmly.'

Mary said, 'Pale as death, he turned. Then his Dad took him home, and good riddance.'

Kasper said he couldn't wait for the next Christmas party. I think I may be gone by then.

Taking a throat swab from a child can be difficult but Trevor had given me a tip: get them to show you how loud they can shout. But Maisie needed no such coaxing. She opened wide and didn't gag and while we waited for the test to show she stood right by my side with her hand on my knee. She was a sweet little thing. The test showed negative. I prescribed iced lollies and gave her a smiley sticker for being a brave girl.

Her mother said, 'What do you say to the nice doctor?'

Maisie lisped, 'thank you' and gave me a kiss.

Paediatrics was one of my weaker areas and I'd already decided to try and attend a few clinics at the Children's Hospital, but that day didn't seem an auspicious one to ask Helen for time off. You never know with Helen, though. Her moods are like April showers. By the time I got back from house calls she was feeling sufficiently well-disposed to offer to make me a coffee. We talked shop a little. She said she was holding off making any staffing decisions because there was only a week to go till Mac's tribunal.

Bruce Macdonald was a doctor of previously good standing but with the business of his buying Hilda Ruck's house there was clearly a conflict of interest and even if Miss Ruck hadn't felt under any pressure, an important boundary had been crossed. He couldn't be her physician and the son she'd never had. The tribunal had to decide whether his fitness to practice was impaired. If it was, he might get a suspension, maybe six months or a year. But he might be permanently struck off the register.

Helen said a lot depended on Mac's attitude. If he showed some insight, some willingness to acknowledge that his behaviour had been less than professional, he could walk away with just a warning. That was what she hoped would happen.

She said, 'I think he's learned his lesson. I think he'll soon be back on the team.'

I said, 'I hope so. I don't mind taking on more work, but I do need prep time for my MRCGP. I'd like to go to some out-patient clinics, fill a few gaps.'

She was quiet for a moment. Sometimes I think she forgets I'm her trainee. Then she said, 'Excellent idea. Let me know if you want me to make any calls.'

The storm had passed, though not for long.

Moira brought in the files for afternoon surgery.

She said, 'He got himself a job, then. And not before time.'

'Who?'

'Dr Helen's lad. He's starting a job.'

'That's good news. What's he doing?'

'Sandwich deliveries, for Crusts & Co. I suppose she'll be expecting us to order from them. Bump business up for him.'

Beverley Knight was a 67-year-old retired shop assistant, slim, brisk, smartly dressed. She'd been experiencing palpitations and episodes of feeling light-headed, but suspected she was wasting my time. She was teetotal, only drank decaf and as far as she knew had no family history of heart disease.

'I was adopted,' she said. 'So your guess is as good as mine.'

She hadn't had any blackouts or chest pain. She was active, did a salsa class twice a week, had no swelling in her ankles. I said we'd take some blood, to check her thyroid function, and do an ECG. I knew Nurse Chris was on duty and she's aces at ECGs. I took Beverley through to the nurses' room.

Chris said, 'Do you want to stay and do it, Dr Talbot?'

I said, 'No, you do it and I'll get on and see my next patient.'

She gave me an old-fashioned look. She knows I take forever, checking and double-checking the leads.

Victor Bellhanger was my next patient. His wife had brought him in. He had a lesion on the side of his nose.

'Dragging me in here,' he said. 'It's only a pimple.'

'It's not a pimple,' says Mrs Bellhanger. 'It's an eyesore and you will keep picking at it.'

It was another of those situations where we use a checklist. How long had he had it? Had it grown? A week or two, he said. 'More like a month or two, she said. Did it itch? He said not. She said in that case why did he keep scratching it?

Victor's lesion was red, 7 or 8 millimetres across, crusting. My money was on a basal cell carcinoma. The question was, whether to funnel him into the urgent, 2-week referral queue or let him take his chances with the normal waiting list.

His wife said, 'Can you nip it off, Doctor?'

'No, he bloody can't, woman,' says Victor. 'How would you like somebody nipping at your nose?'

'Wouldn't bother me,' she said. 'I've gave birth to three babs.'

I said, 'Don't worry, Victor, it's not a job for me. You need to see a dermatologist.'

'Oh yes?' he said. 'And how long's that going to take?'

Decision time. A male, in his late 70s. Mr Bellhanger was in a high-risk category. Did he warrant an urgent referral? I thought he did.

Nurse Chris brought Beverley Knight's ECG trace for me to look at.

'See the shape of the base line?'

'Saw-tooth.'

'Yes.'

'Atrial flutter?'

'Yes, classic.'

'Send her back to me. I'll refer her for a cardio appointment.'

Beverley said, 'Is it serious?'

'It needs investigating.'

'I've always kept myself fit.'

'Sometimes it's just wear and tear. Three billion beats in a lifetime. When you think about it, it's little short of a miracle.'

'Is there anything I can take for it?'

I was going to say I'd leave that for the cardiologist to decide, then I hesitated. I asked her to wait while I checked something with Helen.

Helen listened to the history. With atrial flutter there is the risk of thrombosis. Should I prescribe warfarin?

'Yes. No.'

'So it's a no?'

'It's a tricky one. Leave it to the cardio. Start her on low-dose aspirin, as a precaution. Can you work on Good Friday?'

'I thought we were closed.'

'Used to be, under Trevor's regime, but I'm sure it was only because that's what his father did. Anyway, our waiting time for appointments is getting too long so I've decided we'll have to work. We'll give you the Tuesday off in lieu, if that helps.'

'I don't know. We're going down to my folks for Easter but Chloe's working that Tuesday, so we'd have to be back Monday night anyway.'

Big sigh.

'Then Vaz'll have to cover. He'll just have to forgo his religious stuff.'

'On Good Friday? He'll be upset about that. Okay, I'll work till 12.00.'

'Brilliant. You'll have Trevor for backup.'

'You going away?'

'Chester. A spa break. Golf for Cliff and pampering for me.'

So Beverley Knight got a referral to cardiology, Victor Bellhanger got a referral to dermatology and Vaz's holy day got salvaged from Helen Vincent's vandalism. A good day's work, and I wasn't finished. When I have an evening shift at Out of Hours, I usually make myself a bite to eat and catch up on paperwork until it's time to set off.

Vaz and I were in the kitchen. He'd been for a second interview with a practice in Wolverhampton and was very

81

optimistic. Teresa works at a school in Wednesfield so that was where they planned on buying a house. Everything was falling into place for Vaz. Even his wedding was sorted. Registry office at 12.30, then everybody round to a brasserie for lunch, sixteen people max. Vaz and Teresa were booked on an evening flight to Dublin, picking up a hire car and driving down to Wexford. They were having a honeymoon week in a cosy cottage so they could visit Teresa's Nan who wasn't well enough to travel to the wedding. I quite envied him.

Trevor came in. It was late in the day for him to be around.

'Ah,' he said, 'our future guardians of the nation's health. You may wish to hang around for some breaking news, or you might prefer to slip away quietly.'

'Not good news?'

'No. So if you're staying, probably time to put on your hardhats.'

He tapped at Helen's door and went in.

Vaz said, 'What is a hardhat?'

Then Kasper arrived. He's never around on a Thursday. It's his day for the other practice.

I said, 'What's up?'

He shrugged and went into Helen's office. I called Sterling to tell them I was running late. I couldn't leave without finding out what was going on. I walked past Helen's door a couple of times but couldn't hear anything. There were no raised voices. No blood seeping under the door. It was just before seven when the meeting broke up. Vaz had given up and gone home.

Kasper was first out. All he said was, 'Tell you tomorrow.'

Then Trevor.

I said, 'Shit? Fan?'

'Black Bear. Large Scotch,' he said, and left.

Helen said, 'Why are you still here?'

'I've got an Out of Hours shift. I'm just leaving.'

'Right. Well you may as well know, Mac's leaving us.'

'He had his tribunal?'

'No. But there have been two more allegations. He's decided to take early retirement.'

'More Hilda Ruck scenarios?'

'Yes. A woman in the Waterdene nursing home who'd sold him an apartment on the Algarve, allegedly. The family are saying he got it for well under its true value, but you know people often delude themselves about what property's worth. They have these big expectations.'

'What does Mac say?'

'He's not denying it. He's had enough. Holding his hands up and walking away. I didn't even know he owned that place on the Algarve. I thought he rented it, the sneaky bastard.'

'What's the other allegation?'

'A crappy little terraced house that belonged to some old lady who was in Sunny Arbour.'

'Where's Sunny Arbour?'

'It closed down a couple of years ago. The company who ran it went bust. See, word gets around, people have heard about the Ruck business. These relatives, why didn't they raise their concerns before?'

'But three properties that belonged to patients? It's not right, is it?'

'One was a gift Dan, and he bought the other two. And where were these relatives when that happened? If they think he didn't pay a fair price, why didn't they speak up then? No, this is a case of kicking a man when he's down. Mac's a bloody good doctor. Anyway, he's going. Nothing I can do about it. His mind's made up. We're dissolving the partnership.'

'And will you look for a new partner?'

'Might do. It's all a bit messy with Trevor still clinging on. I might just hire a salaried doctor.'

'Or two? With Vaz leaving?'

'Yes, or two. Are you interested?'

'Me? I'm not even registered yet.'

'But you will be by the end of the year.'

'I don't want to count my chickens.'

'Okay. But think about it.'

Which I did, all the way to the Sterling call centre, every time the phones were quiet and when I woke in the night and couldn't get back to sleep. If I passed my MRCGP, did I want to stay on at the Lindens. Thirty years from now, did I want to be like Trevor Buxton? There were worse prospects. In spite of everything he seemed a contented man. His patients loved him and those he didn't love back, he at least found entertaining.

Chloe wouldn't like it though. She wanted me to work somewhere leafy and genteel. Edgbaston was on her radar. Or somewhere like Leamington Spa, where her Orde-Sykes grandparents lived. And what did I want? When I joined The Lindens I'd seen it as a challenge, as the kind of medicine where I could really make a difference with good, solid primary care, guiding patients towards a healthier lifestyle.

What had Trevor said? 'Our patients don't have a lifestyle, Dan. Not on Brook Glen and Cherry Tree. Booze, drugs, dumb, impulsive choices. Chaos is the word.'

He wasn't wrong. And was I growing a little weary of the Kyle Bibbys and Amber Evanses?

Chloe was talking in her sleep. 'Apple sauce,' she said. 'Chair covers.'

Vexed wedding dreams.

Chapter 10

The week before Vaz's departure for his new job we got back to full staffing strength at the Lindens. Jean and Harold Boddy, a husband and wife team, joined the practice. Pam Parker thought it was a good thing. Trevor thought it was a very good thing.

'Just what the practice needs,' he said. 'Two steady pairs of hands. No dramas, no shouting matches. Mind you, Helen could start a fight in an empty room. And Brook Glen won't faze the Boddys, the things they must have coped with.'

Jean and Harold were in their early fifties and recently returned from Africa. They'd been in the Congo, Democratic Republic of, for nearly twenty years and had come back to England to care for Jean's elderly father. Within a week of their arrival he'd died, which left them at a loose end. I asked Harold whether they'd thought of going back to Africa.

'We considered it,' he said, 'but frankly Jean's had enough. She's tired. It takes its toll.'

Which was pretty much what Jean said, except that in her version it was Harold who'd had enough. She said their work out there had been like trying to carry water when there's a hole in the bucket. I knew there was a big problem in Africa with HIV and AIDs.

She said, 'That's more in Kinshasa and the other cities. The women gravitate there to be sex workers. They see it as a career opportunity. But we were out in the sticks, dealing with their orphans.'

'Is malaria a problem?'

'A big problem. Malaria, dengue, yellow fever, Ebola occasionally, malnutrition. But malaria's the main killer, especially with the kids.'

'We've got a patient with malaria. She went to Nigeria without taking any prophylaxis.'

'People do. I've stopped underestimating their recklessness. Harold's more forgiving than I am.'

I told her we see a lot of cases of progressive incurable stupidity. She laughed.

'That's exactly what Trevor said.'

Yet another indication that I might be turning into a Trevor Buxton.

Legend Busby looked a bit better, but he still wasn't right. It takes time to recover from glandular fever and I thought he looked very slightly jaundiced. His Mum wanted him to go back to school.

She said, 'It's getting on my pippin having him at home all the time.'

I examined him. His lymph nodes were still up. He flinched when I palpated his spleen. That was a new development.

I said, 'Have you been resting, like I told you?'

'Mostly,' he said.

I looked across at his mother but she was checking her phone. I did a Trevor, folded my arms and waited until I had her attention.

'What?' she said.

'Has Legend been resting? Properly resting?'

'Yes.'

'He's not been out with his mates? I know he misses his football.'

'Ledge,' she said, 'have you been going out when my back's turned?'

Legend was zipping up his jeans and looking at the floor.

All he said was, 'Mum! You know I never.'

A 15-year-old boy, cooped up for weeks, or his care-worn mother, who are you going to believe? I had a strong inclination to go with Legend. I couldn't say why.

I said, 'Well here's the thing. I'm concerned that his lymph glands are still enlarged so I think we'll do some blood tests today. Sit tight and I'll see if the nurse is free.'

Chris was on duty. Perfect. She has teenage boys herself. I told her the story, asked her to take her time over the bloods and chat to Legend, see what he'd been up to. I kept his mother in with me. Karen Checkitts. Legend's surname is Busby so I suppose there was a Mr Busby at some point.

I said, 'I think his spleen has taken a knock. Could he have been playing football?'

'I'll bet he has,' she said. 'I mean, I can't watch him every minute. I'm working.'

That hadn't occurred to me. It's a rare Cherry Tree resident who goes to work. She said she was a dinner lady at Ocker Hill Secondary.

'He's at home alone quite a lot, then?'

'Craig's there.'

'Who's Craig?'

'My partner.'

'Legend's Dad?'

'No.'

'He's not working?'

'He's got Fatigue Syndrome.'

'So he's around, to make sure Legend rests properly?'

'He can't be there all the time. He might have to go out to the shop, get something for us dinners, or go fetch his benefit. He's not a babysitter.'

Nurse Chris delivered Legend back to us.

'All done,' she said, 'and he didn't feel a thing. I resisted the temptation to cause him pain, even if he is an Albion fan.'

Chris and her family are Wolves supporters so West Bromwich Albion are regarded as the enemy. Legend gave her a shy smile.

'And I've told him, no footie, no contact sports of any kind until the infection's burned itself out. He'll never make it into the Premier League if he's ruined his liver.'

Chris and I talked later.

'Nice kid,' she said. 'He swore he hadn't been playing football but there had been a bit of rough-housing with the mother's boyfriend.'

'Rough-housing?'

'He called it wrestling.'

'Okay. What do you think?'

'Lads do like to wrestle. It's probably good for them. Natural, like. My three are always play fighting. And my husband. He's the biggest kid of all. I'll bet you were the same.'

I wasn't, really. Da's not the wrestling type. Grandad Talbot used to do a spot of rugby training with me, but he died when

I was eleven. And my brother hated anything like that. Some days Adam'd have a fit if I even looked at him, let alone touched him.

Chris said, 'I'd just keep an eye. He's not a strong boy, not a lot of muscle on him for his age. For all we know the boyfriend could be Son of Big Daddy.'

Good Friday dawned bitterly cold. There was snow forecast for some regions but in Oldbury we just had horizontal sleet. Chloe wasn't happy about me having to work till lunchtime. For her it was another reason not to be a GP. The Arden Clinic where she worked was closed till Tuesday. Its patients scheduled their consultations to the mutual convenience of themselves and the doctors and Easter was a good time to get out onto the golf course.

There were three of us on duty. Me, Pam Parker and Harold Boddy, plus Nurse Linda. When I got in there was a little conference going on in Reception.

Pam said, 'Have you heard? We're changing our name. New sign going up next week.'

'We won't be The Lindens?'

'Never no more. Care to guess what we're going to be? Don't bother. Life's too short. We'll be the Tipton Road West Medical Centre.'

Mary was on Reception. She shook her head.

'After more than seventy years,' was all she'd say.

'Doesn't exactly trip off the tongue, does it?'

'It doesn't. And think of the opportunities it's going to afford the sign monkeys. All those extra letters to play with.'

'What does Trevor say about it?'

'No idea. I hope he's been kept informed. I hope Helen broke it to him gently.'

Mary said, 'How are we meant to answer the phone with a blummin' great mouthful like that? And the patients won't remember. They'll still think of us as The Lindens. It'll be such a muddle.'

Pam said, 'Don't worry, pet. Just go along with it when Helen's within earshot. I suppose we have Mac to thank for this.'

And as she said his name, the man himself appeared. He'd come in to pick up his things, thinking the place would be empty and he'd be able to slip in and out unnoticed.

'What's this?' he said. 'Working on Good Friday, ye poor beggars?'

It was the first time I'd seen him since he'd announced he'd retire rather than be struck off. Why did I feel embarrassed? Mac didn't appear to be.

Pam said, 'Yes, we are working. We don't all have an ill-gotten property portfolio we can live off. Your bits and pieces are in a box in the Filing cupboard. Right, into the fray.'

And she walked away.

Linda started crying. She said, 'It doesn't seem right, Mac. You should have been given a fair hearing.'

'Didn't want one,' he said. 'I'd sooner jump than be pushed. Helen's not in, I hope.'

Mary said, 'She's gone away for Easter. Gone to dream up some more barmy changes.'

Linda held out her arms for a farewell kiss from Mac. A 'goodbye huggle' she called it.

'Away with ye, woman,' says Mac, and gave her a peck on the cheek.

So, the Lindens was about to become the Tipton Road West Medical Centre. Helen felt that recent events had tainted our previously good name. First there had been the sad case of little Usman Okeke, a baby who bled to death after a botched circumcision on someone's kitchen table. We weren't in any way culpable. Trevor had referred the mother to our local hospital. I'd witnessed it myself. But she'd chosen to ignore his advice and the Lindens' name got dragged into the drama. We'd even had TV cameras outside for a few hours. And then there was Mac's scandal hanging over us. Helen wanted a new identity for the practice, her practice, as she now saw it.

There was an unexpected name on my list. Peter Allsop. I'd met him before but not as a patient. Only as the begrudging husband of Glenys, our liver transplant success story. Glenys Allsop's story is one of those that if ever I have trainees under me, I know I'll recount. It was a classic case of a patient failing to mention something because they're embarrassed. I'd have missed it but Trevor, for all his bumbling, seemingly unfocused ways, he'd detected it and allowed Glenys those vital extra seconds to get around to mentioning the colour of her stools.

Pete Allsop came straight to the point.

He said, 'It's Glenys. I'm at my wits' end.'

I hadn't actually seen Glenys since her surgery because she was still getting aftercare from the hospital, but from everything I'd been told she was making a brilliant recovery. I asked Pete if there had been a setback.

'Not the kind you mean,' he said. 'But she's not my Glenys anymore.'

He counted things off on his fingers. She'd become loud and silly. She took unnecessary risks.

'Such as?'

'Going on Oblivion.'

'What's that?'

91

'Roller coaster at Alton Towers. Her sister took her. Mental, the pair of them.'

Pete still had an unlabelled finger raised.

'Anything else?'

'Sex.' He said it very quietly.

I said, 'Well she is still recovering from major surgery.'

'No,' he said, 'that's not what I mean. She's gone sex-mad. And some of the things she comes out with. I mean, she was brought up strict chapel.'

It was hard to imagine little beige Glenys demanding wild sex but who's to say.

Pete pulled his chair up closer to the desk.

'Want to know what I think?' he said. 'She's possessed. That liver they gave her? It's got a demon in it.'

I was at a loss. What did Pete want me to do about his new-style wife? He told me.

'You need to talk to the hospital. They should have her in, whip that liver out and give her one they can vouch for. I mean, we don't know who hers came from. I've asked and I've asked but they won't tell me.'

'There are reasons for that, Pete. You have to bear in mind, whoever Glenys's new liver came from, it was some family's loved one. It's only been a few months. They'll still be grieving. Your gain has been their loss.'

'But has it been a gain?

That did it. I should have been well on the way to Wales for my Easter break but instead I was sitting in Tipton listening to the ravings of an ungrateful whiner whose wife, gravely ill not so long ago, now wanted more sex.

I said, 'Of course it's been a gain. Glenys had progressive biliary cholangitis. Without a transplant she would have become very, very sick and died.'

He was silent. Had I been too harsh? Then he said, 'So you say.'

'More to the point, so said the liver experts. Which means that instead of facing a future without her, you've had your wife restored to you, and in good health by the sound of it. Count your blessings, Pete.'

That got rid of him. His final words were, 'She's possessed, I'm telling you. You needn't think you've heard the last of this.'

My phone had been buzzing in my pocket. Messages from Chloe. What time would I be home? Should she pack a hot water bottle? And what about wellies? I called her.

'Wellies, yes, why not. No need for a hottie, though. Mam keeps a warm house. I've got two more patients to see and I want to have a quick word with Trevor, then I'll be on my way.'

'Must you? He'll drag you to the pub. At this rate it'll be dark by the time we get to Abergavenny.'

'So what? They do have street lights, you know.'

Chloe's first visit to the place I grew up. Just an ordinary little house on an ordinary street in a nice little town. And only her second time of being with Mam and Da. Though she wouldn't admit it, I think she was slightly nervous. I certainly was. I wanted everyone to like each other.

Trevor answered on the second ring.

'Young Dan Talbot,' he said. 'Do you need me to come in? I can be there in ten minutes.'

He was quite disappointed that I wasn't looking for a second clinical opinion.

I said, 'I've just had a conversation I thought you might enjoy.'

'Ooh good,' he said. 'I'm sitting down. Fire away.'

'Pete Allsop. Glenys's husband?'

'Plonker Allsop. Go on.'

'He says Glenys has undergone a change of personality since she got her new liver. It sounds as though she's become more vivacious and adventurous.'

'Of course she has. She'd been feeling crap for ages, then she got a death sentence. Now the cloud has lifted.'

'He says she wants sex all the time.'

'Lucky man. He came in to tell you that?'

'He came in to complain. He thinks she's possessed by some kind of transplant demon, from the donor, I suppose.'

'And he wants his money back.'

'Something like that.

He laughed.

He said, 'Well not to pour too much scorn on Pete, you do hear stories like that about heart transplants. You know, people changing, developing interests they never had before? But livers? I don't think so. When are you off?'

'Now.'

'Have a good one.'

Pam Parker walked out of the building with me. She said the only plan she had for Easter was to work her way through a stash of chocolate eggs.

She said, 'They're in the linen cupboard in our bathroom. The only person who ever looks in there is my cleaning lady and she's gone to Gdansk for the week. I'll be able to lock myself in and eat them without getting any reproachful looks.'

Trevor called me as I was pulling in at home.

'Dan,' he said, 'I've been thinking about Glenys Allsop. Did it ever cross your mind whose liver she might have been given?'

'Not really. Nobody on our books, that I know of.'

94

'Not on our books, but not a million miles away. A member of the wider Bibby-Dearlove tribe?'

'You mean Chad Dearlove?'

'The dates would be about right.'

'Yes.'

'Not that we believe for one minute that Chad's soul could still be hanging around in his recycled liver.'

'No.'

'Gradually colonising her brain cells. Turning her into a Chad Mark II, but in a cardigan and pleated skirt.'

'No.'

'Interesting possibility though, isn't it? Have a nice weekend.'

And he was gone.

Chapter 11

We got to Abergavenny at around five. Mam had been watching out for us and came running out with an umbrella. Da was on the doorstep. There was a funny little shuffle between Mam and Chloe, not sure whether they should kiss or hug, and I'm pretty sure I saw Mam stifling the urge to curtsey. Then she bundled Chloe indoors and Da came out to help me with our bags. He was wearing his old slippers, not the ones I'd bought him for Christmas.

I said, 'What happened to your Sean the Sheeps?'

'In the wardrobe,' he said. 'Too good to wear.'

Which Mam confirmed.

She said, 'He's keeping them for best.'

I hadn't discussed sleeping arrangements with Chloe. I knew Mam was uncomfortable with us sharing a bed in her house before we were married. I was quite expecting to bunk down on Aunty June's air bed. But then Mam made an announcement.

She said, 'Now what it is, I've put you both in Dan and Adam's old room because I know that's how it's done these days, only I don't want your Nan to find out because she'd be scandalised. So you'll see June's Li-Lo pumped up on the landing, just in case Nan goes upstairs to use the lav and starts poking around. Which she probably won't because she's not too good on the stairs these days. She generally crosses her legs till she gets home. But there we are. There's no sense pretending you don't sleep together when you're at home so me and your Da decided we'd better move with the times.'

I said, 'I thought you were the generation that did away with all those old rules?'

Da said, 'No comment,' and Mam said, 'Now who'd like a cup of tea?'

I took our bags upstairs. Not only were we being allowed to share a room, but the two singles had been pushed together and on each pillow there was one of those individually wrapped Raffaello sweets. Since she and Da had been on that romantic Cotswold hotel mini-break she'd evidently decided to raise the bar on hospitality at 17 Northcrest.

Chloe and Mam were in the kitchen, getting the measure of one another. Da was trying to think of something to say to me. We'd already covered traffic on the M50, roadworks on the A40 and the price cull ewes had fetched at the Builth auction. I asked how Nan was.

'Fair to middling,' he said.

'And she'll be coming here? Sunday roast?'

'Sure to,' he said. 'But your Mam has all the particulars.'

She did. She had an itinerary mapped out.

'Now tomorrow,' she said, 'you'd probably like to show Chloe around. There's a craft fair, might be nice. Aunty June's going to pop over in the afternoon and I told Adam we'd be in any time after 3.00. He's doing the Three Peaks.'

'Adam? Has he actually said he'll drop in?'

'He said he might. What it is, I thought he'd be glad of a nice hot bath. He's only got a shower in Cardiff.'

The Three Peaks is a tough 20-mile hike. Adam had done it before.

'Is he going for Gold level this time?'

'Platinum. They start over at Llantony.'

The Platinum Challenge. That was very Adam. When he decides to do something, mere success doesn't satisfy him. Next time he wants to do it faster or better. Like eat more Weetabix than me or collect more milk bottle tops than anyone else in the school, the town, Wales, world, the Universe.

'Then on Sunday,' Mam continued with our schedule, 'I know you'll want to go to church so I thought you could pick up your Nan on your way back and we'll have a nice Easter roast. A nice leg of Welsh lamb.'

I said, 'Oh, didn't I tell you Chloe's a vegetarian?'

And Chloe stepped in before Mam's face fell too far and said, 'He's kidding. Roast lamb is one of my favourites.'

She was doing well with my folks. She bonded with Mam over the merits of a long soak in a Radox bath and coaxed Da into demonstrating his auctioneer's chant. 'Bid 20, now 5 now 5, bid 25, now 5 now 5 now 5, bid 30, now 5 now 5, now 5, no bid, all done, bid 30, sold.' He even stood up to perform, with a rolled-up copy of the Monmouth Beacon for a gavel, the old flirt.

Saturday the Adam question hung over us. I knew he wouldn't come and I think deep down Mam knew it too, but she always puts on a hopeful front. We went down to the

Cwtch cafe mid-morning, for coffee and cake, then Mam and Chloe hit the craft fair and I went with Da to visit Nan. I wanted to see for myself what 'fair to middling' meant. It had been three months.

Nan Talbot never looks any different. My earliest memories of her, she'd have been in her fifties, but even then she was white-haired, with an old lady perm and extra-wide shoes. She gave me one of her awkward Nan kisses and let me hold her hand while we talked, but I noticed she always glanced at Da before she said anything. She wasn't sure of herself, maybe wasn't sure who I was, and Da was her reference point, her true north.

I slipped in a few test questions. She couldn't remember who the Prime Minister was, only that she didn't trust him. Nan's always been Labour. She called me Ed and she called the kettle 'the tea thing', but she counted backwards in sevens from a hundred faster than I could do it and she knew the price of milk.

'Rowlands's or Tesco's?' she said. 'Because Tesco's is cheaper but Rowlands's is handy and they'll help you unscrew the thing on the thing before you bring it home.'

'The thing on the thing?'

'Yes. The plastic thing.'

Da said, 'She means the bottle top.'

The thing on the thing. The tea thing. Nan had signs of anomic aphasia. But her flat was neat and tidy and so was her appearance. She could still nip to Rowlands corner shop for a carton of milk, still go to the Thursday Friendship Club. As old age goes, hers wasn't bad.

I said, 'When you come over, tomorrow, you'll be able to meet my Chloe. The girl I'm going to marry.'

'Well I don't know as I'll be able,' she said. 'Because I'm going to Ed and Eirwen's for dinner.'

'Me too, and Chloe. We'll all be there.'

'Champion,' she said. 'And my grandson will be there. Daniel. He's a… what am I trying to say?'

'Doctor?'

'No, not a doctor! He's only knee high to a grasshopper. But he's a very good…. a diller, a dollar.'

'Scholar,' says Da.

'That's the one, says Nan. 'Daniel's a very good scholar.'

We were driving home. Da said, 'It'll put years on your Mam.'

'What will?'

'Having your Nan to live with us.'

'So, you've decided? When do you plan on moving her?'

'Back end of the year. Your Mam's due to retire in October. I reckon we'll have a little holiday, then tackle it. Get a downstairs toilet put in and give her the dining room. We don't use that table anyway these days. High days and holidays and sometimes not even then.'

'Have you told Nan?'

'I'll cross that bridge when I get to it. We'd best get home now. Adam's expected.'

'You don't really think he'll come?'

'No. But we have to pretend.'

We watched the Llanelli-Pontypridd match on the telly while Chloe and Mam looked at a thousand photos of me as a child and we waited for Adam not to come. Occasionally Mam'd go to the window. I suggested phoning him, but she said if he was still hiking he probably wouldn't have a signal. Then she started saying, 'This isn't like Adam', which really annoyed me because it was exactly like him.

At half past five Mam said, 'Ed, run down to the Red Cross Hall and make sure he got back all right. They had somebody with a twisted ankle on the Sugar Loaf one year, had to be brought down by the Mountain Rescue.'

Da said, 'I'm not chasing after him. It's raining sticks out there' and then he added, 'if he's fallen and broken his neck we'd have heard by now.' Mam teared up.

Chloe said, 'We'll go and look for him.'

And Mam said, 'Dear girl, you are.'

The stewards were packing up at the Red Cross Hall. The Three Peaks was all over for another year. Adam had checked in at the end of the hike and gone straight home. Of course he had. I called him.

'Alright then?'

'Alright then? Four hours and 59 minutes.'

'Well done. Were you doing it for a charity?'

'No.'

'Mam's been on red alert all afternoon, waiting to run you a hot bath.'

'I didn't promise. I only said I might.'

'I'm down for the weekend with Chloe. It would have been nice if you could have met, before the wedding.'

Silence. That's what Adam does when he wants to terminate a conversation. Clenches his jaw, masseter muscle dimpling in and out, gazes off into space, tunes out. I could just picture him.

'It would have been nice if you could have behaved like a normal son, given Mam a call, told her you wouldn't be coming.'

'It wasn't anything definite,' he said. 'She knows that.'

End of conversation.

Chloe said, 'Gosh, poor Eirwen. She'll be so disappointed.'

We told Mam he'd had to dash back to Cardiff before the rain came on any heavier because one of his headlights was out.

Da said, 'On a two-year-old Ford? He should ask for a refund.'

Which wasn't entirely helpful.

I usually go to St Mary's church when I'm back in Abergavenny but Mam had other plans for Chloe.

'Give her a proper Welsh Easter,' she said. 'Take her to chapel.'

So we went to the Castle Street Methodists and as Chloe was inclined to be delighted by everything that weekend, she loved it, especially when some of the older ladies remembered me. I was Deryn Talbot's grandson, who went away and now he's a doctor. Chloe loved that.

She said, 'I've never lived anywhere like this, where people remember you.'

'There must be people in Bishop's Wapshott.'

'No. I can't think of anyone there who'd know me.'

Chloe went away to school, then to university, and the Chummery is outside the village, fairly isolated. No neighbours leaning over the garden gate.

'What about school reunions?'

'Yuck. Flo's been to a few. Her crowd are the type who don't have anything better to do. Ladies of leisure.'

'I don't think running a farm and raising three children is a life of leisure.'

'Flo doesn't run anything. Henry does the pig stuff and the girls do as they please. That's why Daisy was allowed to come to Daddy's birthday lunch in a fairy costume and snow boots. Is there a hospital here?'

'Nevill Hall, where Mam works. Why, are you not feeling well?'

'Is it a proper hospital? Does it do Cardio?'

'Yes, it's a proper hospital. It's got a sweet shop and a coffee bar and everything. Why? Are you thinking of moving here, Dr Swift?'

'Just asking. There'd be worse places.'

My opinion too, but I never thought I'd hear Chloe say it. She even used to talk about applying for jobs in London but somehow, since she got her MRCP, the wind has gone out of her sails.

A text message from Mam. WHAT IT IS, DA WILL FETCH YOUR NAN IN CASE SHE DOESN'T REMEMBER YOU. Manically laughing emoji.

Second message from Mam. SORRY. MEANT TO USE THE SAD FACE. THIS BLUMMIN PHONE.

As soon as we got home Chloe disappeared into the kitchen with Mam. A wedding discussion, she said, and I wasn't required. Then Aunty June arrived, so there were three of them in there, talking a mile a minute. I went up to my old room. You can see across to the Sugar Loaf from that window.

All those things Mam had kept from when we were kids. Cassette tapes, Adam's Etch-a-Sketch, an ancient calculator, a

Slinky. I took a couple of old games downstairs. Hungry Hippos, and Operation, which needed a new battery.

Aunty June is the same age as Mam but she looks older. Mam says that's because June's done more living: two husbands, one dead, one whereabouts unknown, probably Bristol, and three daughters, all with babies. She seems to help out a lot with the grandchildren, but she has osteoarthritis and she was waiting for her first knee replacement. She'd been on a diet.

'Had to,' she said, 'I've lost 8 kilos. What's that in real numbers?'

Mam's got used to metric, weighing babies every day, but June's still stuck on pounds and ounces.

She said, 'Nice girl, your Chloe. You can tell she's got a touch of class but she's in there with Eirwen, sleeves rolled up, rinsing the greens. No side to her.'

'No side to her' is about as big as compliments get coming from Aunty June.

'How are your knees?'

'Shocking.'

'We'll organise a wheelchair for you for the wedding.'

'You will not. I'll manage. Have they told you they're bringing your Nan to live here when your Mam retires?'

'She is getting forgetful.'

'But Dan, your Mam and Da should have a bit of time to enjoy their retirement. She's not an easy woman, your Nan. She's been too used to ruling her own roost, and that's how it'll be. She'll forget this is Eirwen's house and start laying down the law. And your Da won't say 'boo'. Like this pantomime over my airbed, pumping it up, pretending you and Chloe aren't bunking down together, just in case your Nan looks into the sleeping arrangements. In this day and age.'

'I don't mind. Things were different in her time.'

'No they weren't. They crack on that they didn't have the opportunities, but they made opportunities. All those country walks they used to go on?'

'Speaking of which, Adam didn't put in an appearance yesterday. He did the Three Peaks and went straight home.'

'I know. He can't help it, you know?'

'Why not?'

'He's got a screw loose. Always did have. I'd never say it to your Mam, but he's not quite right.'

Nan was very quiet at lunch. She kept looking from Mam to June to Chloe, and back to Mam, trying to work out who was who. She didn't eat much either.

'Too much for me,' she said.

I had seconds, Chloe and Aunty June had thirds. Da declared it a tidy roast. High praise.

June said, 'Are you looking forward to Dan's wedding, Mrs Talbot?'

Nan said she supposed she was. I asked her about her own wedding.

'Chapel,' she said. 'August 1949.'

She'd worn a dress she'd made herself and Grandad had worn his demob suit.

'And where did you go afterwards?'

'Afterwards? Home, for a cup of tea.'

'No honeymoon?'

'Honeymoon! Edwin had to be at Ruthin market on the Monday morning.'

Grandad Talbot was an auctioneer, same as Da.

June said, 'Anyway, you probably didn't need a honeymoon. All those country walks you used to go on before the war. Plenty of kissing and carrying on.'

Mam gave her a warning look, but Aunty June had had three glasses of rosé wine and there was no stopping her.

Nan said, 'There was no carrying on. We were scouting for wild flowers.'

'Well,' says June, 'I've never heard it called that before. And what about all the Americans you had in town? Didn't you walk out with any of them?'

'I did not. Me and Edwin had an understanding.'

Chloe said, 'Why were Americans here?'

'Waiting to ship out to France. There was a war on. We had Eyetalians too, up at Mardy. Prisoners of war. They didn't really keep them locked up. Any work needed doing, digging or suchlike, they were allowed out. And we had Rudolf Hess.'

'Who was he?'

'Adolf Hitler's deputy. Only he bolted. Came over to our side.'

'Gosh.'

'They kept him at Maindiff Asylum, as used to be a loony bin. And he wasn't kept locked up either. We'd see him in town with his guards, sauntering around, bold as you like. He had terrible bushy eyebrows.'

'What happened to him?'

'Can't remember.'

Da said, 'They took him back to Germany at the end of the war, put him on trial. He spent the rest of his life in prison.'

Mam and Aunty June and Chloe played Hungry Hippos. Da fell asleep. Nan dozed for five minutes. She took my hand.

She said, 'That girl? Who is she?'

'That's Chloe. We're getting married in July.'

'Are you? Have you broke it off with Eirwen?'

To Nan we were getting to be like shuffled picture cards. Me, Da, probably Grandad Talbot too. She knew she knew us, but she wasn't always sure of the name, rank and number.

'Look at those things out there,' she said. She was looking out at the garden.'

'What things?'

'The green things, jiggeting about in the wind.'

Leaves. Nan had forgotten the word for leaves. But she could still remember Rudolf Hess's eyebrows.

Chapter 12

I went out on a house call with Vaz on his last day, for old time's sake. My instructions were to make sure he was out of the building till at least 1.30, to give Linda and Moira time to decorate his room with helium balloons and a banner. They'd cleared his afternoon list, dividing his patients between Jean and Harold Boddy. His fiancée, Teresa, was coming over for tea and samosas. Strictly no booze.

Vaz had been asked to visit Connie Riley. She'd been having dizzy spells. I knew Connie. She and her husband, Jimmy, had been patients of the Lindens all their married life and when Jimmy died, Trevor and I were with him, my first and so far my only experience of a death at home. It was something I don't think I'll ever forget.

Connie lived alone now, and therein lay a potential problem. We'd been asked to check on her by a neighbour, Harry Darkin, and Connie wasn't expecting us. I was also afraid that she might resent Harry's interference.

Vaz said, 'But surely she will be glad of her good neighbour?'

I said, 'It's complicated. Connie was widowed last year and Mr Darkin is a widower. I think he'd like to get to know Connie better, if you understand what I mean?'

He didn't. Vaz sees people in very simple terms. Vulnerable old lady. Concerned neighbour. I suggested he let me do the talking, at least for a start.

'Why?' he said. He was laughing. 'Doesn't Mrs Riley like darkie doctors?'

Connie took a while to come to the door.

I said, 'It's Dr Talbot. From the Lindens?'

'Yes,' she said. 'I know who you are.'

'Dr Vaz and I were passing so I thought we'd look in on you, see how you're doing.'

She let us in, took us through to the kitchen. I looked into the living room as I passed. It was just as it had been the day Jimmy died, except there was a space where his hospital bed had been. The rest of the furniture was still pushed up against the walls.

How to broach the dizzy spells? Not even worth the effort. Nothing gets past Connie.

She said, 'This is Harry Darkin, isn't it? I told him, I'm alright.'

She allowed Vaz to check her blood pressure.

She said, 'I haven't seen you before.'

I said, 'And you won't see him again. Today's his last day with us. Dr Vaz is moving to Wolverhampton and getting married.'

'Very nice,' she said.

Her BP was 85/55. A bit on the low side.

'Would you tell me about these dizzy spells?'

'Nothing to tell. Everybody gets light-headed sometimes.'

'True, but when you live alone it's more of a concern. We don't want you crumpling onto the floor. Is your son still working abroad?'

'Roger. Yes. Derek's in West Bromwich.'

'And how often does he get over to see you?'

'Sunday's, generally.'

'There you are then. If you were to take a fall on a Monday you could be on the floor for a long time. So it's no bad thing to have Mr Darkin watching out for you.'

Connie's dizziness usually came on after she'd had a meal. I'd seen it before. Post-prandial hypotension. Old ladies jumping up to wash the dishes before the gravy set on the plates and coming over faint.

Her hands were cold. I asked her if I could listen to her heart.

'Go on then,' she said. 'Seeing as you're here.'

I'm not great on heart sounds. Chloe's brilliant. You can play her a load of recordings and she can tell you exactly what's what. Connie's heart sounded okay to me.

Vaz said, 'Now perhaps try aortic area?'

I moved the stethoscope. There was a clear murmur, like the sound of tearing wet cardboard.

'And upwards a little?'

Vaz was spot on. The murmur was radiating into her neck. Aortic stenosis. Connie's heart was getting old.

I said, 'Would you think of getting an ultrasound, if we arranged it for you?'

'What for?' says Connie.

'I think one of your heart valves is getting a bit stiff.'

'I'm not having no operations.'

'No? Well think about it.'

'I have thought about it.'

'Never say never.'

'That's what Harry Darkin says. At his age.'

Vaz advised Connie to keep her meals small and light and to rest for a while after she'd eaten. Also to consider having an echocardiograph although we both knew she wouldn't.

I said, 'You still not using your living room?'

'It needs sorting out,' she said. 'Derek's going to shift the furniture, when he has time.'

Jimmy had been dead four, five months. Moving Connie's sofa and chairs was the work of five minutes. I know because Vaz and I did it, with Connie twittering in the doorway, saying, 'You doctors shouldn't be doing that. You've got better things to do.'

Leaving Connie Riley with a comfortable place she could sit with her memories and her telly was possibly the most satisfying thing I did that day. It cheered me up when I found myself doling out yet another diazepam prescription to smelly Kevin Hodge and explaining, yet again, to Raquel Yeomans why she was unlikely to get breast augmentation on the NHS.

Vaz and I drove back to the surgery. I told him I was going to miss him. He said he felt sad to leave The Lindens too, in spite of everything.

'The business with Mac?'

'Not only that. Many things have changed.'

'You mean now Helen is in charge?'

'She is a very fine doctor.'

That was what everyone said. It was shorthand for, 'she's also a moody cow who prefers committee meetings to seeing patients and whose personal life is a miserable mess.'

He said, 'Mrs Riley is a lonely old lady.'

'Yes. Her sons could be more attentive.'

'In my country this would not happen.'

'But you're over here. Who'll look after your parents when they need it?'

'Already they need it. My sisters care for them. They are all in one same building. First floor, Daddy and Mummy, second floor my sister Bernadette, third floor my sister Dolores.'

He didn't notice Teresa's car tucked away behind Helen's giant Peugeot so his surprise farewell party was a genuine surprise. Leaving presents were usually the responsibility of Moira and Mary and the default choice for anyone getting married seemed to be a toaster. But I'd pointed out that Vaz and Teresa probably each had a toaster already. Mary went into a brief huff and I was told that if I thought an IKEA gift voucher was a better idea, she'd leave the matter in my hands.

Trevor made a little speech before he handed over the envelope. He said he'd had the gravest doubts about employing Antony Vaz because of his highly suspect dress sense and indeed his fears had been well-founded. He produced in evidence a photograph of Vaz in his skin-tight robin sweater at our Christmas party and another of his red anorak, bought from the Women's rail in a charity shop.

'Nevertheless,' said Trevor, 'beneath the vile, mustard-coloured cardigan he wore to his interview, Helen and I detected the makings of a fine family doctor. And so it has proved. His patients will run rings around him, but they will be lucky to have him.'

Teresa was dashing back to work.

She said, 'Has he explained about everything for the 20th?'

'Holliday Street registry office, 12.30.'

'Yes, but you're a witness so you should be there by 12.00.'

'What about the ring?'

'Rings. I'll have them.'

'Anything else?'

'I was wondering, would you be able to pick him up and drive him in? And help him with his tie?'

'Of course.'

'And make sure he's not wearing odd socks. And that he hasn't left the iron on.'

Vaz and Teresa hadn't been together long, but she had his measure.

Ron Jarrold's biopsy results had arrived. A stage IV prostate tumour with pelvic bone metastases, Gleason score 8. Not good news. I needed to get Ron and his wife in for a difficult conversation. When to call them? Early evening, when Ron got in from work? But what if Ron wasn't home and I got Freda? I knew what she was like. She'd want to be given all the particulars over the phone so she could get on the Internet and be ready to tell me my job.

I ducked out of it and asked Moira to give the Jarrolds a call and ask them to come in.

'Urgent or non-urgent?'

'Non.'

It depended on your point of view, really. Ron's cancer wasn't curable. We'd be talking about palliative care and a few days here or there weren't going to make any difference. If I had a serious cancer diagnosis, would I want to be told as soon as possible? Would I come out fighting, or would I roll over and make peace with my fate? I never have any answers to these questions. Perhaps no-one does, until the moment is upon them.

Chloe doesn't ponder such things much. To her, the Ron Jarrold situation was a no-brainer: throw every possible therapy at it.

'But what if you'd reached a certain point in your life and you just wanted to enjoy whatever time you had left?'

She didn't get it. I told her about Connie Riley. How I'd checked her for heart murmurs but I'm never very confident about identifying what I can hear.

'You just need more practice. You need to be systematic. Is it a systolic sound or diastolic, and where can you hear it? Start on the right, second intercostal space, then the same but on the left, then 4th space, then over the apex, for mitral sounds. It's best if the patient is lying on their left side.'

'Mrs Riley was sitting at her kitchen table, and she wasn't that keen to be examined in the first place. Anyway, atrial stenosis, I'm 90 percent sure. Vaz left today. I'm going to miss him.'

'He's so old-fashioned.'

'That's one of the things I like about him. By the way, Teresa's asked me to chaperone him to the registry office. Make sure he's appropriately dressed.'

'It'll be a bit late for that, on the day. Maybe you should take him shopping beforehand. Your Connie woman needs a new valve.'

'But she doesn't want one.'

'Why?'

'Because she's in her eighties, her husband's dead and her kids are too busy to look after her.'

'So?'

'Do you ever think about getting old?'

'No.'

'What about your parents, or mine? If they get frail, we'd have to look after them.'

'Not mine. They'll book themselves into somewhere like Granny and Grandpa's place. Or they'll move in with Flo and Henry. They've got stacks of room.'

114

'What about mine? Adam probably won't be much help. Vaz's sisters look after his parents.'

'That's because they're very, very holy. Dan, must we talk about this now? Why do you dwell on such things?'

'Because time flies. My Nan's getting pixilated. And when she goes, everybody else in the family moves up the queue.'

'Queue for what?'

'Mortality.'

'Stop it. I refuse to listen to you when you're in such a gloomy mood. Let's go to bed and play doctors and nurses.'

And as I'd been on short rations lately, I abandoned my plan to watch Gogglebox and think about what I was going to say to Ron Jarrold.

Chapter 13

Paul Styles was one of Trevor's more interesting patients. His file bore a Buxtonism: TMS. Too many symptoms. He wasn't a pest of the Kyle Bibby ilk or a workplace hazard like Amber Evans. Just a lonely man who'd lost his job when the metal castings factory closed down and at 57 was unlikely to find another one. He spent his days noticing little things. The odd twinge, or a previously undetected blemish.

Sometimes he came in with a diagnosis of his own, something rare, gleaned from a medical textbook. But he was a mild man. He didn't demand expensive scans. As long as you listened to him, reassured him, and maybe occasionally threw in a routine blood test, he went away happy.

Paul said he was having difficulty swallowing. Anything else? No. That in itself was unusual. With Paul I'd have expected at least two more symptoms.

How long had it been going on? A few weeks. Had he lost weight? He didn't think so, but I noticed his watchband seemed loose. He'd last been seen in December, by Trevor, when he'd come in about vertical ridges on his fingernails, floaters in his right eye and night-time tingles in his feet. Trevor had prescribed Ovaltine before bedtime and volunteer work, to keep the mind from dwelling on little things.

Was the problem with all swallowing or just with solid food? He wasn't sure. I gave him a glass of water and asked him to drink it while I checked his blood pressure. His shirt collar was loose too. Paul always wears a tie and a sports jacket. I think a doctor's appointment is quite an occasion for him.

How were the night-time tingles? Much better. And was he managing to keep busy? Yes, he was doing two sessions a week at the Heart Foundation shop, sorting donations and occasionally working on the till, if required. He said he was more of a behind-the-scenes person.

He drank the water, no problem. I went to the kitchen to fetch a biscuit. Helen was in there with Kasper. They moved apart, quickly. At least, I thought they did. I wasn't sure what I'd seen. Or almost seen.

'A bit early for elevenses,' says Helen.

I said. 'Just doing a custard cream swallow test on a patient.'

Kasper shot past me, went into his office and closed the door. Had I interrupted something meaningful or was he glad of an excuse to escape?

Paul nibbled on the biscuit. 'There,' he said. 'See, it starts to go down and then it gets stuck. Right there.' He tapped his chest.

I said, 'Paul, I'm going to refer you to a specialist.'

His eyes lit up.

'Will that be for one of those barium meals?'

'They might just do a simple swallow test first.'

'Probably be months, I suppose, till I get an appointment?'

'It shouldn't be too long.'

It wouldn't be long at all because I was going to make it an urgent referral, but I didn't tell him that. Late fifties, with dysphagia and possible weight loss. Not quite a red flag but definitely not to be ignored. We had a few patients like Paul and as Trevor Buxton always said, you have to be vigilant and not get so bored by their hypochondria that you switch off, because some day they may really be sick.

Mary said, 'Dr Dan, when you've finished morning surgery would you be so kind as to step into Mr Kowalski's office for a quick word?'

I have an easy relationship with Kasper. We're almost the same age and there's no big difference in rank. Trainee GP and a practice manager still finding his feet. Besides which, I like his style. Unlike his predecessor, Stephanie, he doesn't look for problems or push for major changes. He just aims to keep the practice ticking over smoothly.

He seemed nervous.

He said, 'Earlier? It might have looked a bit strange, but Helen had something in her eye.'

I laughed. I couldn't stop myself.

I said, 'Kasper, the only thing Helen gets in her eye is available younger men.'

He blushed.

He said, 'It's a really difficult situation.'

'I know.'

'You too?'

'Briefly. It was something and nothing, but it did catch me off guard.'

He said, 'I like to keep things strictly professional. Maybe I've been too friendly? Too informal?'

'Not necessarily. If Helen sees something she fancies, she helps herself to it. I think she just likes casual sex.'

'Did you sleep with her?'

'No, only a totally unexpected fumble in her office. Followed by the threat of a slow dance at the Christmas party but I wriggled out of that. Anyway, I have a girlfriend.'

'So do I. And Helen's old.'

'But quite attractive.'

'Do you think so? I don't. How did you put her off?'

'I was in the middle of suggesting that it wasn't a good idea, and then we got interrupted anyway.'

'And that was that?'

'Pretty much. Then you came on the scene. She hasn't patted my backside since you arrived.'

'Is there talk?'

'Nothing much.'

'What are they saying?'

'Not so much saying as exchanging looks. Kind of, "here she goes again" looks.'

'Shit. Any advice?'

'You could get your girlfriend to drop by. When Helen met my Chloe, the temperature dropped by several degrees.'

Jean Boddy reported another case of measles, the latest addition to Nicola Willetts' tribe. Nicola was a confirmed anti-vaxxer and she'd given Jean a lecture on the dangers of MMR. How, according to her, it caused autism. Jean had pointed out that that idea was based on discredited research and that some schools were considering making vaccination compulsory, for new admissions. Nicola didn't care. She said it was all the same to her and if that happened, she'd home school her kids.

'She said it's a big government cover-up.'

Trevor appeared. 'Who says? And what are they covering up?'

'Nicola Willetts. Reasons not to vaccinate for measles.'

'Nicola is a crackpot. As was her mother before her. Nicola's mother was a placenta-eater.'

Harold put down his liverwurst sandwich.

Trevor said, 'I hate to say it, but it's going to take a child's death to stop this nonsense. Now, Dan Talbot, are you busy for the next hour?'

There was no point mentioning paperwork. There's always paperwork.

'Come with me,' he said. 'Sounds like we might have a patient to section and it'd be good for you to see how it's done. Also, if the lift's out in her building I'll need you to do CPR on me by the time I've climbed the stairs. Follow me in your own motor, in case you need to get back here for surgery. There's no telling how long this'll take.'

Harold offered to go instead but Trevor wanted to do it. He said he'd known the patient since she was a child. Toni Swinton.

I'd never met her, but I remembered Vaz going out to see her. A neighbour had reported that she was barricaded inside her flat and refusing to answer the door, but by the time Vaz got there not only had she opened the door, she'd also left the building.

We parked outside Karim's Kabin. It wasn't that our cars were safer there, more that Karim was a civically minded bloke who'd at least be a witness if anyone tried to break into them. It was also a bit early in the day for crime on Cherry Tree. As Trevor observed, the locals were mainly night workers. We walked round to Miss Swinton's building.

Trevor said, 'It's a sad history. She has bouts of paranoia when she hides behind the sofa, bouts of mania when she's out on the street screaming at people. Part of the problem is that she's alone in the world. Parents gone, sibs all gone, God knows where. Boyfriends come and go. There's no-one to make sure she takes her meds.'

'What about a slow-release antipsychotic?'

'That's what she's been on. Abilify Maintena. Maybe she missed an injection. Or maybe it's just not doing the job for her. Tower C. Abandon hope all ye who need to go higher than the third floor.'

The lift was actually working, for a change, though the stench of urine took my breath away.

'Who are we meeting here?'

'The mental health nurse, I hope. If it's anybody else, prepare to hear a load of jargon and jabberwocky.'

In fact there were two women waiting for us in Toni Swinton's flat, both social workers. The younger one, Leanne, introduced herself as Toni's key worker. The other one was her crisis resolution team leader, Pat.

Trevor muttered, 'See? Pure jabberwocky.'

Toni herself was curled up on a stained mattress, eyes open, blinking, absent. Catatonic. But earlier in the day she'd been out on the walkway threatening her neighbours with a knife. Trevor spoke to her, asked if she'd like some help. There was no response.

He said, 'Would you like to go to Dudley Road, pet? Have a bit of a rest?'

Team leader Pat remarked that the crisis seemed to be over.

'Do you think so?' says Trevor.

People who don't know him see this kindly grandad figure, but I knew that when Trevor says, 'do you think so?' it means he's about to tell you how sadly mistaken you are.

She said, 'It's our policy to aim for resolution with the least possible restrictions placed on a client.'

'Is it?' he said, very pleasantly. 'Well then why don't you come over here and discuss it with Toni?'

She didn't. She held back, motioned to young Leanne to do it.

Leanne perched on the edge of the mattress. Trevor moved across to his bag and opened it. As he passed me, he whispered, 'on your mark, Dan.'

Leanne was very young.

'Ms Swinton?' she said. 'Is it okay if I call you Toni? We're just discussing your care plan. Would you like to give us some feedback? On your care plan?'

You could hear the neighbour's television through the wall. Toni's blinking stopped and she reared up so suddenly it made me jump. She let out an unearthly growl and grabbed Leanne by the throat.

Trevor said, 'Pin her arms, Dan. I'll inject into the deltoid.'

I don't know how long I was restraining Toni. She wasn't a big woman, but she was strong and it felt like hours. Trevor said it took him less than minute to get a shot of Largactil into her shoulder. She relaxed, gradually, and we settled her back on the mattress, covered her with a grubby blanket.

'Now,' he said. 'Let's get transport organised.'

Pat was already outside, summoning an ambulance.

Trevor said, 'That might not come any time soon. Let's get the forms signed. You alright, sweetheart?'

Leanne was far from alright. She was in shock.

Trevor said, 'Make yourself a cup of tea. No, second thoughts, don't. Seeing the state of this place I doubt you'd find a cup that's not growing mushrooms. Get yourself down to

Karim's. He's got a coffee machine. Tell him Dr Buxton'll pay him later. And put plenty of sugar in it.'

He went through his options with me. If he used Section 2, Toni could be kept in hospital for up to 28 days but was then quite likely to be sent home.

'If she had family to look after her, I'd probably go that route, but there isn't anyone.'

Pat had come back in. She started to say something about community support. Trevor cut her off.

'Community support, my eye. There are young children living along this walkway. We don't want her back here a month from now, brandishing a damned carving knife. No, I'm inclined to use Section 4.'

Under Section 4 Toni could only be held for 72 hours but she'd be seen by a psychiatrist as a matter of urgency. She could then be recategorized and taken to a secure ward, if necessary.

Team Leader Pat said, 'I should warn you that our Rapid Assessment Interface is at breaking point. It's the cutbacks.'

'Yes,' says Trevor. 'Tell me something that isn't. But I'm going to write all over this form that Toni is unpredictably aggressive and a danger to herself and others. As Leanne can testify. How long for an ambulance?'

'Could be an hour.'

He said I should go.

'What if she needs restraining again?'

'She won't.'

Toni was in a deep sleep.

'Anyway, I'm not completely helpless. No, you clear off. I'll stay here with Mrs Team Leader. Might be fun. See if I can learn a bit more jabberwocky.'

Leanne was just coming out of the Kabin with a coffee. She said she was feeling better, but she was still trembling. It was her first close encounter with schizophrenia. Mine too, apart from a brief Psych rotation when I was at the Queen Elizabeth.

She said, 'He's nice, isn't he? Dr Buxton?'

'Most of the time.'

'He doesn't like Pat.'

'It's nothing personal. He's old school. He just doesn't like all the jargon.'

A moped stopped behind me. Something made me turn. Crusts & Co sandwich deliveries. On Cherry Tree? The rider was taking off his helmet. It was Helen's son, Miles. Then over Leanne's shoulder I saw another familiar figure loping towards us. Kyle Bibby. He stopped in his tracks when he recognised me, pretended to study the whitewashed window of Karim's Kabin. No customary cheery greeting.

By the time I turned again, Miles had his helmet back on and rode away as fast as his 50cc would carry him. Kyle sidled off the way he'd come. I called after him. He stopped.

I said, 'Did I interrupt something there, Kyle? You and the sandwich man?'

'Sandwich man?' he said.

'The guy on the Honda. I didn't realise he delivers around here.'

'I wouldn't know nothing about that,' says Kyle. 'I'm just going home. I need some Rizlas but I come out without any money.'

An eventful lunch hour. A paranoid schizophrenic sectioned, Kyle Bibby uncharacteristically reluctant to chat, and Miles Vincent spotted acting suspiciously. What with one thing or another I hadn't had time to dwell on my 5 o'clock appointment with Ron Jarrold.

Ron was walking with a stick. He had Freda with him. Either they'd already worked out the seriousness of the situation or Freda didn't trust Ron to ask the right questions. She pulled out a notepad and pen. I started.

'So we have the biopsy results.'

'Is it cancer?'

Don't shilly-shally, Dan.

'There's a malignant tumour in your prostate.'

Ron cut straight to business.

'How long have I got?'

Freda interrupted, which gave me a bit of time to think what to say.

She said, 'That's not the right attitude, Ron. Men can live a long time with prostate cancer, isn't that right, Doctor?'

'They can, yes. It depends on several factors. How aggressive the tumour is, for instance. Whether it's spread to other areas.'

Ron said, 'So what's mine?'

Ron's Gleason score was 8. Not good. His tumour was aggressive and he had bone metastases in both hips and the head of one femur.

'Yours is a Stage IV tumour and it has spread, which explains your back pain and your problems walking.'

He said, 'I told you, Freda. I knew I shouldn't be feeling like this.'

Freda shushed him.

She said, 'So they'll operate, to take it all away.'

'You'll need to talk to the hospital team about that. Did they give you a follow-up appointment?'

'Week after next. And then they'll have him in, to operate?'

'My guess is they'll offer radiotherapy first. There's also a hormone treatment, if the tumour is hormone sensitive.'

'Hormones!' says Ron. 'I don't want them turning me into a woman.'

'There are a lot of treatment options. Ways to shrink the tumour, ways to slow the bone damage.'

Ways to control the pain. I didn't say. And none of them are cures. I didn't say. They just make the best of a bad job, for whatever time you have left. Which was Ron's repeated question.

'How long?'

'Hard to say. Could be three years.'

He nodded. Three years seemed acceptable to him. It depends where you are in life, I suppose. If you were young, you'd probably start bargaining with God.

'As your treatment progresses, they'll be able to give you a clearer idea.'

'Well,' he said, 'That's a bit of a bugger.'

Freda thought three years was ridiculous. She said they had a neighbour who'd lived to 90 with prostate cancer.

She said, 'You mustn't take this lying down, Ron. When we go to the hospital, we'll tell them you want an operation. I'll do the talking.'

I said, 'They're the people who can best advise you. Of course, prostate surgery can have major consequences.'

'So can being dead three years from now,' she snapped.

Ron said, 'He means urination, dear.'

'I know what he means.'

'And married life.'

Freda said, 'I don't care about married life. I care about you giving up the ghost too easily.'

If you had told me, six months earlier, that I'd feel warmth and sympathy towards Ron Jarrold, I wouldn't have believed it. He'd been an officious little prick who dragged out Patient Participation Panel meetings far too long with his points of order. Now he was a sick man, worn down by pain and beleaguered by a wife who was going to make him clutch at every slender straw she could find on Google. She hadn't given him much of a write-up in the sex department, either.

Chapter 14

I called Vaz, as instructed, to check that he had everything ready for Saturday. Wedding rings? Teresa had them. Passport? Yes. Outfit for the ceremony? Yes. I knew his clothes were Teresa's main concern. She herself wouldn't have minded if he'd turned up in a grandad cardigan but she didn't want to give her family any ammunition. There had apparently been some sniping from her two sisters that she'd only known Vaz for five minutes and he'd be dragging her off to India for the church ceremony when they could just as well have gone to Our Lady of Good Counsel.

I wasn't sure Vaz's blithe assurances were enough, so I probed a bit further.

'We're wearing suits, right?'

'Yes. I have bought new suit.'

'Good. And a shirt?'

'Yes, I have new white shirt, also new tie.'

I'd told him I'd pick him up and drive him to the registry office. Just as well. He'd been planning on going on the bus. I thought 11.00 sounded plenty early enough but Chloe, who was treating our own wedding like a military operation, said I should get to him by 10.00. She cited heavy traffic and wardrobe emergencies.

Vaz was still in his bathrobe when I got there. He'd cut himself shaving. He said he was suddenly very nervous.

He said, 'I will forget my words.'

'Relax. The registrar will feed them to you. You just repeat what they say. And even if you fumble them, people will understand. Everyone gets nervous. Now you should get dressed, so I can inspect you.'

After their brief honeymoon in Ireland, Teresa was moving in to his flat. Chloe had given me a list of things to do. Put fresh sheets on the bed, give the bathroom a quick wipe, and make sure the fridge contained a split of champagne, a Ready Meal and a carton of milk, for their return.

I gave the champagne a miss. Vaz and Teresa aren't drinkers. By the time I got back from the all-hours with the milk and the chicken tikka, Vaz was dressed. My heart sank. His new suit swamped him. And it was black.

He said, 'You don't like it?'

I said, 'It's a bit big for you.'

'Yes,' he said. 'Trevor told me I always wear clothes too tight. This is better. Also it was half price.'

I'll bet it was. They probably didn't get many short, wide undertakers shopping in Sootz. His shirt was a slightly better fit. His tie was a mustard yellow abomination, kipper width. Knowing Vaz's sartorial cluelessness, I'd brought a spare tie with me, but when it came to it, I didn't have the heart to make him change. It was his day, and I was pretty sure Teresa wouldn't care about his tie.

He was padding around in slippers.

I said, 'We're leaving here in fifteen minutes. You can't keep a registrar waiting and you definitely can't keep Teresa waiting. Get your shoes on while I change your sheets.'

'Why must you change my sheets?'

'Because brides are fussy about these things.'

'Thank you, Dan,' he said. 'You are so wise.'

Fond as I am of Vaz, I was starting to regret taking on the job of chaperone. His bathroom needed more than a wipe. Bristles in the sink, musty towels, a toilet bowl that hadn't seen bleach in a while. I did what I could. When I emerged, Vaz was at the front door with a little wheelie suitcase, ready to go. He was wearing battered old suedes.

'You don't have any formal shoes? Black leather?'

'Yes. I can't find them.'

'Where have you looked?'

'Everywhere.'

I panicked and called Chloe.

She said, 'Look in bloke places. Under the bed, behind the sofa. Bear in mind they might still be in their box.'

'In case we don't find them, when you get to the registry office will you find Teresa and warn her?'

'You mean, like, "hi, I'm Dan's girlfriend. He's asked me to let you know Vaz has lost his wedding shoes but you shouldn't let it ruin your day."? I told you you should have stayed over with him last night.'

We did one last sweep of the flat. No black leather shoes. Vaz didn't seem in the least concerned that he'd be getting married in bouncer black and what my Da would call brothel-creepers. He'd bled onto his shirt collar too. As a groomsman I was feeling pretty rubbish.

The wedding party comprised Teresa's mother, her two sisters with their husbands, Ervin Gul, who was Vaz's new boss, and four teachers from Teresa's school. The Buxtons had been invited too. Teresa looked lovely. She didn't seem at all fazed by Vaz's appearance.

Vaz and Teresa were summoned into a room to go through some formalities before the ceremony. Trevor arrived, alone.

'Mrs Buxton not coming?'

'No, she's not a morning person. Are those the outlaws? They look a bit grim.'

'They think Teresa's marrying in haste.'

'Well it has all been a bit fast, but she seems a sensible girl and Vaz doesn't have a bad bone in his body.'

A door opened and Vaz peeped out, beckoning to me.

'Dan,' he said, 'perhaps the black shoes are in my suitcase.'

'Are you sure?'

'Perhaps they are.'

'Do I have time to run back to the car?'

'I think so.'

'Is the case locked?'

'No. Yes. But no key. It has code. Code is 1981. Or 1891.'

They were just going in for the ceremony as I got back. I was in a muck sweat but at least Antony Frances Xavier wasn't wearing duffed up old suedes when he married Teresa Anne.

We all piled round to Côte afterwards and with a few drinks and Vaz and Teresa's 150 watt smiles the atmosphere lightened.

Teresa's mother, said, 'Well at least he's a Catholic,' and one of the brothers-in-law said, 'Handy to have a doctor in the family. Somebody to pull a few strings. Waiting lists are getting terrible.'

Trevor told me that Toni Swinton had been admitted to a secure ward in Small Heath.

'Not for the first time,' he said, 'and not for the last, I fear. But it was a useful one for you to see, particularly with Mrs Team Leader. The mental health nurses generally still speak plain English but even they're going the same way.'

'I saw the young social worker as I was leaving.'

'Yes, she said. Toni gave her a fright, lunging at her like that. Poor blighter. How old was she, would you say?'

'Early twenties, I suppose.'

'She looked about ten.'

'Something odd happened, actually. I was talking to her, outside the Kabin, when Miles Vincent pulled up, on his delivery moped.'

'Delivering three quid sambos to Cherry Tree? You could get two sausage rolls for that kind of money.'

'That's what I thought. Then Kyle Bibby hove into view. I'm pretty sure it was a planned rendezvous.'

'You mean, Kyle was picking up his avocado wrap?'

'As soon as they saw me, they both scarpered. I did speak to Kyle but of course he acted dumb.'

'It sounds like Miles might be running his own business on the side. Mother's Little Helpers available alongside the egg and cress.'

'Should I say anything to Helen?'

He thought, scratched his ear.

'Best leave it to me. You know what she's like. There might be blood and guts on the walls and you have your whole life before you. Tell me, is it an Indian custom to wear a shiny black suit to a wedding?'

'No, just a Vaz thing. Do you know his new boss?'

'Dr Gul? Only by reputation. Quack quack.'

132

'Really?'

'They probably say the same about me.'

We had apple tart and ice cream and drank a toast to Vaz and Teresa. Then their taxi came to take them to the airport. Teresa's mother actually gave Vaz a hug. Three glasses of fizz had done their work. Alcohol can have its uses.

I whispered an apology to Teresa, about the shoes and tie.

She said, 'Don't worry. It was all very Vaz.'

'Are you really going to call him Vaz?'

'I might as well. Everybody else does. Mind you, when we go to India I'll have to remember to call him Antony. Anyway, you got him here on time, that's all that matters. I'll take over the clothes shopping from now on.'

Chloe said it was the absolute worst wedding she'd ever been to. I had to challenge her on that. We'd been to two of her family's weddings that were unforgettable: her cousin Hugo's, where the bride and groom were barely speaking, and her cousin Lulu's where we both got food poisoning.

I said, 'Well I thought it was lovely. It was simple, sincere and very happy. What more can you ask?'

It was a rhetorical question, but I knew I'd get an answer.

She said, 'I'm going to send Rob a checklist and tell him if he doesn't make sure you're perfectly turned out at our wedding, I'll personally kill him.'

On Monday morning Glenys Allsop came to see me. It was the first time I'd seen her since she got her new liver. She was a woman transformed.

She said, 'I'll tell you what, Doctor. I hadn't realised how poorly I'd been feeling until it was over, know what I mean? I'm going back to work next week.'

133

Glenys was being seen regularly by the liver unit. She was on cyclosporin, a reducing dose of prednisone, and an immunosuppressant, Myfortic. I reminded her to give any source of infection a wide berth. Sick friends and relatives, dog licks, cuts and scratches.

'No gardening, neither, that's what they told me at the hospital. Pete's not best pleased. I've always done the weeding.'

Pete. Did she know he'd been to see me?

I said, 'But I'm sure he'd rather have an untidy garden than a sick wife.'

'Yes,' she said. 'I know he would really.'

'You've been through a lot, both of you. A transplant is a lifeline, but it takes its toll. There's the anxiety before you get it.'

'Terrible,' she said. 'We had one false alarm, you know? They phoned us, we were just going to bed, but they said to go straight in because they'd got a liver for me. Then after we'd been there for a few hours they sent us home again, said it wasn't suitable after all. So that was a setback.'

'My point exactly. You've been through all that, and all the aftercare.'

She was picking at the clasp on her bag. I did a Trevor, shuffled some papers, let the silence hang.

She said, 'Pete says I've changed.'

Let it hang a while longer, Dan.

She said, 'Pete thinks I've got the devil in me.'

'Does he? And what do you think?'

'I don't know.'

'What is it he doesn't like?'

'Going out. I like going out. I never used to be bothered but I enjoy it now.'

'What kind of things do you do?'

134

'Dancing. Swing and modern jive.'

'That sounds fun. Dancing's good, as long as you don't over-tire yourself. And does Pete go with you?'

'Not to dance. He only comes to keep an eye on me. He thinks I'm going to take up with men.'

'And are you?'

'Dr Talbot!' she said. 'I'm a married woman. It does take the shine off it though, Pete sitting at the side scowling. I mean, you need a partner. Not anybody special, just a partner. Any road, I can't sit at home like an invalid.'

'Quite right.'

'You do wonder though. This liver they've given me, it belonged to somebody else. And now they're dead.'

'And your body has accepted the liver. So now it's yours.'

'What I mean is, you feel you'd like to say thank you to someone, only the hospital won't tell you where it came from.'

'Sometimes the donor's family prefer it that way.'

'Be funny if it was somebody you knew. Be funny if it was somebody you never liked.'

'Another good reason not to know. And it could have come from anywhere.'

Which was perfectly true although, since Trevor had planted the idea, I couldn't help but wonder whether Glenys had been the lucky recipient of a liver from Chad Dearlove, petty thief and Elvis impersonator, late of this parish.

Kyle Bibby was my last patient of the day. He likes a late slot. He thinks if he catches me when I'm tired, I'll give him what he wants so I can be rid of him, pack up and go home. How little he knows of my working life. I had an out-of-hours shift at Sterling, and a pile of revision to do for my Applied Knowledge Test.

Kyle thought he might have broken a finger. He'd had an argument with a wall. I asked him who'd started it, him or the wall.

He said, 'It's Jade. She's doing my head in.'

Jade Shotton is his on-off girlfriend.

'You're back with her?'

'No. That kid she's having. No way is that mine.'

'Jade's pregnant again? I didn't know.'

'She goes to the lady doctor. The chubby one.'

'Dr Parker. So Jade is pregnant, she says you're the father, you say you're not, and then you punched the wall?'

'Yeah.'

'Doesn't solve anything, does it, Kyle? There's still a child coming into the world and I daresay the wall's still standing. Let's have a look at your finger.'

There was no swelling, no deformity, a normal range of movement.

'I'd say it's just a bad sprain.'

'It don't half hurt though. And she's giving me brain ache, says I've damaged her wall.'

'Her wall? So you do still see Jade?'

'A bit.'

'But you haven't had sex with her?'

'Not much.'

I didn't have the time or energy to talk Kyle through the basic facts of life.

I said, 'In my opinion your finger isn't broken. You could go to A&E if you want it X-rayed.'

'Naah,' he said, 'I don't think I'll bother. You can be there for hours. I could do with a few temazzies while I'm here, though.'

I wrote him a prescription.

I said, 'Funny bumping into you outside Karim's Kabin the other day.'

'Did you?' he said.

'Yes, we spoke. There was a guy on a moped? I thought you might have been buying something from him.'

'No, don't remember.'

'You need to be careful. You're already taking what we prescribe. If you're buying stuff on the street as well, it could end badly. Remember what happened last year.'

Kyle had been hanging around with much younger kids, sniffing lighter fuel with them. He'd suffered a cardiac arrest and the only reason he'd survived was that it had happened while he was in the back of an ambulance. If he'd arrested in the alley behind the Kabin, it would have been curtains.

'Bloke on a moped, you say? No, can't say as I noticed. But I'll keep an eye out. We don't want people selling dodgy gear on Cherry Tree.'

I'm never sure with Kyle, is he sincere in his own befuddled way, or is he mightily taking the mickey?

Chapter 15

There was the sound of laughter as I opened the front door. I was bone tired. I wanted to shower and go to sleep. But Chloe had company. She and her mate Dee were down to the last inch of a bottle of white.

Dee and I have never actually quarrelled, but I only endure her for Chloe's sake. She's loud, she can be pretty crude, and she thinks I'm boring. Still, I felt obliged to greet her with a kiss. Chloe notices that kind of thing.

She said, 'There's another bottle in the fridge.'

I said, 'I'm for bed, but don't let me break up the party.'

'You won't,' says Dee. 'We're just getting going.'

Dee had made senior registrar. She's an obs/gynae. I congratulated her.

She said, 'How's life, ministering to the swamp-dwellers?'

There it was, in a nutshell, Dee's opinion of my work.

'Endlessly interesting,' I told her. 'Because I get to deal with more than one set of organs.'

I left them to it, took a glass of milk to bed, tried to sleep, failed. Then I tried revising. A 46-year-old male with sudden onset, unilateral hearing loss. On examination the canal appears clear and the tympanum appears normal. Likeliest diagnosis? Well a bit more information would have been helpful. Any history of ear infections? Or shingles affecting the facial nerve? My best but not very confident guess had to be otosclerosis. I picked another question at random. Posology. Not my strongest suit.

You are prescribing prophylactic trimethoprim for a 3-year-old with recurrent UTIs. The suspension contains 50mg per 5 ml, the recommended dose is 2mg per kg body weight and the child weighs 12 kg. What instructions do you give regarding dosage?

Dee's shrieks of laughter had made it impossible to concentrate. It was after midnight when Chloe slid in beside me.

I said, 'I hope you put her in a taxi. She must have had quite a skinful.'

'No need,' says Chloe. 'She's sleeping on the couch.'

So not only had Dee deprived me of my rest, she'd also still be there in the morning. I wouldn't be able to wander around in my boxers or leave a smell in the bathroom.

I said, 'Not great timing. I need to go in early tomorrow, catch up on letters. I'm sitting in on an asthma clinic tomorrow afternoon and I'm seriously behind on my revision. Don't expect me to tiptoe around Dee. She'll no doubt have a thick head, but it'll be lights on, radio on and coffee brewing, as per.'

It was a brave speech which Chloe didn't hear because she was fast asleep.

The sound of the bathroom extractor fan woke me. It was 6am and Chloe was dead to the world. Dee had beaten me to the shower. I took my time, got a clean shirt out, thought up a few withering remarks I could make. When I emerged from the bedroom, she was standing in nothing but a towel, looking to see what we had in the fridge.

She said, 'You need a new showerhead.'

'Anything else not up to standard?'

'Why do you buy this skimmed milk? What's the point?'

For once I agreed with Dee, but I wasn't going to let her know that.

I said, 'Chloe's a cardiologist. She sees potential fatbergs everywhere.'

By the time I'd showered, Dee was dressed and ready to leave. She said she'd just have a quick coffee. She didn't look at all hungover.

She said, 'This is some mega wedding Chlo's organising.'

'It's what she wants.'

'Outdated institution, if you ask me.'

'So why are you coming?'

'For the booze and the dancing and the chance of a hook-up. A wedding's a great place for no-strings sex. You'd have to be a total dog not to get any action at a wedding. Is Chloe taking today off?'

'I don't think so.'

'Poor kid's in such a funk.'

'What about?'

'This catheterization training she's doing. She didn't tell you? It's probably the instructor's fault. With a procedure like that, you need somebody to boost your confidence. Anyway, tell her "hugs and don't let the bastards grind you down". I need to fly. It's hunt and destroy day.'

Hunt and destroy. Abortions. She only told me that to try and get a rise out of me. She knows I think she's far too casual about it, like she's just unblocking a U-bend, removing a small

140

inconvenience. Maybe that's the only way she can face her morning's work, but I don't think so.

She said, 'See you on Execution Day. What are her folks like?'

'They're okay. Are you staying at the Chummery the night before?'

'Yeah. It sounds amazing.'

'It isn't. It's big and draughty and if the Aga dies there's no hot water.'

'Wild. I saw a photo of her olds one time. I thought her Dad looked quite cute.'

Laurence Swift is certainly not cute. Trevor Buxton knew him at Bart's when they were both students and described him very accurately as having a head like an Easter Island statue.

Dee left. She'd eaten the banana I'd planned to have with my granola.

So, it was the cardiac catheterization training that was troubling Chloe. I thought it was just pre-wedding stuff. I should have been more attentive, like I was when she was preparing for her exams. I'd been so wrapped up in my own worries, I'd overlooked the fact that she's still learning too.

Catheterization is a delicate procedure. You have to localise the septal artery and then infuse it with pure alcohol. Effectively you're provoking a minor heart attack. You'd need to be careful but confident. Sooner my working life than hers any day. I had Elsie Turney to look forward to. I'd inherited Elsie from Trevor's list, a lovely old lady with slight hypertension and a very good attitude to life. She always brought us a tin of Quality Street at Christmas.

Elsie came in wearing an eye patch.

'What do I look like?' she said.

She was seeing rainbows out of her right eye.

'Any pain?'

'It's throbbing. I've been lying down with the curtains shut but it's still paining me.'

'Let's have a look at it.'

The white of her eye was inflamed, the right pupil was unreactive. If my diagnosis was right, the eye patch and the darkened room had only made things worse.

I said, 'You're not going to like what I'm going to say.'

'Oh dear. Go on then.'

'You need to go to the hospital.'

She groaned.

She said, 'Well I'm booked for the Seniors' trip to Paignton so they'd better not send me an appointment for July. I'm not cancelling my holiday.'

'No, I'm sending you straight to the hospital from here.'

'Get away! Is it serious?'

'I'm going to get one of the other doctors to look at you, but I'm fairly sure you've got a blockage that needs dealing with immediately.'

'A blockage? Well if you say so. I don't want to be any bother.'

I caught Harold between patients, told him I thought I had an acute glaucoma, but I'd like a second opinion. He came to have a look.

I said, 'This is Dr Boddy. He's one of our new doctors.'

'New to the practice but not new to the job,' he said. 'Can I have a look at your eye?'

'Yes,' says Elsie. 'There's no charge today. So where did they find you?'

'Africa,' he said. 'We've come home from Africa.'

142

I said, 'Elsie's been a patient here since Trevor's father was in charge.'

'That's right,' she said. 'I've been under two Dr Buxtons. How is he? Still smoking himself to death?'

'He's cut down. Still doing a bit of work.'

'And what's this new name you've got on the sign?'

'Tipton Road West. It's Dr Vincent's idea.'

'I don't think it says Tipton Road West.'

Harold agreed with my diagnosis.

'Good catch,' he said. 'What's your plan?'

'Pilocarpine drops and then straight to A&E?'

'Yes. Maybe give them a call, tell them she's coming. I imagine she's the kind of patient who'd sit in the waiting room all day without a murmur.'

I fetched the eyedrops from Nurse Chris, explained to Elsie that they'd narrow her pupil and reduce the pressure until an ophthalmologist could examine her.

'Before I put these drops in, you're not pregnant? Not breastfeeding?'

She laughed.

I said, 'Now, Elsie, who can we get to take you to the hospital?'

'Well, my Leonard, I suppose. What a lot of fuss over an eye.'

I called Leonard Turney

'Dear, oh dear,' he said. 'Will she go blind?'

'Not if we get her treated fast.'

'Tell her I'm on my way.'

'What a pity this had to happen on a Wednesday,' she said. 'It's Leonard's day for bowls.'

143

Mary made her a cup of tea while she waited for her son to come. I called Sandwell and spoke to the on-call ophthalmologist. You can't hang about with acute glaucoma.

I went out for a word with Leonard when he arrived. He was an old man. In his sixties, I suppose, but you could easily have believed he was Elsie's husband, not her son. How strange must that be, to watch your own child grow old? He took his Mum off to the hospital.

Arthur Gee was a patient I hadn't seen before although his file dated back to the late Sixties. There was no helpful Buxtonism scrawled on its cover. Arthur was 79, smartly dressed, collar and tie and tweed sports jacket. He had a rash between his fingers. Dermatology never interested me when I was in medical school, but I should have paid more attention. When you're in general practice you spend a lot of time examining skin.

Was it dermatitis? Had he been using any chemicals? Painting the house, maybe, or gardening? He couldn't think of anything. Did he have the rash anywhere else? Arthur seemed on edge.

'A bit,' he said. 'Down below.'

It was more than a bit. He had the rash in both groins and around his waist. That was where I noticed the clincher, a clear track mark where the culprits had burrowed. Arthur had scabies.

'I feared it was,' he said. 'I had it when I was a kiddie, when I was evacuated. Well that's terrible.'

He looked devastated.

I said, 'It's nothing to worry about. I'll give you a prescription for peremethrin cream. You'll need to apply it everywhere, head to toe, and then shower it off after 12 hours. One application should do it. It's caused by mites, so you'll need to hot wash things like your towels and bedding, to get rid of them.'

He put his head in his hands.

I said, 'Arthur?'

He shook his head, couldn't speak. He was crying.

I said, 'There's no shame in scabies. It's like head lice or fleas, anybody can get them.'

Then he said, 'How am I going to explain this to the wife?'

I could hear the spirit of Trevor Buxton whispering, 'give him time, lad. Give him time to cough it up.'

There are various ways a person might get scabies. Sleeping in infested bedding or close contact with someone who has the mites on their body. Those are the most likely sources. But Mr Gee was immaculately turned out. He blew his nose.

He said, 'The only thing I can think is, there's this lady I see.'

I left it for a beat or two, then I said, 'You know anything you say in here goes no further?'

'Oh yes,' he said. 'I know that. She's very clean, the lady I go to. Very nice. I can't think how this has come about.'

'This lady? Do you have sex with her?'

He nodded.

He said, 'You see, my wife's not a well person. Hasn't been for years. I couldn't trouble her in that department. I do still have my needs though.'

Poor Arthur. Having to pay for sex at his time of life. I told him I thought it showed great consideration and good sense.

'But now this,' he said. 'She must have caught it off one of her other gentlemen.'

'You'll need to tell her. She'll need to clean all her bedding too.'

145

'I should hate to stop seeing her. She suits me very well.'

I said, 'I don't see any reason for you to stop. And as long as we nail the scabies, there's no need for your wife to know. If she doesn't already. Women do tend to know things, without being told.'

He said. 'When I see this lady, I tell Norma I'm going to a meeting. Table tennis committee. It's a white lie. I mean, I wouldn't ever want to upset her. We've been married 55 years.'

I suggested he stop off at a supermarket on the way home and buy a non-biological washing powder.

'Tell your wife Dr Talbot thinks you might have developed an allergy to your usual powder, so to try a different one.'

Another white lie, to spare Mrs Gee.

'That's an idea,' he said. 'You've been very helpful. I always used to see Dr Buxton. I heard he was dying. Has he gone yet?'

'Far from it. He's just taking things a bit easier these days.'

He went to shake my hand.

I said, 'I won't, if you don't mind.'

He smiled, thanked me, said it had been a relief to talk about it, man to man. His friends were mostly dead, he said, and those that weren't were only interested in their allotments.

He said, 'I tried that phone sex one time, when Norma was at the chiropodist's, but it's not the same. It's not value for money.'

You just never know. Leonard Turney, probably around the same age as my Da, seemed old before his time, lawn bowls and a cardigan. Arthur Gee, nearly 80, was still eager for a full gravy dinner.

Pam Parker and Helen Vincent were in the kitchen. Helen asked if by any chance I was going to minimarket.

146

I said, 'No. I'm heading off to Dudley Road. I'm sitting in on a clinic this afternoon.'

'Oh,' she said, 'did I know that?'

'Yes, I told you.'

'Who's taking your afternoon list?'

'I am,' says Pam. 'I'm taking half and Harold's taking half.'

Helen wasn't happy.

Pam said, 'Dan's a trainee, remember? Your trainee, strictly speaking. He needs to get out and about.'

Helen said, 'We're just so short-handed at the moment. Jean's off sick. Trevor's only doing nursing homes.'

Pam said, 'Yes, well, it's not Dan's fault if you keep disappearing to committee meetings. You ought to be encouraging him to spread his wings not complaining about it.'

She can say these things to Helen. Pam doesn't care what people think of her, although funnily enough she's well-liked.

I said, 'I hear Jade Shotton's pregnant again.'

'She is. Who told you?'

'Kyle Bibby. Who denies being the father but I'm not sure Kyle has a firm grasp of what conception actually requires. He said he had had sex with her but not much, whatever that means.'

'Bless him. As I recall he was in the frame for the previous one, until it was born with the wrong skin tone. Definitely not the Bibby couch-potato pallor. We'll have to wait and see what shade this next one turns out.'

I set off for Sandwell. Elsie Turney had been right about the surgery sign. The letters had been rearranged to say SNOT DRIP WET MEDICAL CENTRE.

The waiting room for the asthma clinic was packed. Standing room only and a lot of children. The clinic nurse said they might

147

not start on time because ward rounds were running late. The consultant was away at a conference and one of the housemen wouldn't be in because his wife was in labour. I felt a bit spare but eventually the respiratory medicine team arrived and they put me in with a registrar, an Australian, Brett Noble.

He said, 'GP eh? Not sure how much you can learn from us. A lot of what we do is sorting the sheep from the goats.'

'The real asthmatics from the non-asthmatics?'

'And the life-threatening from the slightly debilitating.'

'I have a lot of trouble getting patients to use their inhalers properly. I've even had one who swapped her Ventolin for a Qvar because she preferred its colour.'

'Yes,' he said. 'Got that T shirt.'

It was a long and tiring clinic. When I look through my files before a surgery there are always some names I recognise. Brett had no recollection of having seen any of his patients before. The children had been tested for allergies. An allergen is almost always the trigger for childhood asthma. I remembered my brother having a skin prick test done in our GP's surgery but I'd never been asked to do one at the Lindens, at Snot Drip.

When I was in medical school there was an allergen blood test called RAST but that had been superseded. They do a hi-tech test now, read by microchip. All they need is a few drops of blood and they can identify more than a hundred allergens. Brett said a lot of the kids he saw were living in a perfect storm for asthma. Parents who smoke, bad housing with mould on the walls and a dog with dander.

'Damage control,' he said. 'That's all we can hope for. The mother won't give up her cigs, the dog can't quit shedding and slobbering, and no-one's going to rehouse them. Personally, I prefer the adult-onset referrals. There's usually something useful you can do for them.'

148

'Such as?'

'Get the diagnosis right, for a start. Unless they've just started a new job, handling chemicals for instance, chances are they don't have asthma at all. It's more likely to be bronchitis, or heart disease or COPD.'

It was after six when the last patient left and Brett switched off his computer.

'Any the wiser?' he said.

I was, but not quite the way he meant it. I'd had confirmation that hospital work, with its conveyor belt clinics, wasn't for me. I might not get much excitement in my job but from the way Brett was yawning, neither did he. At least I could tell you the name of every patient I'd seen that day. Which made me think of Elsie. I wandered along to ophthalmology, to find out what had happened to her. The lights were off, no-one was around. But at the ticket machine for the car park I was hailed by her son, Leonard.

He said, 'Have your ears been burning?'

'Is she cross with me?'

'No. Praising you to the heavens. They told us, if you hadn't sent her here, quick sticks, she'd have lost the sight in that eye.'

'So she's okay?'

'They've kept her in, just for tonight. She's none too pleased about that. But she should be home tomorrow. They've given her something to stop her eyes making tears, only temporary, and then they'll do a little operation, with a laser. Something beginning with I.'

'Iridotomy.'

'That's the one. They're going to do both eyes and then she should be as good as new.'

'And fit to go to Paignton.'

'Oh yes. It wouldn't do for her to miss that. She helps them look after the cripples, you know? The poor old dears, as she calls them. Well I'd better get off. She needs me to bring her a nightie and her tuthbrush.'

Chloe was working late. I looked in at the Black Bear to see if Trevor was in his usual seat. He was.

'What news on the Rialto, Dan Talbot?'

'Very little. I'm just not in a hurry to get home.'

'You'll have to do better than that. You must have something interesting to tell me.'

'Elsie Turney presented with an acute-angle glaucoma. Now stabilised and having bilateral iridotomy tomorrow.'

'Good. Next?'

'Kyle Bibby has another paternity claim against him, which he's disputing.'

'Jade Shotton again?'

'Yes.'

'Of course, she's not playing with a full deck.'

'Kyle says the baby can't be his because he's only had a bit of sex with her.'

'One of these days we should stun him with Ketamine and give him the snip, do the West Midlands a favour. About Mrs Buxton's birthday party. May 18th. It's a Saturday. Buffet lunch. I hope you'll come.'

'Definitely. Shall I bring Chloe?'

'Of course.'

'What should we bring, for a present?'

'Nothing.'

'What are you giving her?'

'No idea. To be decided. So, nothing else of import from Snot Drip?'

150

'You saw the sign, then.'

'I did. I dropped by to tell Helen her son had been seen acting suspiciously on Cherry Tree.'

'What did she say?'

'That his sandwich delivery round covers a very wide area and why don't people give Miles a break and mind their own fucking business.'

'Maybe I misread the situation.'

'All right, we'll leave it at that. You told me, I told Helen. Nothing more we can do.'

'Someone was asking after you today, wanted to know if you'd died.'

'That's nice. Who was it?'

'Arthur Gee.'

'Arthur Gee. Nice old boy. Pretty spry, or at least he used to be. Invalid wife, though, with terrible arthritis. What was ailing Arthur?'

'A washing powder rash.'

'And they say general practice is boring. I wonder if he's still using that knock-off Viagra. He used to get a friend to order it on the computer. I offered to prescribe it, but he didn't want it on his records.'

Chloe didn't get home till nine o'clock and not in the best of moods. She'd had another training day on cardiac catheterisation. From what Dee had told me, she was fine practicing on the training simulator, but then she'd bottle it when it came to performing it on an actual patient.

I offered to make dinner. 'Couldn't eat a thing', she said, but as usual when Chloe says that she then spent the rest of the evening snacking. I did some revision, she had her wedding files spread out on the floor. I suggested we were due an earlyish night.

'Why?' she said.

'Because you and Dee were partying till late last night and I didn't get much sleep either.'

'Partying? We were discussing wedding stuff.'

'Okay. Still, I'm tired, you're tired. But sex might be nice.'

'Dan,' she said, 'you do realise the invitations need to go out this week. You seem to think weddings organise themselves.'

'Can I help?'

'No, you'll ask too many questions. By the time I've explained everything I could have done it myself.'

'We could elope.'

'Very funny. Go to bed and leave me in peace.'

It occurred to me that Arthur Gee might well be enjoying more action than I was.

Chapter 16

I'd never been to Trevor's house although I'd driven past it several times. We have a few patients in Wombourne. Brook House is on the edge of the village, a detached property, set on a ridge above the road. Chloe was impressed.

She said, 'He's done all right out of a little mouse shit practice. Will we be getting something like this?'

'Trevor inherited it from his father. The surgery used to be here, in one of the downstairs rooms, until the Seventies.'

'Quaint. Nice house though.'

'Do you think you'll inherit The Chummery?'

'Should do,' she said. 'Slow's got his Shag Pile. Flo and Henry have the farm and anyway he'll do okay when his olds die off. The Senior Packwoods are loaded. Shit, look who's here. You didn't tell me they'd be coming.'

We'd pulled in behind Helen and Clifford Vincent. Cliff was reputed to be quite a ladies' man and Chloe's brief encounter with him at the Christmas party had confirmed that. He'd actually propositioned her. The fact that Helen had propositioned me was in a completely different league. We worked together and feelings can run high in a small practice.

With Helen it had been a silly slip in a fleeting, dangerous moment. But Cliff had given Chloe his phone number within half an hour of meeting her.

Helen jumped out of their car.

Chloe said, 'Bitch Face is very dolled up. I thought this was a casual lunch?'

Helen trotted over. She was wearing heels and a very nice dress. There was no denying, moody cow she may be, but she has great legs.

'Don't block us in,' she said. 'We're only staying for half an hour.'

I parked beside them. Clifford was putting on a jacket. He gave Chloe a second look.

'Oh. My. God,' she said. 'Look at his feet. He's wearing tights.'

'What do you mean?'

'Instead of socks, he's wearing sheers.'

'How can you tell?'

'The colour, Dan. Englishmen don't have Sombrero Tan feet. Englishmen wear socks with their loafers. Welshmen too, I'm sure. I wonder who the red convertible belongs to?'

My guess was the Buxtons' son, James.

There were about twenty people at the party, some I knew. Pam Parker and her husband, Bob. Our receptionists, Mary and Moira. The rest were neighbours and family. Mrs Buxton's sisters, who seemed to be the bane of Trevor's life. They looked exactly like her. They could have been triplets. James was easy to spot. He was a taller, smoother version of Trevor. Very Harley Street.

The Buxtons had brought in help from the village for the party. Two women were ferrying food. A pimply boy in a waistcoat was circulating with a tray of drinks. We found

154

ourselves in a lovely, light-filled room. The French doors were open and people had spilled out onto a terrace. Pam had been to scope out the lunch arrangements.

'It's a serve yourself buffet but there's a big table as well, so we can sit down, thank heavens. You never get a proper meal if you're trying to eat standing up.'

'Do you think the daughter will come?'

'Alice? She's here. Her and the demon dyke partner. They're probably out the back having a row.'

Chloe said, 'I wonder if we'll get to find out Mrs Buxton's name today? Her sisters surely can't call her 'Mrs Buxton'.'

'They don't,' says Pam. 'I heard them call her Baby, but that can't be her real name.'

Mrs Buxton was holding court. We'd bought her, well, that is to say, Chloe had bought her a silk scarf. So had several other people. She was sitting in a low armchair, so I just kissed her hand.

I said, 'I'm Dan, from the surgery.'

'I know you are,' she said. 'You're the nice young doctor who's been helping my Trevor.'

She pulled me closer so she could whisper.

'I wish he hadn't let that Vincent woman take over.'

I said, 'She's here, you know?'

'Yes, Trevor said we had to invite her. You see, I wish he could have held on, until somebody like you could take over.'

'That'd be a long wait. I'm not even registered yet, and Trevor needs to ease up.'

'I know,' she said. 'But he's always loved going to work. There's not many who look forward to Monday mornings.'

She had a gin and tonic in her hand and from her breath I'd say she'd already had a few.

Chloe had been cornered by Helen's husband, but Chloe's very capable of handling men like Clifford Vincent. James Buxton was pacing around, talking on his mobile. I joined Mary and Moira. I find old ladies easier to chat to than blokes who drive 100k's worth of wheels.

Mary and Moira are sisters. The Marys, as Trevor calls them, as though they're a unit. Well, I suppose they are, in a way. They do seem to own identical cardigans. They live in Sedgley with their very old mother and job-share on our reception desk. Maybe they cardigan-share as well.

The Marys are much more than receptionists though. Amazons, Trevor reckons, who defend us from impatient patients and chancers and drug reps. They've been with the practice as long as he has, but their memories are sharper. If you want to know some random fact about a patient you could pull the file and wade through it, or you could just ask the Marys.

They don't hide their prejudices either. If they like you, you can get away with anything. If they dislike you, there's no court of appeal. They don't like Helen. They loathed our old practice manager, Stephanie. And they didn't have much patience with Vaz. I think it was his accent. His English was perfectly good but they'd squint at him, as though he was speaking Malayalam. They loved Mac, and still do, in spite of his transgressions. And as for Trevor, they worship him, but they conceal their feelings by bossing him around. They seem to like me too.

I asked after their Mum. Not so good, they said. Bed-bound, incontinent and profoundly deaf, but at least they still had her. A neighbour was sitting with her for an hour or two, so they could come to the party. Women like Moira and Mary amaze me. They're not young, and their days are shaped by caring for

156

their mother, but they don't complain. Did they ever have other lives? Did they have boyfriends and hobbies and holidays? I never felt I could ask. It might sound like I was suggesting their current lives were less than peachy.

They gave me an unofficial tour, showed me the room where Trevor's father used to hold his surgery. It's Trevor's snug now, with a nebuliser and a giant ashtray and a view of the garden.

Mary said, 'Patients used to wait in the front hall. There was a line of chairs.'

'No receptionist?'

'Not till he moved to The Lindens. You see, you wouldn't have needed one. People would just wait their turn. All you had to do was remember who was there before you. And you wouldn't have had kiddies running around, creating havoc. In those days you sat nicely and waited for the doctor to call you in, or you'd get a wallop.'

'Trevor told me his mother acted as doorkeeper and nurse.'

'She did. She ran everything. Old Dr Buxton was a lovely man, but he wasn't an organised person.'

'Like father, like son.'

'Yes,' says Moira, 'only Trevor couldn't have relied on Mrs Buxton to run things. She was too busy getting her hair done. A shampoo and set, every single week. I ask you!'

I said, 'And she was bringing up two children.'

'Yes, well.'

The little things that can get you judged for life: a weekly appointment at the hairdresser's.

The Vincents were leaving. They had a wedding to get to in Stourbridge.

Mary said, 'They didn't stay long. Well, there's no love lost. And did you notice? He was wearing stockings.'

I said, 'According to Chloe they're called ankle-highs. I think it's a look. Sort of Mediterranean summer casual.'

'What?' says Moira. 'In Wombourne?'

A tiny figure stepped into the lee of the French doors, trying to light a cigarette.

Mary said, 'And that one's got some nerve, showing her face.'

'Who is it?'

'Alice's lady friend. You'd have thought she'd have had the decency to stay at home.'

Trevor's daughter lives in North Wales with a woman called Micky. It's a bad relationship, according to Trevor, violent sometimes, and yet Alice refuses to leave.

I said, 'That's Micky?'

'That's her. I'm not saying anything about, you know, what they are? Live and let live, I say. But how a woman can hit another woman. It's not natural.'

'But she's tiny. She doesn't look capable.'

'She knocked Alice's front teeth out last year. Broke her arm too, a few years back. They said it was an accident, said it got caught in a car door, but we're not daft. We didn't ride down on the up train.'

'And which one is Alice?'

'The one talking to Pam Parker's husband. She's put up a bit of weight since we last saw her. Wearing slacks too, at her mother's birthday. You'd have thought she'd have made more of an effort.'

I sat down with Pam to eat lunch.

She said, 'So now you've seen the Buxton tribe. Have you filled in the blanks?'

'Alice's partner was a surprise.'

'You mean her sex or her size?'

158

'Size. But it sounds as though she packs quite a punch.'

'I'll say. Alice needed a partial plate after the last lover's tiff. Trevor showed my Bob the X-rays.'

'But Alice won't leave.'

'She says all her money's tied up in the business. They've got a souvenir shop, her and Micky. But she could walk away. I would. She could come down here, live with Trevor and Mrs B till she's back on her feet. Did you talk to James?'

'Every time I look at him, he's on the phone.'

'I know. Glued to his ear. He's okay. He has some commitment issues. Always looking for a trade-up with cars and girlfriends, but he's all right. Alice and her mother hardly speak. Trevor can't stand the sisters-in-law, but Mrs Buxton can't function without them. A fairly normal family, you might say.'

'How's yours these days?'

'Averagely dysfunctional.'

'Is Bob's father still with you?'

'He is. I don't know how long we'll be able to keep him living at home but at the moment he's less trouble than two teenage girls. Have you heard of Thinspiration? Or Pro-mia?'

I hadn't.

'They're websites. You should look at them, educate yourself. Handy online hints on how to starve yourself.'

I'd met one of Pam's daughters.

'When I saw Melissa a few months ago she didn't look anorexic.'

'They don't. They wear baggy clothes to fool you. And Melissa's bulimic, so she's always stuffing her face. All my lovingly cooked dinners get flushed down the bog. It took us a while to cotton on to what she was doing.'

'What can you do?'

'Pray. Send her to live somewhere people are genuinely starving. I don't know. That salmon was damned good. Shall we get seconds or move on to the puddings?'

I needed to get home. Only five days till my exam. Chloe was talking to Trevor and his daughter. Micky was at Alice's side.

Chloe said, 'Trevor and Daddy were in the same year at Bart's. Isn't that fun? I can't wait to tell him.'

'I already did. They weren't friends or anything.'

Trevor said, 'Same year, different crowd. Laurence was always destined for greater things. The tonsils of the rich and famous.'

Alice said, 'You're from south Wales?'

'Abergavenny.'

'Dad couldn't remember. "Aber something" was the best he could do. Wales is a mystery to him.'

Trevor had his arm around her shoulder, a father just plain happy to be with his daughter. When she smiled my eye was drawn to those front teeth. Slightly too perfect dentures, thanks to little Micky.

We conducted the post-mortem on the way home. Chloe thought Mrs Buxton might have Parkinson's. I think she has an essential tremor.

'Explain your diagnosis, Dr Talbot.'

'It's just one hand that shakes, and it's not pill-rolling, like with Parkies, plus her head wobbles. Her gait's normal.'

'Okay, I'll buy that. The son has halitosis.'

'You got that close to him?'

'I didn't need to get close. Did you see Clifford Vincent hitting on me again?'

'I did. He's persistent, isn't he?'

'Not really. He'd actually forgotten that he'd met me before.'

'That can't be true.'

'It is. He introduced himself, gave me his card, told me to give him a bell if I fancied a discreet dinner some time. It was like we'd never met.'

'Did he use the words 'fine dining'?'

'He did. Same script, just different hosiery.'

I was laughing so much I had to pull into a lay-by.

'So now you have two Clifford Vincent business cards. Is he attractive? I mean, even slightly attractive?'

'He's quite good-looking I suppose, but his m.o. is so repellent. So blatant. I mean, Bitch Face was almost within earshot.'

'Trevor says Helen has affairs too. She probably doesn't mind what Clifford gets up to.'

'Right. And what about the goblin who was glued to Alice's side?'

'That was Micky. They run a gift shop in Snowdonia and Micky beats her.'

'That figures. I noticed every time Alice spoke, she shot a little sideways look at the goblin, checking she wasn't stepping out of line, I suppose. Why doesn't Trevor do something about it?'

'Such as?'

'Take a contract out on the goblin. Get someone to shove her off a mountain.'

'Trevor's strategy is to keep the door wide open. Any time Alice decides to leave, she knows she has a place to run to. I was talking to Pam Parker. Both her girls have eating disorders.'

'Hm. Teenagers with an obese mother? I can't imagine why they'd have food issues. And fancy Trevor knowing Daddy. He's such a sweetie. Even if he does smoke. I can see why Mrs

Buxton fell for him. By the way, you didn't tell me one of your receptionist women is ill.'

'They're not. Which one?'

'White cardigan.'

'They were both wearing white cardigans.'

'No, Dan. One was white and one was more like parchment. White cardigan had petechiae on her ankles. Don't tell me you haven't noticed.'

'I don't look at their ankles. They're old ladies and they're almost always behind the desk. Petechiae? Tell me what you're thinking.'

'What would she be, late sixties? Any weight loss?'

'Not that I've noticed. I wonder which of them we're talking about. Moira has a chipped front tooth.'

'Couldn't say. I didn't talk to them. Still, whichever one she is, White Cardigan should get a full blood count.'

'That will be an interesting conversation. Excuse me, but my girlfriend happened to notice suspicious marks on your ankles, probably nothing to worry about but let's look at your blood anyway. I think I might pass that one to Trevor.'

But I'm afraid to say I was so worried about my exam that I clean forgot about Moira's ankles. Or were they Mary's?

Chapter 17

The Applied Knowledge Test is a computer-based exam. You have about 200 multiple choice questions to answer. Sometimes I knew how to work out the answer, sometimes it felt like a guessing game.

How soon is a patient deemed fit to drive after successful elective angioplasty and stent insertion? a) Immediately? b) A week? c) A month? d) 6 months? e) At the discretion of the DVLA? It was a good question. I didn't know the answer.

The patient is a 50-year-old female with a BMI of 29 and a family history of Type 2 diabetes. How do you interpret her HbA1c result of 40 mmol/mol? a) Impaired fasting glycaemia? b) Impaired glucose tolerance? c) Type 2 diabetes? d) Pre-diabetic? e) Normal?   Those test results used to be expressed as a percentage and I haven't quite got used to the new mmol per mol system, but 40 was a low figure. Whatever else, this woman does not have Type 2 diabetes.

A 23-year-old female on Day 14 of a 28-day menstrual cycle requests emergency contraception, having had unprotected sex on Day 13. She also wishes to start Combined Hormone contraception.

Will she require additional protection for a) 24 hours, b) 5 days, c) 7 days or d) 14 days? I was pretty sure the answer was 7 days, although if she was my real live patient I'd err on the side of caution. I chose answer c).

I came out of the exam feeling cross, exhausted and absolutely convinced I'd failed.

The surgery sign had been tampered with again. SNOT DRIP had become RAT POND. Mary was on reception. That was when I remembered about the ankles.

I said, 'At Mrs Buxton's party, what colour cardigan were you wearing?'

She looked at me.

'Why?'

'My girlfriend wasn't sure which of you was which. She said one of you was in white and one was in parchment.'

'Buttermilk, not parchment.'

'I'm hopeless with colours.'

'Our Dad was colour blind. He wanted to be an electrician, but they wouldn't have him, in case he mixed up the wires.'

'What did he do instead?'

'He worked at Danks's, in the boiler-making.'

'So, just to clarify, who was wearing the buttermilk cardigan at the Buxtons?'

'I was.'

'Thank you.'

She said, 'That Amber Evans is in the waiting room. She was angling to see you, but I told her, it's Dr Boddy or whistle.'

'You do mean Jean Boddy, not Harold?'

'Of course. I wouldn't let her anywhere near my gentlemen doctors.'

As soon as I got into the office, I wrote it down. Moira, white cardigan, petechiae.

So Amber Evans was still on the prowl. She was a trier, there was no denying. Amber was a notable feature of our patient lists. She had a long history of gynaecological adventures and was usually seen by Pam Parker, although I'd had a couple of encounters with her. It was me she'd first consulted when her fliptop phone got wedged in her vagina, and it was me she'd stalked one dark winter's night out in the car park. She'd offered me a blowjob in exchange for a lift home.

When I was being interviewed for the trainee position, Helen and Trevor had both had some concerns that I might attract unwanted attention from some of the female patients. It was very flattering, but actually, apart from Amber, the only approach I'd had was from Helen herself, so maybe I wasn't that attractive after all.

Amber called out to me as I passed the waiting room door. She may have a careless attitude to her private life, but she doesn't miss a trick. She was on her feet, ready to follow me into my room.

I said, 'You're on Dr Boddy's list today, not mine.'

'Pity, though,' she said. 'I only need five minutes and I've got to get down the housing office.'

They're like rubber balls, patients like Amber Evans and Kyle Bibby. You tell them 'no' and they just bounce back and come at you from a different angle. It doesn't make any difference if you're short with them, or even cross. Back they come, still smiling.

She said, 'Thing is, if I have to see a new doctor, it brings on my anxiety.'

'Anxiety?'

'Yes. I get it really bad.'

'If anxiety's your problem, Amber, you're in luck. That's one of Dr Boddy's areas of expertise.'

Jean Boddy herself appeared.

She said, 'What area of expertise is that?'

'Anxiety, particularly about new situations such as consulting a doctor you haven't seen before. This is Amber Evans. I think she's on your list?'

'Well, Amber,' she said. 'Let's you and me go and have a nice, relaxed chat.'

'Oh,' says Amber, 'I heard you was African. You don't look African.'

I saw Jean at the end of surgery.

'How did it go with Amber?'

'She told me the story of her life. I never did find out why she'd asked to see a doctor, but she seemed to go away satisfied.'

'You know her history?'

'I looked through her file. Pam's notes make very amusing reading. I hope Amber never asks to see them. We might have to do a bit of filleting.'

'Funnily enough, that topic came up on the test yesterday.'

'Your AKT! How did it go?'

'I really have no idea. You can only answer the question with one of the options they give you so even if you'd like more information, you're stuck with what they've given you. There was a question about confidentiality.'

'Go on.'

'A patient with a history of alcohol abuse comes to you for a medical report in support of his application to be rehoused. You write the report, the housing authority rejects his application and the patient comes back to you, angry, demanding to see what you wrote about him. Do you have any grounds to refuse?'

'What were the options?'

'Could you justifiably withhold the report because a) it contained factual errors, b) its contents would upset the patient and put the author of the report at risk, c) it revealed information about a third party or d) the housing authority hasn't agreed to disclosure.'

'Okay. Who does the report belong to? The patient or the housing department?'

'The patient, I suppose.'

'Right. Therefore d) is irrelevant and a) is ridiculous. But c) definitely and b) arguably.'

'I think I chose c). I hate that kind of test.'

'You'll be better suited to the Clinical Skills Assessment. From what I've heard, you don't have a lot of time to think but you can use your own common sense, and you can ask for more information. When are you taking it?'

'September or October, assuming I've passed the AKT.'

'We'll give you some practice sessions. Me and Harold.'

'That'd be great.'

'Pam too. I'm sure she'd be willing, and Trevor. He'd enjoy dreaming up a few cases for you.'

'How do you think he seems?'

'Hard to say because we didn't know him before, but full retirement is probably a death sentence. Okay, so he puffs and wheezes but he's still a good doctor. The patients love him. They all ask after him.'

'Helen's supposed to be my training supervisor, but I've learned far more from Trevor.'

'That's no surprise. She's never here. You stick with Trevor. When's this wedding of yours?'

'July 6th.'

'When you get back from your honeymoon, we'll organise some clinical skills sessions for you. Put you through your paces. Where are you going, by the way?'

'Zanzibar.'

'Very exotic.'

'Chloe's choice. Any advice, health-wise?'

'Anti-malarials, definitely. The rest depends on how intrepid you're going to be.'

'We're not. We're staying at a resort. What about yellow fever?'

'Yellow fever and typhoid are pretty low risk if all you're going to do is lounge on a beach and eat in a hotel. You might think of getting a Hep A/B shot, if you've not had one recently. Some people like to cover themselves for every possibility. Belt and braces. But don't mess around with malaria. Malarone's a good option. Start it 48 hours before you set off and keep taking it until you've been back for seven days. With food. Without fail.'

'A cottage in Pembrokeshire would have been a lot easier.'

Jean laughed.

She said, 'Zanzibar might be an adventure, before you settle down to married life. We did it the other way around. Honeymoon in Weymouth, then off to the Congo.'

'A lot of adventures there?'

'Too many. No, I take that back. Enough adventures.'

'Do you miss it?'

168

'A bit. The people. The mangoes. The night skies. It was time for us to come home, though, even if my Dad hadn't got sick. There are people who stay on, decide to live out their days there, but it doesn't always have a happy ending.'

Moira was on duty the next day. She had dark circles under her eyes. they Had they always been there?

She said, 'What are you studying? Have I got egg yolk on my chin?'

'You look tired.'

She said they'd had a bad night with their mother. I went behind the desk, to check if Chloe had been right about her ankles, but Moira was wearing trousers.

'And now what are you up to, snooping around in my Reception?'

'I thought I'd pick up the files for surgery.'

'The files for surgery are already in your office, same as always. Now stop cluttering up my place of work.'

I apologised for invading her territory.

'All right,' she said. 'So long as it doesn't happen again. Have a toffee.'

Trevor looked in, mid-morning. He'd just been to the Sorrento nursing home to certify a death. Clarence Bliss, the man I'd found with pressure sores. He'd died of aspiration pneumonia.

He said, 'He was 97, poor old blighter. And that's about all he weighed as well. He looked like a skinned cat. No family either.'

'It was nice to meet yours on Saturday. Did Mrs Buxton enjoy her party? You must be pleased Alice came.'

'Oh yes. God only knows when we'll ever see her again and we could have done without Micky, but we're grateful for whatever crumbs they toss us. So, what are you doing, sitting idle at 11 o'clock on a Wednesday morning?'

'I had a no-show and then Barbara Humphries phoned to say she's running late.'

'I haven't seen Barbara since her op. Would you mind if I sit in?'

'I'd be glad. Especially if she has her husband with her. He phoned me after her amputation and gave me a right ear-bending. He seemed to think it was all my fault. There's something else I'd like to ask you about. Do you think Moira looks okay?'

'I can't say that I've paid her much attention. Why?'

'Chloe noticed she had lower leg petechiae. At your party. I was hoping to have a discreet look myself but she's wearing trousers today.'

'Well I'm certainly not going to ask her to take them off, or even roll them up. We'll just have to wait till she comes to work in a skirt.'

'She does look a bit washed out. She says she's tired from nursing their mother.'

'Bound to be. But thanks for mentioning it. We should keep an eye on her. You know what women like Moira are like, trudging on, never complaining. Mind if I use your phone?'

He called Ladbroke's and placed a couple of bets.

Barbara Humphries burst into tears when she saw him. He gave her a hug, sat her down, pulled up a chair beside her. It was as though I wasn't there. She said they'd given her a temporary prosthesis, but she couldn't wear it. The stump of her leg was still slightly swollen, she was getting flashes of pain

170

from the foot that wasn't there and she felt life wasn't worth living.

Trevor said, 'You're grieving, sweetheart. I know it sounds daft to grieve for a foot, but it's still a loss when all's said and done. What do you think, Dr Dan? Try a bit of amitriptyline?'

It was a good idea. An anti-depressant might ease some of the pain as well as lift her mood. He asked her about her daughter's wedding.

'It's in August,' she said. 'But I've lost all interest in it.'

'Then you definitely need some amitriptyline. Mother of the bride, not interested! Mrs Buxton'd give anything to see our Alice married. Have you bought your hat?'

'No. I don't want people looking at me. Looking at where my foot used to be.'

'Nobody'll be looking at that, you silly billy. You get yourself up to Rackham's and spend some of Ken's hard-earned money. Or there's that place in Himley. Eileen Prior runs it.'

'RSVP.'

'That's the one.'

'I heard Eileen Prior's got multiple sclerosis. And her husband left her.'

'Yes. All true. But she still needs to earn a living and you need bucking up, so go and see her and buy a hat. And get yourself one of those TENs gadgets for your pain. They sell them in Boots. When Mrs Buxton had sciatica, she swore by hers.'

Barbara said, 'I think my Ken owes you an apology, Dr Talbot. I know he shouted at you, after they took my foot off.'

'No apology needed. It was an emotional time for both of you.'

'It still is,' she said. 'He looks at me different since this happened.'

171

'Another thing they don't teach you about in medical school,' Trevor said, after she'd left. 'Collateral damage.'

When I have an evening shift, I like to make myself tea and a sandwich before I set off for the Sterling call centre. The kitchen door was closed. The kitchen door is never closed.

Harold said, 'I'd leave it if I were you, Dan. High level conference going on in there.'

There was a raised voice. Helen was shouting at someone.

'Do you know who's in there? Is it her son?'

I knew it couldn't be Pam Parker. Pam would never stand for it. She'd be out of there, or raising her own voice.

He said, 'I could make an educated guess, but I'd prefer not to. I'm off home. Jean's roasting a chicken.'

I fetched my coat and bag, turned off the computer. Just as I was leaving, the kitchen door opened and Kasper emerged looking flushed and furious. He patted his pocket, found his car keys and headed for the front door. I followed him, asked him if he was alright.

He said, 'I can't do this anymore.'

'Trouble with Helen?'

'I'll have to quit, Dan. I don't want to. The job suits me. But she's impossible. I can't work with her.'

'Is it the actual work or the unofficial extras?'

'Unofficial extras!' he said. 'That's exactly right. I don't know which bit of "I don't want to have an affair with you" she can't understand. If it was me chasing her, I'd be in deep trouble.'

'It'd be a pity if you felt you had to leave. You're doing a great job.'

'Yes, well,' he said. 'I'm off now till Monday. Maybe she'll have cooled down by then.'

By Monday Helen had not so much cooled down as changed tack. She followed me into the nurses' room just before morning surgery.

'Dan,' she said, 'you and I should talk about how your training's going. Come for a drink one evening?'

I made what I hoped was a non-committal noise, a kind of okay-but-not-sure-when fob off.

She said, 'Nice wedding invitation, by the way. It arrived on Saturday morning.'

Her hand was resting warmly between my shoulder blades.

'Another fit young stud gone,' she said, and her hand slid down my back. 'What a shame.'

She left.

Linda said, 'Did she just pat you on the bum?'

'Possibly.'

'What is she like? A woman of her age. You know she's tried it on with Kasper? I mean, as if. It's pathetic. She must be fifty if she's a day.'

I said, 'I'm told fifty is the new forty.'

'That doesn't make it any better,' says Linda. 'Forty's old. I got my wedding invite too. Very nice. Is it, like, only for me, or can I bring a date?'

'Does it say "plus one"?'

'Don't think so.'

'Are you seeing someone?'

'I might be, by July.'

'You'll have to make a last-minute application to Chloe, to see if she has any spare places. Or you might get lucky at the wedding. Chloe's got a couple of cousins who are single. Wealthy too.'

'Now you're talking. I'll come on my own.'

I looked in on Kasper.

I said, 'I think you're off the hook. I just had my backside squeezed.'

He smiled.

'Who's next in line, do you think? Harold? The MediVan delivery driver?'

Trevor came by at lunchtime. Helen was out, Kasper had left to go to his other practice, the rest of us were in the kitchen.

'Moira, my lovely,' he said.

'Enough of the flannel,' she said. 'What do you want?'

'A drop of your blood. I don't like the look of you.'

Moira said, 'And I don't like the look of you. Never have.'

Trevor was in earnest though. He said he'd noticed she was looking pale and he wanted to check she wasn't anaemic.

She said, 'I'm not. I eat my greens.'

'Humour me, woman,' says Trevor. 'Or are you scared of needles? I can get Linda to do it if you don't trust me. She's got a light touch.'

Moira said she wasn't scared of needles and anyway she always looked pale, but she agreed to let Linda take a blood sample.

'Only because I don't want you niggling on about it,' she said. 'Blood tests! Whatever next?'

Linda was waiting for instructions.

'Complete cell count, plus diff,' he said.

I asked him what had made him decide. Moira was in trousers again so there was still no way we could check, casually, whether Chloe was right about the marks on her ankles.

He said, 'I don't know. Call it instinct. When you see somebody almost every day, year in, year out, you don't always notice things. If your Chloe's right, it might be a very important

174

observation. And if she's not, no harm done. Except I'll never hear the end of it from Moira. You are sure it was Moira?'

'Yes. Identified by the cardigan she was wearing. To Chloe they were completely different colours.'

'Aren't women amazing?'

I said, 'Just one thing. How are you going to handle the results? If they come back tomorrow, Mary will open the post. If they come back on Wednesday, Moira will be on duty.'

'All this is true,' he said, 'but they wouldn't know what the numbers mean and anyway, I'll make sure I'm here, hanging around, making a nuisance of myself. Right, Now, I've got one visit to make to a UTI in Dovecote, then I'm going home to watch the racing from Redcar.'

Chapter 18

Moira's blood results didn't come on Tuesday or Wednesday or even Thursday. When I got to work on Friday morning, Trevor was behind the reception desk with the day's post in his hand.

'Dr Dan,' says Moira, 'will you please take Dr Buxton away and make him a cup of coffee. He's getting under my feet.'

'Only trying to help,' says Trevor.

We went to my office, sorted through the envelopes and found Moira's report. Trevor sat down in my chair, his old chair, to read it. There's not a lot can be done for his breathlessness but if he leans forward, very slightly, and braces himself against the edge of a table or desk, it can make his breathing less laboured.

Well,' he said, eventually. 'I don't like the look of this. I don't like the look of this at all.'

Moira's platelet count was low, her haemoglobin was at the low end of the normal range, and her white cell count was elevated, notably neutrophils and lymphocytes, with a very high proportion of blast cells. It made sense of Chloe's fleeting observation of little skin patches of haemorrhage on her legs. Something was seriously amiss with Moira's blood.

I said, 'What do we do now?' She's not our patient.'

'Fuck. She and Mary are with the Joshi practice in Coseley. You'd better call them.'

'Me? Wouldn't it be better coming from you? They know you. They'll understand. Stubborn old lady. Valued employee. Concerns over her health, etc.'

'Yes, I suppose you're right. I'll have to tell Moira first, though. That's the tricky one. Getting the tone right.'

'You mean you don't want to alarm her.'

'I mean I want to alarm her slightly. You know what she's like. She'll tell me off for interfering. Then she'll promise to see her GP and do nothing about it.'

'But once you've spoken to her and her doctor, it's out of your hands. And if it is what it looks like…'

'Acute myeloid leukaemia.'

'If it is AML, isn't it up to Moira how she deals with it? She's a grown woman.'

'How did you get so wise all of a sudden, Dan Talbot?'

'I've had a few lessons from an old hand.'

Trevor said he'd speak to Moira at lunchtime, when things were quieter. Except that on that particular day things weren't. I'd had one house call, to Marion Flitwell. Marion is one of our morbidly obese shut-ins. She had intertrigo in her skin folds and it wasn't responding to treatment. It was a frustrating visit because Marion had managed to lose weight, the previous year, when her husband was in hospital. Terry was Marion's feeder, so as soon as he got home her weight piled on again. I hated seeing her go back to her old size but that was their deal, their chemistry. Terry liked Marion fat and Marion liked keeping Terry happy.

177

I calculated I had time for a lukewarm meat pie and some paperwork before afternoon surgery. As I pulled into Rat Pond a woman stepped out right in front of me, pushing a supermarket trolley. I had to stand on my brakes. She hardly noticed me, she was so intent on pushing the trolley across our car park. She was wearing carpet slippers. We reached the front door to the surgery at the same time. That was when I realised there was a human being slumped in the trolley. A girl.

I said, 'We're closed till 3.00. What do you need?'

'Look at her,' she said. 'She's ever so badly.'

It was a warm day, but the girl was wearing a thick, padded jacket. Her face was grey, her pulse was weak. I thought I recognised her.

I said, 'Is that Tegan?'

'Yes,' says the woman. 'She's my bab. Are you a doctor?'

We pushed the trolley into the surgery. It was the dead hour. There was nobody around apart from Nurse Chris who came out of her office to see what the noise was.

'Wow,' she said. 'Mini-market delivery. This is a first. Patient not ambulatory, then?'

'Tegan Strange. This is her mother.'

Chris helped me lift Tegan onto the examination table. Tegan was out of it, speech slurred, no idea where she was. Her mother said she'd been a bit fluey the day before and then suddenly felt too weak to walk. They'd just been to the Wavy Line to buy a Lottery ticket when she collapsed.

We got Tegan out of her jacket.

'Hmm,' says Chris, 'Something doesn't smell good.'

She pulled up the sleeve of Tegan's pyjamas and the problem was revealed. Her forearm was an oozing, septic mess and as I was fitting a blood pressure cuff on her, the story came back to me. The tattoo, GERG AND TEEG 4 EVAH. Gerg, or rather, Greg, hadn't stayed the 4 evah course, so Tegan had wanted the tattoo removed at the tax-payers' expense, I'd sent her away, and now this had happened. She'd tried to gouge off the tattoo herself.

Trevor and Helen both appeared. The room was getting crowded.

Helen said, 'Why is there a trolley in my surgery?'

Tegan's Mum said, 'I haven't got no money for taxis.'

Trevor said, 'What's up?'

'Tegan. She's got an infected wound, she's clammy and breathless and her BP is through the floor.'

Helen shouted to Moira to call for an ambulance. Moira didn't reply. Mrs Strange started wailing. Tegan was rambling.

Trevor shouted, 'Tell them it's urgent. It looks like a case of sepsis.'

Still no response from Moira.

Helen said, 'She must be in the loo. I'll do it.'

Mrs Strange asked what it all meant. Was Tegan going to die? 'She's my only bab,' she kept saying.

Trevor said, 'She'll survive. She's made a right old mess of her arm, though.'

'It's not her fault,' she said. 'She come here, to see about getting the tattoo lasered off but they said she'd have to go private and we haven't got that kind of money. I told her, if you cut yourself a bit, tell them that tattoo's giving you bad nerves, then they'll have to do it because it's your mental health. But she would keep poking at it.'

Helen returned. 'Twenty minutes for an ambulance,' she said. 'Let's get her into the shock position. Moira was in the back office, asleep. Napping on the job. It's time she retired.'

179

'You mean napping on her lunch break,' says Trevor. 'I've been known to do it myself. But leave it with me. I need to have a word with her anyway.'

'Have a word?' says Helen. 'That won't get us anywhere. You get too attached to people, Trevor. You've never sacked anyone in your life.'

Trevor was checking Tegan's blood pressure again.

I said, 'The thing is, Helen, we've reason to suspect Moira's ill.'

'We?' she said. 'Who's 'we'?'

Trevor said, 'Twenty minutes? Do we believe them? This lass could do with a vasopressor, but I'd rather let them administer it once they've got her in the wagon. Helen, I'll tell you about Moira later.'

The ambulance was with us in fifteen. I'd met the crew before. Chelle and Vic were the team who'd attended when Kyle Bibby collapsed in the street. I reminded them.

'That's right,' says Vic. 'The lighter fuel sniffer. Did he make it?'

'He did. He bounced back.'

'I dare say we'll be seeing him again one of these days. A returning customer. Are we about set, Chelle?'

'Are you going to give her dobutamine?'

'No. Just fluids i/v and the blue flashing light. Dobutamine's above my pay grade.'

As I wheeled the supermarket trolley outside, Pam Parker was arriving for work.

'Such a promising medical career,' she said, 'and then he ended up working for Wavy Line. What are you doing, Dan?'

'Obeying Helen's orders. We just had a sepsis case delivered by trolley. The patient's on her way to A&E and I've been told to tidy up.'

Back inside, Helen and Trevor were having a barney, but hissed and low so Moira wouldn't hear. Helen said he'd had no business checking Moira's bloods and strictly speaking she was right. Freelancing, she called it. Making up his own rules. Blurring professional and personal boundaries. Then she softened a bit.

She said, 'Call Dar Joshi now, then you can drive her over there. She ought to be seen today. And you'd better call Mary as well.'

'Good idea. Moira would want her there.'

'No, I don't mean for Mary to go with you. I mean get her in here, to take over on reception.'

I said, 'But what about their mother? She can't be left.'

Helen said, 'They left her to come to Mrs B's birthday. I have to have someone answering my phones.'

Nurse Chris said she'd cover reception as best she could.

Pam Parker said, 'Give me a shout if you get desperate, Chris. Anything for a break from cervical smears. And what exactly is the emergency with Moira?'

'Platelets at 20,000 and a raised blast count.'

Pam grimaced. 'And she's a stubborn old duck. Trevor'll have his work cut out getting her to put her coat on and go.'

But he didn't. Moira went without a fight. She knew something was wrong with her. The only argument she gave him was about calling her sister.

'No, no,' she said. 'There's nowt she can do. Any road, Mother needs her more than I do.'

Somehow, we got through the afternoon Moira-less. The phone rang unanswered a few times but as Pam said, all we were doing was implementing unavoidable triage. If it wasn't urgent, the caller would try again later. And if it was something really urgent, there was still the option of calling 999. By 5 o'clock Pam had finished her list and was sitting at the front desk, chain-eating Moira's toffees.

'Dan,' she said. 'You've seen the Hastilows.'

'Have I?'

'Maisie. Six years old. You treated her for tonsillitis.'

'Yes.'

'Anything strike you?'

I tried to rerun the Maisie consultation in my mind. The fact that I remembered it at all was possibly significant. We see an awful lot of sore throats.

'Don't think so. Why?'

'The mother brought her in because she's started bed-wetting. I only checked her throat because of her history. She's got oral lesions and they looked to me like genital warts.'

'No! And I missed them?'

'Not necessarily. They were on the floor of her mouth, and they might be a recent development. I gather there's quite a rapid turnover of 'uncles' in the Hastilow residence.'

'Did you ask the mother?'

'Pas devant les enfants, Dan. The mother's either clueless or complicit and anyway, this is an area for experts. I've made an urgent referral to a paediatric clinic and voiced my strong suspicions. The child's started stool-holding as well so God knows what's been going on.'

'Did you examine her?'

'Down below? No. I suspect the poor scrap has been poked enough.'

182

I called Sandwell to get an update on Tegan Strange. In ICU, they said. The waiting room was empty, but Pam Parker was still sitting at Reception.

'I like this job,' she said. 'You can try out different voices when you answer the phone. You can even read a book when there's a lull.'

Trevor came shuffling in.

'We're closed,' says Pam. 'Go home. Take paracetamol. There's a three week wait to see Dr Vincent, but I might be able to slot you in with one of the other charlatans next week.'

'What about Buxton?' he said. 'I heard he's a good doctor.'

'Buxton!' she said. 'Forget it. He's for spare parts only. So, what's the Moira story?'

Trevor had just taken Moira home.

'They're having her in tomorrow morning for bone marrow aspiration and biopsy.'

'That's quick.'

'It needs to be. If it is AML, her age is against her.'

'Does she realise?'

'I think so. It's hard to tell with someone like Moira. She keeps herself buttoned up. And of course, her main worry is their old mum. How Mary'll cope on her own if she's going to be out of action.'

'We'll be in a fix here too, if she's off sick.'

'Let's leave Helen and Kasper to deal with that headache. Any news on the sepsis girl?'

'Sedated and intubated. Do you know the Hastilows?'

'Vaguely.'

'Maisie,' Pam said. 'Six years old with very suspicious oral lesions. I think somebody's been getting his rocks off with the poor little mite.'

183

Trevor groaned.

I said, 'I've remembered something from when I saw her.'

'Go on.'

'It's probably nothing.'

'Say it anyway.'

'At the end of the consultation I gave her one of those stickers, for being a brave girl. And she kissed me.'

Pam and Trevor were both looking at me.

'On the lips, though. Was that a bit weird?'

'Oh Dan,' says Pam. 'My alarm bell is ringing loud and clear.'

Chapter 19

It was our weekend for meeting the Rector of St Botolph's. Chloe had tried to wriggle out of it with the 'busy doctor' ploy. Laurence and Vinnie had tried to buy him off with a donation to the altar linens fund. To no avail. If we wanted the Reverend Spedlow to marry us in his church, we were required to attend a pastoral Preparation for Marriage session with him. Chloe was furious. Vinnie was furioser. She said she had a good mind to ask for her twenty quid back.

The plan was to drive over to Bishop's Wapshott on Saturday morning, spend an hour with the rector, then head to the Chummery for lunch and an afternoon of wrestling the she-brats into their flower girl outfits. Dee was also coming, to try on her dress and receive instructions regarding her wedding duties.

I wasn't looking forward to the day. What with the prospect of one of my future mother-in-law's lunches, plus being in a confined space with potty-mouth Dee, plus Chloe's insistence on referring to the rector as Reverend Spud-u-Like, I had a humdinger of a stress headache by the time we set off. What I knew, but Chloe didn't, was that facially the Reverend Spedlow did slightly resemble a potato.

For all her bluster in the car, Chloe barely said a word while we were at the rectory. Reverend Spedlow saw us in his study. Mrs Spedlow brought in a tray of coffee and biscuits, then disappeared.

He said he wanted to remind us of the 4Cs that are vital in marriage: communication, commitment, conflict resolution and constancy. Marriage was a marathon, not a sprint, he said. Chloe nodded a lot. I found myself thinking about the time she left me, about her unrequited Jamil interlude. Did she still think of him? Did she have any reservations about marrying me? Her career had gone off the boil. What if the same thing happened with her feelings for me?

Reverend Spedlow read from 1 Corinthians 13. The 'Love is patient, love is kind' passage. Chloe seemed never to have heard it before.

'Oh,' she said, 'that's so lovely. I think I'd like that for our service. Who did you say wrote it?'

She knows just about everything there is to know about cardiac emergencies but very little about anything else.

We drove round to The Chummery. Flo's muddy Range Rover and Dee's sparkling Mini Cooper were parked out front. We were the last to arrive. There was a smell of hot food, not a thing you can always rely on with Chloe's mother.

'I've roasted a chicken,' she said.

Chloe said, 'A chicken? One chicken? There are nine of us and I'm starving.'

'Ne te fâche pas,' says Vinnie. 'There are oodles of veg. How was the vicar?'

186

'It was dead easy,' said Chloe. 'Just coffee and biscuits and a pep talk about not letting the sun set on a quarrel. Where's Dee?'

'In the garden. Daddy's showing her round.'

Flo was in the kitchen, with two of her girls, Poppy and Daisy.

I said, 'I'm told we're having chicken?'

'A sparrow, more like,' says Flo. 'I'm doing extra oven chips to eke it out. Why don't you drive over to see Henry? He's doing a fry-up.'

Poppy wanted to come with me, but she wasn't allowed. She had to stay for a dress fitting after lunch. The mention of this brought on a fit of pretend retching. Laurence came in from the garden. Dee was dressed for the country, denims, riding boots, a waxed cotton jacket. She had Lily hanging round her neck like a lanyard. I got a peck on the cheek.

She said, 'Cheer up, Popster. I'll tell your Aunt Chloe to let you wear trousers.'

Popster! She'd been there five minutes and she was already giving people nicknames.

Laurence said he'd join me if I was going over to see Henry.

'Damned good idea,' he said. 'Leave the girls to their big heap wedding pow-wow.'

Packwood Grange is about five miles from The Chummery. It's a rather fine house but also a working farm with puddles and fence holes blocked with sheets of corrugated iron and gates held shut with baler twine. Two lurchers ran out to escort us. Henry was in the kitchen, cooking, oblivious to the bleeping of the smoke alarm.

'Ah,' he said. 'Tactical withdrawal? Jolly sensible.'

He lobbed some more rashers and slices of black pudding into the pan and opened a bottle of red. Two cats wandered in and out, followed by a hen.

Laurence said, 'Did you know you have poultry in the house?'

Henry was busy wiping mushrooms.

He said, 'Is it a Lincolnshire Buff?'

'No bloody idea,' says Laurence. 'Not terribly hygienic, one imagines. Poultry shit on the kitchen floor.'

Henry said, 'If it's a Lincolnshire Buff, it's Daisy's. She's training it to count.'

We sat down to a feast. Henry talked about ammonia emissions. He was planning to install a tank for his pig waste.

'Pump the slurry in, add sulphuric acid, emissions problem solved.'

I asked about Charlie. Discussion of her brother's brush with the law was a no-go area with Chloe. I'd have expected his case to be heard by now, in spite of the family's insistence that it would never come to court.

Laurence said, 'All's quiet on that front. Of course, we've retained a very good brief. In law as in medicine, one gets what one pays for.'

Henry winked at me.

I said, 'That's all very well for those with money, Laurence. But I like to think we give the rest of the population a good standard of care.'

'I'm sure you do your best,' he said. 'And never forget, we in the private sector ease the pressure on the NHS.'

Henry said, 'Except for doctors who play at both ends. Cousin of mine is a surgeon. One hears of horrendous waiting

188

lists, but Gerald seems to carve out plenty of time for his private patients.'

It was the most I'd ever heard Henry say on any non-pig subject.

Laurence said, 'That friend of Chlo's is a livewire. I wonder we never met her before. Australian. Cracking girl.'

I explained Dee to Henry.

'I said 'bridesmaid' doesn't seem like quite the right word for Dee. She swears like sailor and drinks like one too. According to Chloe she's bi.'

'Mmm,' says Laurence, 'there's a lot of it about.'

Chloe phoned to say they were nearly done.

'How's it going?'

'Nightmare. Dee's out of control.'

'True to form, then.'

'Poppy's refusing to wear the dress and Dee's encouraging her. And Mummy keeps calling sage green snot green. What are you and Daddy up to?'

'Drinking Henry's very strong tea and eating fruit cake.'

'Well I need you to get back here so we can leave ASAP.'

'Half an hour.'

'Please. Any longer and I'll probably kill Flo.'

'Why, what's she done?'

'Nothing. Absolutely nothing. That's my point. She just sits there, showing zero interest.'

I called at the Horn and Trumpet on the way back to The Chummery, to check on our booking for July. Rob and I are staying there the night before the wedding, plus Da and Mam, and Nan Talbot and Aunty June in the ground floor annexe, to avoid any stairs. Everything was confirmed. All in all, I felt we'd had a good day. The Reverend Spud-u-Like was satisfied,

Poppy believed she might be excused the flower fairy dress. And I'd had a good lunch. Chloe wasn't happy though.

I said, 'Does it really matter if Poppy wears cricket whites? She'll just look like a boy with long blonde hair.'

But it wasn't the Poppy thing that was bugging her. It was Dee, who apparently looked too fabulous in indigo.

'I thought one of the reasons you chose her was because she'd look good?'

'Forget it,' she said. 'You clearly don't understand anything.'

By Monday morning Moira and Mary's mother had been taken to Dovecote for respite care, and we had an agency temp on Reception, a middle-aged woman called Carol. The first thing she told me was that she'd be leaving at 5 o'clock sharp.

Trevor emerged from Helen's office. I heard him say, 'All right, my dear. Keep me posted.'

I asked him about Moira.

'She's had bone marrow aspiration and a trephine biopsy. Now we have to wait.'

'How long?'

'Couple of weeks. It might not be AML. But if it is, the therapy's brutal. Seven days on cytarabine, three days on anthracycline. It's not for the frail and our Moira's not young and she's not so strong as she used to be. Step outside with me a minute. I'd like a quiet word.'

He wanted to tell me Helen's news. Miles had been arrested on Saturday night and charged with possession and intent to supply.

'Benzos?'

'And party pills. Piperazine. All Class C, I gather. He's at Dudley Magistrates this afternoon.'

'Will his Dad get him off?'

190

Trevor said, 'Not entirely, I hope. Clifford's a lawyer of limited talents and Miles would benefit from a cold shower.'

'Is he likely to get a custodial sentence?'

'I very much doubt it. And much as I'd like to give the little prick a sobering lesson, I don't think prison would help. He'd fall in with a crowd of career idiots and come out worse than he went in.'

'I'm still waiting for the shoe to drop regarding Chloe's brother. The Swifts all seem confident that he'll get a suspended sentence. But that was cocaine, so I'm not so sure. Are we all meant to know, about Miles?'

'Officially, no, but given that you can't break wind behind a closed door at the Lindens without Nurse Linda's closest twenty friends hearing about it, yes. Just use your discretion. And don't give Helen any pitying looks.'

'I still think of this place as the Lindens too.'

'Of course you do. Bloody Tipton Road West. Ridiculous name. Do you ever hear from Vaz?'

'Yes. Married life is wonderful and he's blissfully happy.'

'Bless his saggy little socks. I'm glad somebody is.'

I saw several hay-fever cases that morning and a couple of lower backs. I like to take my time with back pain, particularly since Ron Jarrold. Paul Styles came in as well. His oesophageal endoscopy was all clear, but he was still worried. What to do with him? He was clearly having problems swallowing. I'd seen it for myself. Could it be psychological? Some patients get very offended if you even hint at such a thing.

I said, 'Paul, I think we could be in a vicious circle with this. It may be your gullet just goes into spasm and the more anxious you get about it, the more it does it. How about we try you on something to take the edge off your anxiety?'

191

Paul has great faith in doctors. If I advised him to stand on his head in the window of Topman, I believe he'd do it. He was all in favour of taking off the edge. I gave him a prescription for Tofranil, told him to report back to me after a few weeks.

Helen came in at the end of surgery. She never knocks.

She said, 'I suppose you've heard about Miles?'

'Yes, Trevor told me. You'll be going to court with him?'

'Of course. We just have to hope there's nobody on the bench today that Cliff has ever annoyed. You haven't done a surgery with me for a while.'

'I haven't done a surgery with anyone for a while. I'm getting used to working solo. But I'm observing at a dermatology clinic on Thursday, at Sandwell, and a paediatrics clinic next week.'

'Good. Fine. Tell Trevor. He'll be delighted to take your list. Have you had anything of interest lately?'

'I've got a patient with oesophageal spasm. Endoscopy didn't reveal anything, so I've prescribed Tofranil. Any other suggestions?'

Then I wished I hadn't asked. She sat down in the patient's chair to think. Helen makes me nervous, particularly when the door is closed. She wasn't looking at her best, little wonder with a son due in court on drugs charges, but there was still something about her that was very sexy.

She looked at me, shoved her glasses on top of her head.

'Not long till your wedding.'

'Yes.'

'We should have that drink.'

'Yes?'

'Talk about your clinical assessments. Talk about your future.'

'Okay. You remember I'm going to be away for two weeks, after the wedding?'

'Two weeks?'

'I did tell you. We're going to Zanzibar.'

'Zanzibar? Are we paying you too much? What happened to the trolley girl?'

'Tegan. She's out of ICU but she might need dialysis.'

'She's lucky she didn't lose her arm. Viagra.'

'Sorry?'

'Your spasm case? I'm pretty sure I read somewhere about Viagra helping with oesophageal spasm. Might be worth investigating.'

Carol, the temp on Reception, didn't win any friends on her first day with us. She cleared all Mary and Moira's bits and bobs off the desk, sighed when I asked her for some prescription blanks, and told Pam Parker off for walking in without registering.

Pam said, 'I'm a doctor, pet. I work here.'

'Doesn't matter,' says Carol. 'You should still check in with me. What if there's a fire?'

She had her coat on at 4.55 and was on her way out the door at 4.59 even though the phone was ringing. As she left, Trevor arrived.

'I bring good news,' he said. 'Mrs Aldridge loves Dovecote.'

'Who's Mrs Aldridge?'

'The Marys' mother. I don't think she'll want to leave and nor should she. She's not a small woman and they shouldn't be doing all that lifting. It's the biggest wonder they don't both have slipped discs.'

'If the old lady settles in Dovecote, that means Mary can come back to work.'

'It'll depend on how Moira goes on. If she's going to be put through the mill, Mary'll want to be with her. Be nice if she comes back though. Then we can give that clock-watcher her cards. And in further news this evening, Miles Vincent got sentenced to 100 hours unpaid work and a 6-month night curfew, 8pm to 8am. So if you see a pasty-faced lad in a high viz vest cleaning up grass verges, that'll likely be our Miles. Right. Anyone for the Black Bear? I'm buying.'

Chapter 20

Chloe was taking a break from choosing wedding flowers and had a new bone to chew: our honeymoon flights. We'd got our visas and the hotel was booked. Now we just needed to get there and, surprisingly, there seemed to be plenty of options. Fortunately, I looked over her shoulder before she hit any Buy buttons.

She said, 'I think this is the one to go for. An afternoon flight out of Birmingham and it's £300 cheaper than Emirates.'

'Great. How long is the flight?'

'Just under 19 hours.'

I said, 'Chloe, that can't be right. You can get to South Africa in 12 hours. I remember when Matt did it.'

She said the 19 hours probably included time for a connecting flight. I'm sure she pays much closer attention when she's dealing with patients. She peered at the screen.

'We change planes at MAD. Where's MAD?'

MAD was Madrid. But there was a second stop where we'd have to change planes again. ADD.

'Where's ADD? Look it up.'

'You look it up.'

Chloe was losing interest. She's a great one for quick-click buying, then sending stuff back because it's not what she thought it'd be. You can't send flights back, though, or flog them on e-Bay. You're stuck with them.

She wandered off to the kitchen, looking for cheese. I knew there wasn't any.

I said, 'No wonder it's a 19-hour journey. ADD is Addis Ababa. Birmingham to Madrid, Madrid to Addis Ababa, then Addis Ababa to Zanzibar.'

'Okay.'

'No, not okay at all. I am not spending the first night of my honeymoon at Addis Ababa airport and I'm definitely not travelling on any plane with the word Ethiopian on its fuselage.'

She said I seemed determined to ruin everything. First, I'd failed to get more than two weeks off from work, then I'd doom-mongered about malaria, and now I was quibbling over flight times. All true.

'I just want us to have a nice honeymoon, without getting sick or exhausted or stranded because we've missed a connection.'

'You just want us to go to that bloody Welsh cottage.'

'Look, I'd love to go to Barafundle Bay but, being mindful of the advice given to us by Reverend Spud-u-Like, I'm prepared to compromise.'

I got a weak smile out of her.

'How much of a compromise?'

'Hot enough for you to wear a bikini. Not so hot that I don't have the energy to remove it.'

I made us grilled Elvises, like we used to eat, late at night, when we first got together. A peanut butter, bacon and banana sambo is a very useful way of short-circuiting a Chloe sulk. She said she really needed to get her body beach-ready.

'Starting tomorrow,' she said.

I said, 'I promise we'll go to Zanzibar someday. Just not when time and money are limited.'

'You mean when we're old?'

'Probably. When the kids have left home.'

'How many?'

'Kids?'

'No, how many Elvises are you making. I'm starving.'

Tuesday was my good news day. We cancelled Zanzibar and booked a beach holiday in Turkey and I heard that I'd passed my AKT. On Wednesday, the temp receptionist failed appear, but it didn't matter because Mary was glad to come back to work. She said she didn't know what to do with herself, sitting at home. Moira was sleeping a lot. And going to visit their Mum in Dovecote felt like a wasted journey because Mrs Aldridge suddenly had a full social diary. Music Hour, Pet-a-Dog, Armchair Yoga.

The Jarrolds came in, late-morning. Ron looked seedy. They'd started him on hormone therapy, to slow the growth of his tumour or even shrink it, if he was lucky. He said he felt worse, not better. It can happen after the first dose, but things usually settle down. His breasts were enlarged and tender and he was getting hot flushes.

Freda said, 'Now he knows what we women go through.'

I was keen to finish surgery on time because I needed to get to Sandwell, to a dermatology clinic, and there were roadworks on the Expressway, but I gave Ron more than his allotted ten minutes. It seemed he was on short rations of sympathy at home.

'Pomegranate juice,' he said. 'She's got me on pomegranate juice. What do you think of that?'

'Do you enjoy it?'

'No. Flaxseed. That's another thing. She's sprinkling flax seeds on everything.'

'Well, on everything is probably too much.'

'See, Freda? You tell her, Doctor, because she won't listen to me.'

But Freda wouldn't be gainsaid. She was throwing everything she could at Ron's cancer. It was a delicate situation and it would probably have been better coming from Trevor, the older, wiser man, but I said, 'I do think it's important to keep a balance. Yes, Ron has cancer, but you can't let it rule everything you do. You have lives to live too.'

'All very well for you to say,' says Freda. 'He's developed a very defeatist attitude. Some days I feel like I'm the only one putting up a fight.'

Ron said he'd just like to be allowed to eat steak and chips without getting nagged. Suddenly I was a marriage guidance counsellor.

We left it that he'd report back to me after he'd had his second injection of Prostap and in the meanwhile he had my approval to eat a steak dinner if that was his heart's desire and limit the flaxseeds to his cornflakes.

Freda's parting words were, 'Thanks for nothing. Big help, you were.'

I was late getting to the dermatology clinic, but I struck lucky. They put me in with a registrar called Imtiaz, a man who thought skin was the most interesting organ in the world and by the end of the afternoon he'd almost convinced me. The first patient we saw was a middle-aged woman with a rash on the skin under her considerable breasts and belly overhang. A candida infection, according to Imtiaz, but he took a swab anyway, to make sure. He prescribed a topical anti-fungal.

'She'll be back,' he said. 'It's very hard to treat when you have deep skin folds like that.'

'We have an obese diabetic with exactly the same problem. And even if she lost weight, which she's not going to do, she'd still have the loose skin.'

'Right,' he said. 'Depressing, isn't it? Too many biccies. Too many pies.'

Imtiaz was from Bolton. Pies is a very long word when you have a Lancashire accent.

We were just finishing up with a man who had a small, raised blue lesion on his upper back. When you looked at it under a magnifying glass it had a little frill of spider veins around its edge which indicated that a biopsy was in order. Imtiaz's pager beeped. He was required in A&E. I hadn't expected anything exciting to happen at a dermatology clinic, so I went with him.

The patient was a man in his 40s, well-spoken, well-dressed. Colin. His wife had hung his suit jacket over the back of a chair. Colin had flu' symptoms and a blotchy rash. The GP had prescribed a topical steroid cream but that hadn't helped. The odd thing was the location of the rash, on the palms and the soles of his feet. That was why Imtiaz had been beeped.

He spent a long time looking at the rash. Had Colin been overseas recently? Yes, he travelled a lot. Ecuador mainly. Colin was in bananas. Imtiaz asked the nurse if any bloods had been taken.

'Not yet,' she said.

'Perhaps you could go through the admission form with next of kin?' he said and gave her a beady-eyed look until she twigged what he was getting at and ushered Colin's wife out of earshot.

Colin himself was very subdued. He was feeling rotten and I suppose he knew which way the consultation was likely to go. On his travels, had he ever had unprotected sex? Once or twice. Had he noticed any sores or other lesions on his genitals? He didn't think so. Well, he might have.

He said, 'Is it HIV?'

Imtiaz said, 'We'll screen for that, but it's more likely you have secondary syphilis.'

'Shit,' says Colin. 'I thought they'd wiped that out.'

'No, but don't worry. We can treat it with antibiotics. It's not the end of the world.'

'Ha,' says Colin. 'You don't know my wife.'

Imtiaz said, 'In the meanwhile, best not to have sexual intercourse. Would you like a doctor to talk to your wife?'

'No need. We'll just say I've got a bit of an infection, all right?'

Imtiaz went off and made a phone call. I asked him what bloods he was ordering.

'None,' he said. 'Not my field. I know the RPR test and VDLR can give you false negatives and anyway, they're not specific to a syphilis infection. Anyway, I'm leaving all that to the cock doc.'

Colin's wife had rejoined him.

She said, 'Are you keeping him in? I brought his pyjamas, in case.'

'No, no,' says Imtiaz. 'Dr Ang will be down presently. She'll explain everything to you and take some blood and probably give Colin a penicillin shot.'

'What, another doctor?' she said. 'All this waiting around. And it's probably just something he ate.'

200

We went back to the clinic. One of the patients on Imtiaz's list didn't appear when her name was called. Gone walkabout perhaps, or given up hope. He gave me five minutes of potted dermatology for GPs. To refer or not to refer?

'We get a lot of psoriasis referrals. But it can usually be managed by the GP, with a Vitamin D preparation or coal tar. They're both good options. Nothing's a quick fix, though. It can easily take three months. The patient needs to be patient. So don't send them to us unless their psoriasis is really disabling them. Same thing with Molluscum contagiosum. It'll usually resolve, given time.'

'Skin cancers are my biggest worry. Whether a lesion calls for a 2-week referral or just the regular waiting list.'

'If in doubt, fast-track them, but basal cell is pretty easy to spot, nice smooth, curved margins with a pearly sheen. No great urgency there. With melanoma, you're looking for ragged edges, varied pigmentation, itching, bleeding, crusting, growing. Melanomas even look bad. Squamous cell carcinoma can be harder to differentiate, so like I say, when in doubt…'

'The syphilis case was interesting.'

'It was. I had seen it before, but only once. It's very treatable. The marriage might be harder to fix, mind, once the penny drops.'

I was home before Chloe. There was a parcel hanging out of the letterbox, half ripped open. T shirts for Chloe's hen weekend. Dee was organising everything. They were going to London. The original plan had been to go to Amsterdam, but some of Chloe's friends are married now, with children. They didn't have the energy or the inclination for airports or getting expensively blootered or stoned, or both.

201

On the front of the T shirts it said 1 HEN, 6 CHICKS, BRING ON THE COCKS. On the back of one shirt it said BRIDE: FINAL FLING BEFORE THE RING. I waited to see Chloe's reaction before I said anything. She laughed when she saw them.

I said, 'You're not going to wear that in public, are you?'

'Why not?' she said. 'Lighten up. Don't give me that Welsh face.'

'So, if some bloke reads it, he'll think you're available for a quickie.'

'He won't. They won't. It's just a bit of fun. Everyone knows that.'

'That may be what you think. For a guy it's pretty confusing.'

'If you had a stag weekend you wouldn't think twice about having a little flirt. Why don't you? There's still time.'

'Because I don't want to. Rob's not here yet, Matt's a bore and I never see the rest of the crowd.'

'Actually, what are you going to do while I'm away? Organise your sock drawer?'

'I'm going to have dinner with Vaz and Teresa.'

'Wild.'

I said, 'If it's 'wild' you want, you've chosen the wrong man.'

It wasn't that I didn't trust, Chloe. We may have had a slight wobble, over Jamil, but we'd recovered. We were back on track. I did trust her. Basically. It was Dee who was the problem. When she's around, Chloe's different.

We didn't quarrel. I decided to be the grownup. If drinking shots and listening to Dee's screams of laughter was Chloe's idea of a fun weekend, she was welcome to it. I was going to buy my wedding shoes, listen to the Wales/Japan rugby match and have a curry and a catch-up with the Vazes.

Chapter 21

The hen weekend hadn't been a success. Chloe had a persistent Tequila headache and relations with Dee were strained. Not good between a bride and her right-hand woman, a month before the wedding. Dee had apparently had a great time, but at the expense of Hua who had been locked out of their shared bedroom so Dee could have sex with a man she'd picked up in a nightclub called Gorilla.

Chloe called in sick. I left her in bed with Eeyore and went to work.

Though I still think of the practice as The Lindens, I do look forward to driving in and seeing what the vandals have been up to. I wasn't disappointed. The RAT POND sign, only recently restored to TIPTON ROAD WEST MEDICAL CENTRE, had become TIT DROOP.

Trevor said, 'And you all wonder why I'm reluctant to retire. Where else would you get a cheap laugh at half past eight on a Monday morning?'

He came in for a natter before surgery started.

'Good weekend?'

'I saw Vaz. He sent his regards.'

'Has that sweet wife licked his wardrobe into shape yet?'

'I don't think she intends to. She likes him just the way he is.'

'Lucky man. So, any tasty morsels for me, young Talbot? Clinical or otherwise?'

I told him about the Jarrolds, and about man with the syphilitic rash. He wasn't sure he'd ever seen one.

'Were you there when they told the wife?'

'No. I think they were leaving that to someone from the STD clinic. Or maybe to the man himself. What would you do?'

'As a physician or as a patient? No idea. Decide on the spur. Bottle it, probably. Have you noticed a decline in the number of Cherry Tree residents you've been seeing?'

'No. Well, Kyle hasn't been in for a while. Why?'

'They're filming a documentary. Very exciting. Bread and circuses, lad. Kyle'll be busy getting ready for his close-up.'

'Any news on Moira?'

'She's threatening to come in tomorrow. I don't suppose you know where that temp gargoyle hid her panda pencil sharpener?'

'I think she shoved everything in a drawer. Does this mean Moira got the all-clear?'

'Sadly, no. It's galloping AML. They're offering palliative care only, which in Moira's case means coming to work till she drops. Very much my own plan, as you know. She'll probably let Mary drive the desk and she'll just sit at the back and provide helpful comments. Be nice to have her back, though. Right, I'm off to the Sorrento. Tommy Jukes is at the departure gate.'

Helen looked in on me towards lunchtime. She had her coat on, as per. Off to some meeting, no doubt.

She said, 'Did I tell you about Keith Sideaway?'

'No. How's he doing?'

204

'He died. Last week. Tuesday, I think.'

'That was sudden. He seemed stable the last time I saw him. Poor Keith.'

'Don't forget we're going to have a drink one evening.'

'Sure. When's the funeral?'

'I don't know. Why?'

'I'd like to go.'

'Why? He wasn't even your patient.'

'Because I liked him. He had a great attitude. And I was there when he first came in, with his drooping eyelid.'

She shrugged.

'Don't get so involved,' she said. 'Patients die. You could spend all your time going to funerals.'

Nevertheless, I decided I would go, if I hadn't already missed it.

I was out on a couple of house calls when Chloe phoned me.

'So much for Daddy's brilliant lawyer friends,' she started. 'Slow's case is being heard on Thursday.'

Charlie Swift, was about to learn his fate.

I said, 'But isn't that good? To get it over with?'

'How can it be good? It's horrid. I don't see why they even have to have a court hearing. It's not as though he's some big drug baron. They should just fine him and concentrate on real criminals.'

'Which court?'

'Somewhere in London. Snaresbrook.'

'Did you go to work in the end?'

'No. I was about to when Mummy phoned and dropped this bombshell. There's no point in going in now. I wouldn't be able to concentrate.'

From the point of view of patients paying good money to see a cardiologist, this was probably the right decision. Still, if this was what Chloe was like before the hearing, I dreaded to think what she'd be like after it.

When I got back to Tit Droop Mary had tracked down the information I needed.

'The Sideaway funeral. Friday, 12 o'clock. Lodge Hill Crematorium. Family flowers only.'

'Thank you. Did you find Moira's pencil sharpener?'

'I did not.'

'Let me see if I can find you one, on-line.'

She said, 'It's kind of you, but don't bother. They've told us she hasn't got long.'

'I'm so sorry.'

'She's leaving me in the lurch. We were always going to have a little holiday, once Mother passed, but that won't happen now. It looks like Moira's going to pip her to the post.'

All through afternoon surgery I felt out of sorts. Moira was never going to see the Scottish Highlands. Keith Sideaway hadn't made it to Euro Disney. And Charlie Swift's court appearance was going to hang over Chloe like a week of wet Mondays. Then Mary cheered me up.

She said, 'Your 4.30 has cancelled. Is it all right if I squeeze Mr Bibby in?'

Ten minutes with Kyle was just what I needed.

He threw himself into the chair like a man whose last ounce of strength was spent.

'What. A. Day,' he said.

'Been busy, have you?'

'Don't ask.'

'What can I do for you?'

'Just me tammies. Only I've been working.'

'Good for you.'

'For the telly people.'

I took the bait. I was ready for some light relief.

I said. 'That sounds interesting. What kind of work would that be?'

'Started off, I was actually on camera. Local colour, like.'

'What's the programme?'

'Documentary, about the estate. Only then they realised how useful I could be. Nobody knows Cherry Tree like I do. I'm in a bit of a management role as well, you know? For the residents. Making sure they're getting a fair deal. Making sure they're not being exploited.'

He said the word 'exploited' with quite a flourish.

'You have been busy. So, it's a documentary about the residents? And what's the angle?'

'Poverty trap. Health problems. Social isolation. Like my Mum, she's got agoraphobia.'

'Has she? I didn't realise. I've seen her out and about.'

'She puts on a brave face. Then there's my sister. She's got whiplash. Tripped on a loose slab. Caz Dearlove's got mildew and SAD, and then there was our tragic loss.'

'Chad?'

'Chad. A needless death. They should put safety barriers along them walkways. So what with one thing and another, I'm feeling the strain. I reckon I need 30s this week, Doc.'

As soon as Kyle starts calling me Doc, I know it's time to get rid of him. I wrote him up for 20 mgs.

He said, 'It's a pity they haven't interviewed you. Right up your street, when you think about it. Health and that. You must have quite a few patients on the estate. I'll put in a word.'

'No thanks, Kyle. Dr Buxton would be the man for that. Or Dr Vincent?'

'What, the one with a face on her? Not likely. I'll tell you, man to man, women like her make my nuts shrivel.'

I wasn't looking forward to an evening of Chloe's What Ifs about Charlie. I dropped by the Black Bear for a half with Trevor.

I said, 'Did you get a call from your agent?'

'What?'

'This documentary they're filming on Cherry Tree? Kyle Bibby said he'd put in a word with the director, get you on camera, for the health care perspective. He asked me first, but I told him it was more your kind of thing.'

He grinned.

He said, 'Then I shall sleep with this mobile jobbie under my pillow. I wouldn't want to miss that call. How is dear Kyle?'

'Exhausted. He's taken charge of finding locations, negotiating appearance fees, generally keeping his finger on the pulse.'

'Blimey. He could be up for a BAFTA.'

Trevor didn't think there'd be anything amiss with me going to Keith Sideaway's funeral.

He said, 'Helen doesn't hold with it, I know, but once in a while there'll be a patient who gets a little toe hold in your heart. And why not? We're not machines. We're not penny-in-the-slot pill dispensers, though God knows, some days that's what it feels like.'

'It's in Selly Oak. Would you be okay to do morning surgery on Friday?'

'It'll be my pleasure. Unless I'm required on set, of course.'

'Of course.'

'Here, do you think Kyle's got one of those director's chairs with his name on it?'

Chloe said she was thinking of taking the rest of the week off, so she could go down to London, to support Charlie. I suggested that not only was it completely unnecessary, seeing as he'd have Laurence and his lawyers with him, but also inadvisable. She was already taking a generous amount of time off for the wedding and our honeymoon.

I said, 'What about your patients?'

'What about them?' she said. 'We have plenty of other doctors who can see them. The Arden's not like your place.'

Nothing like. We don't have carpet and a fish tank and piped relaxation music in our waiting room. But we do get to know our patients. Best not to mention the funeral I was going to, I decided.

Mam phoned.

'What it is,' she said, 'your brother's probably definitely coming to the wedding.'

'Probably definitely' was about as strong a statement of commitment as you'd ever get from Adam and I didn't really care whether he came or not. I suspected anyway that Mam had edited its content. Adam himself had probably said, 'Dunno. We'll see.'

She said, 'So I was wondering about the catering. Because I know you're having the hog roast.'

Adam is selectively vegetarian. He'll put lashings of Mam's gravy on his dinner and he knows full well she uses beef dripping. It's a power play.

I said, 'Mam, half of Chloe's cousins are vegetarian. Don't worry. Adam won't starve. How's Nan?'

209

'Not bad. She's still doing her own shopping. It's more her personality, Dan. She never used to be so quarrelsome. She's still not speaking to that poor woman next door. The one she thinks stole her floor cloth? But she's going on a mystery trip next week, with the Seniors. To Monmouth.'

'So not really a mystery trip.'

'Well, Evan Coach is driving them, so it could be. You all set then, for the big day?'

Should I mention that Chloe's brother had a big day coming up too? I decided not. Then Chloe demanded to speak to Mam and I was banished to the bedroom and warned not to listen at the door. My mother and my future wife, who had previously circled each other nervously, sniffing the air for traces of disapproval, were apparently hatching a secret together. This made me feel so ridiculously happy that I lay on the bed and nodded off. When I woke, the pink glow of contentment hadn't faded, something the next few days was about to correct.

Charlie Swift was sentenced to 18 months in HMP Coldingley in Surrey. The sentence was roughly what I'd expected but it hit Chloe hard and she spent much of Thursday evening on the phone to her mother. Vinnie herself seemed mainly relieved that he hadn't been sent to a prison anywhere near her golf club.

'Much better to go away,' she said. 'Like fallen girls used to, until they'd podded and had the baby adopted. Otherwise there's bound to be talk.'

'Did Laurence get to speak to him?'

'Only before the hearing. They bundled Charlie away afterwards. It's all just too awful. Laurence is staying in Town tonight. He's too drained to drive.'

I imagined Laurence was not only drained but also busy scraping the hubris off his face.

'You know, 18 months doesn't mean 18 months. He'll probably be out in nine months.'

'Yes, that's what the brief thinks. Now do put poor Chlo on. She must be so distressed.'

Chloe was beyond distressed. When we first heard the news she said, 'When will he have to check in?'

'Check in?'

'You know, register, whatever it is they do.'

I said, 'It's not a conference. He's already gone, checked in, banged up, whatever the term is, and I don't think they'll have given him an orientation pack or a free book bag.'

She said I was enjoying her brother's misfortune. I really wasn't. I was just quietly pleased that Laurence's web of influence hadn't been as useful as he had so confidently predicted.

Chloe said, 'He'll be terrified.'

'Yes, he will. That's part of the plan.'

'What plan?'

'To discourage him from doing it again.'

'I'll bet half of those judges do cocaine at weekends. The first thing we have to do is send him some nice things, sweets and toiletries and stuff, so he knows we haven't forgotten him.'

'He's not been transported to Tasmania in shackles. I bet there's a gym. Probably a library.'

'Slow doesn't do gyms or libraries. Then we have to make sure they know the dates he'll need off. Ideally the Friday, Saturday and Sunday.'

'Dates? What are you talking about?'

'For the wedding, dimwit.'

211

She howled when I spelled it out for her. That prison is prison and you don't get a weekend off because your sister is getting married. She cried and cried. Nothing I said consoled her. She spent the evening on the bed with Eeyore, but even he couldn't cut it. Eventually, quite late, she emerged. She was calm and composed.

'Well,' she said, 'it's pretty clear what I have to. I'm cancelling the wedding.'

Chapter 22

What to do? To ignore Chloe's threat to cancel the wedding? Try to reason with her? Humour her, pretend it was all the same to me if she pulled the plug on months of preparations? I played it cool. Apart from wondering out loud what the second-hand market in wedding dresses was like, I said nothing.

Vinnie was furious, but with me not with Chloe.

'Be firm with her, Dan,' she said. 'Impress upon her the absolute heaps of money we stand to forfeit.'

I said, 'If money's the argument, it needs to come from you or Laurence.'

'No use Laurence calling her,' she said. 'She wraps him round her little finger. Anyway, he's terribly busy. He has Charlie to sort out and he has a very heavy case load at the moment. I doubt if he'll get home this weekend.'

'Laurence is working on a weekend?'

'He has a hugely important client with vocal chord nodules. I'm afraid I'm not allowed to say who.'

I resisted the urge to call Mam and tell her the wedding was off. What if Chloe changed her mind? What if she didn't? I kept myself busy. I was ironing a shirt when Chloe's phone rang. She ignored it.

She said, 'You answer it if you're so interested. My life is in ruins.'

The caller was just about the last person on earth I'd have expected. Her brother-in-law, Henry Packwood.

I said, 'Chloe's not available at the moment.'

'Of course she's available,' he said. 'Put her on. Or do I have to drive up there and tell her a few home truths to her face? Because I will.'

Sweet, meek Henry, normally monosyllabic unless the conversation turned to pigs, had home truths to deliver? I had underestimated the man. I put the phone on speaker, handed it to Chloe and watched her deflate. Her mouth opened a couple of times, but nothing came out. Henry was in full flood. She couldn't believe her ears and I could hardly believe mine. He was magisterial.

'You were ever the spoiled child,' he said, 'though your brother runs you a close second. It's a mere sixteen days until your wedding, an event that has monopolised time, money and energy for as long as any of us can remember. I fear Dan is too careful of your feelings to tell you how immature your behaviour is. Charlie received no more than he deserved and if I know him, he'll emerge from prison as full of bluster as ever. He is not a reason to cancel your wedding to a good and decent man. Relatives, old and young, are looking forward to it. People are travelling from the Antipodes for it. Your hog-roast beast has already gone to slaughter and I have foregone the opportunity to exhibit my prize boar at the Goosnargh and Longridge Agricultural Show in order to attend your nuptials. Pull yourself together, woman.'

214

Who ever knew he could be so passionate? Fit to pop a button on his Harris tweed waistcoat. He'd used the word 'nuptials'. And 'foregone'. But even that didn't raise a smile from her. She went to bed without saying another word. I think she was in shock.

I woke early but Chloe was ahead of me. She was curled up on the sofa with a mug of tea, watching television with the sound muted. She looked at me.

'Why are you wearing a suit?'

'Because I'm going to a funeral.'

'Whose?'

'A patient.'

'Is that appropriate?'

'Are you going to sit in your dressing gown all day?'

'Why are you being horrid?'

'Can't imagine. Oh. Wait. You cancelled our wedding. That'll be it. You cancelled our bloody wedding and when I get home tonight, after two surgeries and a funeral, I'm going to have to phone my family and friends to break the news.'

She mumbled something. I didn't quite catch it.

'I said "no need",' she said. 'I won't cancel. I'll be miserable, knowing Charlie's locked up with criminals, but I won't cancel.'

'Is that your final decision?'

'I think so.'

'You have till tonight to do more than think so. Everyone needs to know, Chloe, one way or another.'

'Henry was vile to me.'

'Not really. He only said what I should have said. You can't mess people around. But don't marry me if you don't want to. Even Henry wouldn't want that.'

215

'He said the piggy already went for the chop. He said 'slaughter' and he must have known I was feeling delicate.'

'He also used the word 'Antipodes'.

'What does it mean?'

'Australia, you numpty. He meant Rob. Get dressed and go to work. We have bills to pay, wedding or no wedding.'

The crisis was apparently over, I did the first two hours of morning surgery, then drove to Selly Oak to pay my respects to Keith Sideaway.

There was huge crowd. It was standing room only in the crematorium chapel. No hymns, no prayers. The Sideaways weren't a religious family. Keith's daughter struggled through a poem she'd written and his boss from Codsall Cables said a few words. About what a cheerful, friendly bloke Keith had been, always willing to take on a job, no matter how shitty, without complaining. Exactly my impression of the man.

I could have slipped away afterwards but it was lunch time, so I was in no hurry to get back to Tit Droop. I joined the long line to offer my condolences. His widow, his two teenage kids, his parents, his in-laws, they all looked stunned. They'd known he was very ill, that he might even die, but they hadn't expected it so soon.

They said it was very nice of me to come. Over and above, they said. And how he'd had nothing but praise for everybody who'd looked after him.

I said, 'He was one of the first patients I saw when I joined The Lindens. I was a trainee, sitting in with Dr Vincent. I hadn't seen Keith for a while, but I'd often thought of him. Wondered how he was getting on.'

Mrs Sideaway said, 'They'd warned us, at the hospital, there wasn't much more they could do for him. We'd told the kids and everything. I thought he might make it to his birthday. August. But you see, he knew. On the Friday he suddenly said "Jackie, I think I'd like to go to the hospice." I said, "wait till after the weekend. You might feel better by Monday". He said, "no, I'd like to go today." So he did. And he was dead by the Tuesday afternoon.'

I'd heard stories like that before. Patients understanding that death is fast approaching, when their relatives and sometimes even their doctors think they still have some time. Keith had sensed how things were and taken control. His wife said the hospice had been wonderful. He'd had a room with a view of the garden and a waterbed, to keep him comfortable, and he'd gone very peacefully.

I was in a sombre mood when I got back to the surgery and the first person I saw, Pam Parker, was looking sad too, not her customary, smiley self. It was unusual for her to be in on a Friday too.

'Just been in for a meeting with Helen and Kasper,' she said.

'Are you alright?'

'I am. But Bob Senior's getting to be a handful. He's started going walkabout. And refusing to shower, giving me a load of lip. And Melissa's fallen off the wagon again. She'd been doing better but I found half of last night's dinner stuffed in the pocket of her jeans, so I think she's relapsed. I need to be at home more.'

Another familiar story. An elderly father-in-law with dementia and a teenage daughter with an eating disorder, and Pam was caught in the middle and feeling the squeeze.

'You won't stop work altogether?'

217

'No, no. I'll still do one surgery a week, Wednesday afternoons. I'll need my fix of surreal gynaecological conversations. Jean Boddy's going to take over my other days. Although I do hope to retain sole responsibility for seeing Amber Evans. You know? For moments of unexpected laughter? What's up with you? You look like you've been to a funeral.'

'Actually, I have.'

'Oh I'm sorry. Anyone close?'

'No. One of Helen's patients, not very old. I'd followed his case.'

'Good. Nice touch. So, not long till the wedding.'

'Right.'

'That wasn't very enthusiastic. You're not getting cold feet?'

'Not exactly.'

'Not exactly? That doesn't sound good. We've got half an hour till surgery. I'll make us a nice cup of coffee and you can tell Aunty Pam your troubles.'

I told her the whole ridiculous saga, about Charlie Swift going to prison, Chloe threatening to call off the wedding, Henry yelling at her, Vinnie yelling at me.

'Did she really mean cancelling. Not postponing?'

'I don't know.'

'Was everything okay between you before this business with her brother?'

'Mainly. I mean, no relationship is perfect, is it?'

'No, but quite nice to start out under that illusion. I don't know, Dan. Given that the wedding's only a couple of weeks away and I've broken in my shoes so I can't get my money back, I think some tough talk is called for. Yes or no, now or never, that kind of thing. She might appreciate it.'

218

'You mean, man up?'

'Yeah. Have another Hobnob. Go on. Since Moira got sick nobody's monitoring the biscuit tin.'

Tegan Strange was on my afternoon list, a girl who was lucky to be alive though she didn't seem to think so. Her mother had brought her in.

'Look at her,' she said. 'Eighteen and all she wants to do is sleep. She used to be out every night but since she come out of hospital, she don't have no interest in nothing.'

I had a look at her arm first. It wasn't a pretty sight. They'd had to go quite deep, debriding the wound, but she was lucky they hadn't had to amputate. And the Gerg 4 Evah tattoo had disappeared, destroyed by sepsis. All that remained was vah.

I said, 'You know this scarring will fade?'

Tegan shrugged.

Her mother said, 'See what I mean? She's lost her mojo.'

I said, 'It's very early days yet. She was in ICU. She was on a ventilator. You don't bounce back from that overnight. What do they say about her kidneys?'

'How do you mean?'

'She hasn't needed dialysis?'

'Oh that. Yes. They've had her in twice and she might have to have one more session.'

'But that's great. It means her kidneys are recovering.'

'She needs something to perk her up. Prozac's good. I've had that.'

I wasn't inclined to prescribe any medication for Tegan. Her body was recovering from a major shock and she might yet need more dialysis. It could take weeks for her to feel any

219

benefit from an anti-depressant and it would just be another burden for her body to bear.

I asked Tegan if she remembered what had happened, how her Mum had wheeled her to the surgery in a Tesco trolley.

Another shrug.

I said, 'You were very, very ill, but you're on the mend. My prescription is for plenty of rest and patience. Simple as that.'

'Well that's no bloody good,' says Mrs Strange. 'She needs tablets. I don't understand it. All these foreigners coming over here, they get anything they ask for.'

'Not at this surgery they don't.'

'Test-tube babies, bigger tits. They just waltz in and help theirselves and here we are, British, born and bred, and we can't even get no Prozac.'

I told her she was free to seek the opinion of a different doctor.

'What here?' she said. 'You're all the bloody same. Tegan come in and begged to have that tattoo took off, which she did need for her mental health, and do you know what he told her? That she'd have to go private.'

'Yes,' I said. 'That was me.'

That got rid of them. I did feel sorry for Tegan, but not enough to back down. And a word of thanks might have been nice. The day Tegan collapsed we'd worked fast, me, Nurse Chris and Trevor. We'd spotted the gravity of her condition and got her to hospital fast. But no. Mrs Strange was a woman with a grievance and when it comes to gratitude, you don't get many Keith Sideaways to the pound.

I felt nervous driving home. It was going to be showdown time with Chloe, and if she said the wedding was off, then what? Was I going to give her an ultimatum, July 6th or never?

220

And if never, would I move out, or would she? The really annoying part of it was that she and her brother weren't even that close. They could go months without speaking and Charlie wasn't a crucial member of the wedding party. Apart from organising a car, he didn't have any responsibilities at all. So, no, I wasn't going to put up with any more hysterics.

There was a smell of cooking and the table was laid for dinner. Candles were lit. A romantic gesture of reconciliation or a condemned man's last meal?

She threw her arms around me.

'Soweee,' she said. 'Everso soweee.'

'You mean the wedding is on? No more melodramas?'

'Pwomise,' she said.

'And you're quite sure? Because today hasn't been the best. I've been to a funeral, I've been abused by a patient's angry mother and I've spent the day wondering what exactly my future holds, so if there's any chance you're going to pull another 'call off the wedding' stunt, tell me now. I've come home prepared for it. But if you do it any nearer the day, my Mam'll drive up here and give you a smack, and that's if Henry doesn't get to you first.'

She cried a bit, but she didn't overdo it. She knew I wasn't in the mood.

'Did you talk to your mother?'

'No. She had a big golf tournament today.'

'How about Flo?'

'God, no. I didn't need a lecture from her. How can she stay married to that monster?'

That made me laugh. Henry, a monster!

'Did you go to work?'

'They said to stay home, until I was feeling better.'

221

'You're becoming a part-timer.'

'Don't you start. Hua's on my case. She says the wedding's distracting me from my career. Dee doesn't see the point of getting married anyway. They're both getting on my nerves. I made a marmalade chicken thing. And millionaire's shortbread.'

We ate dinner, cleared away, I washed, she dried, then we made spoons on the sofa and watched television. All the cares of my day dissolved. Then my phone rang. It was Rob.

'Mate,' he said, 'you're going to kill me and I'm really, really sorry, but I'm not going to make it to the wedding.'

Chapter 23

Suddenly the boot was on the other foot. If Chloe had felt she couldn't get married without Charlie around, how was I supposed to cope without Rob? He was still my best friend even if he was in Sydney. I needed him at my side for the wedding. He was a top bloke, steady but not boring. He could be relied on to give a good speech, but nothing that would offend the grannies.

I said, 'Tell me this is a wind-up.'

'Sorry,' he said. 'Only Kim got us tickets to see the Lions against Australia at the ANZ. Third Test. Best seats in the stadium. It's a big deal, Dan.'

It was a bigger deal than he knew. I had to be gracious. I had to set a calm and phlegmatic example to Chloe. But I had less than two weeks to replace my Best Man.

Chloe said she'd never really liked Rob anyway. That didn't help. She said Charlie would have done it like a shot, if only he'd been available.

I said, 'Your brother is almost the last person in the world I'd have asked. Second only to my own brother.'

'Well then,' she said, 'I suppose there's only one thing for it.'

'I don't think I can. Vaz is a sweet guy but I he's not Best Man material.'

'Vaz?' she said. 'I don't mean Vaz. The man couldn't even dress himself properly for his own wedding. No, I meant that other dipstick you used to live with.'

'Matt?'

'Yes. He's coming anyway. Call him. He might even fit in the suit you've ordered for Rob.'

I said it was a decision I needed to sleep on, which wasn't quite true because there was no way I was going to ask Matt. Give him an inch and he'd take a mile of liberties. He'd have me tarred and feathered and tied to a lamp post outside some Digbeth nightclub the night before the wedding.

Chloe had whipped out her voluminous wedding files and was going through the guest list, naming male cousins who might be prevailed on if Matt wouldn't do it, blokes I'd never met, or if I had, I didn't remember. She wanted to start making phone calls.

'What, and be known evermore as Desperate Dan? No thank you.'

'But you are desperate, let's face it.'

I don't think Chloe ever read the Dandy comic.

She said, 'How can you be so calm? If that was Dee who'd just let me down, I'd be beside myself.'

'I'll deal with it. Trust me. Calm is my optimum physiological state.'

'Just don't ruin my wedding,' she said.

'You mean the wedding you threatened to call off 24 hours ago? And by the way, it's our wedding, not yours.'

When I woke the next morning, I had a clearer idea what my Best Man options were but as I was working two Out of Hours shifts over the weekend, any action would have to wait till Monday. My lack of sense of urgency drove Chloe nuts. I was rather enjoying that.

She said, 'You're causing me so much stress. If my skin breaks out it'll be your fault. What's the point of me having a back peel today if you're going to carry on torturing me?'

'I don't know. What is the point of a back peel? It sounds gruesome.'

Chloe had been having a raft of beauty treatments, all unnecessary in my opinion because she's naturally gorgeous. The back peel was a procedure to remove skin imperfections that might detract from her backless wedding dress.

I said, 'You'll be wearing a backless dress? Will that be okay with the Reverend Spud-u-Like?'

'What's it to do with him?'

'It's just, you know? Church? Backless sounds a bit red carpet. Does it have sleeves?'

'No, it does not. Why would I have worked so hard to tone my arms if I wasn't going to showcase them? Is this a Welsh thing? Getting the vicar's approval for the dress?'

'Rector, actually. Forget it. I'm probably being old-fashioned.'

'Yes, you are.'

The first hour at Sterling was quiet. I was on duty with Neil, the nurse practitioner. I ran my Best Man emergency by him.

I said, 'I've got two candidates.'

'Do they know? That they're contenders?'

'No, right now they're both enjoying their weekend in blissful ignorance.'

225

'Okay. Who have we got?'

'We've got a man who's mature, pleasant and unassuming, but surprisingly eloquent when the spirit moves him.'

'I'd go with him then. He sounds perfect. Why agonise?'

'Because he's currently on Chloe's shit list.'

'And in the blue corner?'

'A man who is also mature, pleasant and eloquent but isn't in the best of health.'

We were interrupted by a call about a possible acute abdomen. An anxious husband said his wife was in terrible pain on her left side. It had come on suddenly in the past hour. Mrs Taylor was 37, a PE teacher, fit and usually in good health. How did she look?

'Pale,' he said. 'Really pale.'

Was she restless?

'No, she can't bear to move.'

'Could she be pregnant?'

'No,' he said. 'We're not able. I've got low sperm.'

The address was in Dudley, not far away. I decided to go and take a look at her. Abdominal pain can signal something as innocent as colic or as life-threatening as a ruptured aortic aneurism and there's a limit to what you can glean over the phone. One thing was clear. Mr Taylor was frightened.

The moment I walked in, I knew I'd been right to attend. She was grey and cold to the touch, her pulse was weak and there was clear guarding when I palpated her abdomen. She was bleeding somewhere internally, and her body was in hypovolemic shock. I stayed with them until the ambulance came.

The paramedic asked if there was any possibility Mrs Taylor was pregnant. Like me she was thinking it had the hallmark of an ectopic pregnancy.

'No,' says the husband. 'How many more times? I already told this call-out doctor. There's no way.'

As he said it, I happened to look at Mrs Taylor, whose face said something different. Perhaps she was pregnant. Miracles can happen. Perhaps she'd kept it a secret from him until she was sure. Saved it up to be a lovely surprise for him. Or perhaps a not so lovely surprise, if someone else had made her pregnant.

I saw them loaded into the ambulance, wished them good luck.

The paramedic said, 'Are you thinking what I'm thinking?'

'Ruptured ectopic pregnancy?'

'Yep.'

'But the husband was told he's sub-fertile so I wouldn't mention it again.'

'Got it. Life's full of surprises, isn't it?'

Back at Sterling, Neil had been thinking about my dilemma.

He said, 'So the choice is between someone who'll really brass off your girlfriend and someone she wouldn't mind, but who might collapse under the strain. Well, it's obvious what you need to do.'

'Is it?'

'Toss a coin.'

And I did it, to humour Neil, but I'd already decided.

Everyone seemed in an irritable mood at Tip Droop on Monday. Nurse Linda had a hangover, Jean Boddy was miffed with Harold because he'd forgotten their anniversary, and Helen was cross with Mary and Moira but didn't feel she could

227

give full rein to her annoyance because how can you berate a dying woman?

Mary had brought Moira to work with her and sat her in a chair at the back of Reception, so she'd still feel part of the team but without any responsibilities. Helen was in the kitchen, giving out about it. She said it looked bad. Unprofessional.

'Patients coming to the surgery, they don't want to see a sick woman propped up in Reception like a Hallowe'en decoration.'

Harold said, 'People probably don't notice. And the older patients might be pleased to see her. How many years has she worked here?'

'Too many,' says Helen. 'Kaz, you're going to have to have a word.'

Kasper said he'd do no such thing.

'Not my job,' he said. 'Anyway, I agree with Harold. And it won't be for long. If Moira gets bored it might only be for today.'

To be fair to Helen, she'd told Mary she could have fully paid leave for as long as she needed it and we'd get in another temp. But I imagined that was one of Mary's fears. The right temp might become a permanent solution and then she'd be left with no sister, no mother and no job.

Elsie Turney was on my morning list. She'd bounced back from her glaucoma surgery.

She said, 'They said I was lucky not to go blind. I mean, if you hadn't phoned my Leonard and made him take me to the hospital, I shudder to think. I said you'd make a bostin' doctor the first time I saw you, remember?'

'I do.'

'And how's Dr Buxton going on?'

'He's all right. He does the nursing home visits.'

'I remember him when he was your age.'

'What was he like?'

'Same as he is now. Allus losing his pen, allus knocking his papers flying. Sharp though. You'd think he didn't know if he was on foot or hossback, but he noticed things. And he'd give you time. He got that from his father. Old Dr Buxton would give you all the time in the world.'

Then she told me her oft-repeated story about giving birth at home and Trevor's father boiling her an egg while he sterilised his suturing needle.

She said, 'It's nice to see the other receptionist lady here. You can tell she's not well, but at least she's got a bit of company, a bit of interest going on around her. A lot of places, they'd have put her out for the bin men, but that's the thing about the Lindens. They look after you. Cradle to grave.'

I passed Elsie's remark on to Helen, although I bigged it up, told her three patients had said positive things about Moira being allowed to sit out her time in her old territory. Helen's reaction was, 'Ha!'

Trevor was actually in the building when I called his mobile. He appeared in the doorway with his phone still ringing.

'A word?'

'Now or Black Bear?'

'Possibly both.'

He sat down.

'Sounds serious.'

'I have a really, really big favour to ask.'

'Sounds like a job for the pub, but go on.'

'My Best Man was supposed to be flying in from Australia and now he can't come. Would you be willing to take his place?'

He said nothing for a minute, just took his specs off and rubbed his eyes. Was he tired, or teary?

229

'Dan Talbot,' he said, 'I'm touched and honoured. Of course, I'll do it. But are you sure, lad? Haven't you got a brother?'

'I'm not sure Adam's even coming to the wedding. I need someone steady and reliable.'

'I think I can manage that. Do I have to make a speech?'

'A short one. I think you're supposed to say something nice about the bridesmaids.

'Shouldn't be hard. And they are?'

'A gobby, bi-sexual Australian doctor, plus Chloe's three free-range nieces. They're supposed to strew rose petals. I think.'

'How charming. You'd better write all this down for me, including any embarrassing anecdotes from your past that you'd rather I didn't mention in my speech. Do you need me on parade the night before?'

'Not really. If you can get to me by 10 o'clock on the Saturday morning. It's only an hour's drive. I'm so grateful.'

'And I'm highly chuffed. I do have prior experience. I was Den Pitkethly's Best Man, back in the Sixties. I think I did a good job. Sadly, you can't ask him for a reference because he's dead.'

'There is just one other thing.'

'I'm braced.'

'We're supposed to wear indigo waistcoats and sage green ties. There's a whole kit ordered for Rob. Would you mind going to the outfitters to see if it fits?'

'I don't know, Dan,' he said. 'Sage green? It's not really my colour. Could be a deal-breaker.'

Chloe was fairly happy when I told her about Trevor.

230

She said, 'You sly old thing. I was sure you were going to ask Horrid Henry and that would have ruined everything. I like Trevor. Will he smell of cigarettes though? Can you spray him with something, before you come to the church?'

'Spray him? With like Hugo Boss or something?'

'Floris neroli is nice.'

'How about Golden Fleece Sheep Dip? My Da can bring some of that.'

She was in a great mood. She'd had a good day at work. Diagnosed a mitral valve prolapse by auscultation and had it confirmed by echogram.

'What were the symptoms?'

'Nothing dramatic. Fatigue, occasional palpitations and breathlessness when supine. Only 42 though, so he was right to come in.'

'Talk me through it.'

'He had a click, mid-systole and a late murmur.'

'Where were you listening?'

'At the apex, obviously.'

'Obviously.'

'Which is located where?'

'Fifth left intercostal space?'

'And?'

'Mid-clavicular line?'

'Correct.'

'What did the murmur sound like?'

'A rough whoosh.'

'What next?'

'Let's have sex and then get a Chinese.'

'I actually meant what's the treatment for your patient. But I like your other idea too.'

'Beta-blockers, for a start.'

'No surgery?'

'It's very unlikely. I'll have salt and pepper squid and crispy duck with pancakes. Phone them now. I'm starving.'

'What if they deliver while we're otherwise engaged?'

'They won't. This time of night they take ages and anyway I'm feeling really hot.'

I told the Happy Wok I'd collect the order myself, and no hurry.

Chapter 24

A week to go and I'll admit I had a touch of nerves. Not about losing the ring or fluffing my vows, but about two hurdles I had to clear before the wedding itself: a long-threatened 'drink' with Helen Vincent, and then the Friday night pre-wedding dinner at the Chummery when Mam and Da would be sitting down to eat with Vinnie and Laurence.

Chloe's parents are nice people and mine are brilliant. It wasn't class friction I was worried about. It was catering standards. No matter how much she denied it, I knew Mam was expecting Vinnie Swift to be a Lady Grantham-type figure, with a well-staffed kitchen running like a ship's engine room. But the Swifts don't have staff. They have a woman from the village, Mrs Pickering, who hoovers once a week and a man with a van who keeps the garden under control.

Food is always an afterthought with Vinnie. Soup warmed up in the microwave. Sardines on toast if she's read another osteoporosis story. Laurence seems to go along with it, but I suspect he eats very well when he stays over in London, something that seems to happen more and more frequently because he's too tired to drive home. I'd asked Chloe to make some gentle enquiries about what Vinnie was planning to serve and the news was encouraging. Prawn cocktail, steak, sherry trifle.

I said, 'That sounds great, although steak for six can be tricky. Is someone helping her?'

'Flo's making the trifle. Mummy's doing the prawns. Mrs Pickering's coming up to supervise the mains.'

Having laid that worry to rest, I was left with the Helen situation. I knew I was probably being ridiculous. I hoped I was. She was my boss, my training supervisor, so-called, and she simply wanted to have a catch-up and a chat over a glass of wine. Our one little 'moment' hadn't amounted to anything and anyway, it was six months in the past. Ancient history. And in the intervening months she'd either been more interested in Kasper or too tired and harassed for anything more than a very occasional hand on my lumbar spine.

We'd agreed to meet at a wine bar in Moseley. Helen had been home and changed her clothes. Over her first glass we covered Moira's prognosis (weeks not months), Miles's community service (she said he was doing really well on graffiti removal) and Pam Parker (a woman wedged between the rock of an ailing father-in-law and the hard place of two troubled teenage daughters). It was towards the bottom of her second glass that we turned to the subject of my plans for the future and I felt Helen's hand on my knee.

Knee, I could cope with. I told her I'd applied to take my Clinical Skills Assessment. Once I had that in the bag, I'd start looking for a permanent position.

She said, 'But you know there'd be a place for you at Tipton Road. Trevor can't keep going forever, Pam's down to one surgery a week. You're already a valued member of the team so why change anything?'

Her hand slid up my thigh. I thought I'd disengage by going to the bar to get her glass refilled, but she was ahead of me and signalled for table service. The time had come. The elephant wasn't just in the wine bar. He was perched on a stool at our table.

I said, 'Helen, your hand is now way beyond my comfort zone. It's very pleasant and very flattering, but I'm not sure what I'm supposed to do about it.'

'Poor Dan,' she said, 'I'm terrible, aren't I? Am I terrible? It's just that you're so adorable and you're about to enter holy deadlock and when you get to my age…'

Her voice drifted off. She was quite tipsy.

She said, 'It's okay for blokes. They can hit on younger women. Look at Cliff. He's got grey hair growing out of his ears. He's got varicose veins. Doesn't affect his score rate. Want to know something really disgusting?'

'Not really.'

'I'm nearly fifty.'

I felt kind of sorry for her. That was the only reason I said, 'So what? Fifty's nothing these days and you're a very attractive woman.'

I should have left it at 'fifty's nothing.'

She said, 'Let's go. Are your wheels outside?'

She allowed me to put her in a taxi but not before the brief tussle she seemed determined to have, with me pressed between her pelvic symphysis and my nearside door handle.

235

Was she satisfied? Apparently. Did I escape with my honour intact? Arguably.

I didn't go straight home. I went to a chipper, sat in the car and ate jumbo haddock and mushy peas, to soak up the Pinot Grigio and dispel the smell of a very sexy woman on heat. That was where I made the slightly regretful decision that I'd move on from Tit Droop as soon as I'd passed my CSA and registered. There were many things about the place I'd miss but Helen wasn't one of them. Chloe would be pleased, and she never needed to know my main reason for leaving.

I wondered if she'd notice anything. Women can sense the damnedest things, but all she said was, 'How was Bitch Face?' and she was so busy with packing her bags and checking things off her wedding lists I don't think she even waited for me to answer.

Chloe left for Bishop's Wapshott on Thursday morning. I had one last day to work. Helen, who I'd hardly seen since our car park fumble, was out at a committee meeting, Nurse Chris was doing the dressings clinic so Nurse Linda could go for a pre-wedding spray tan and manicure.

Chris said, 'Anybody'd think it was her getting married.'

Jean Boddy came in to see me, mid-afternoon.

'Dan,' she said, 'Are you familiar with Trevor's abbreviations?'

She had a file for a patient, Monica Slade. There was a Buxtonism on the cover. RBB. It was a new one on me.

'What's she like?'

'Fiftyish, rough-looking. She's in the waiting room.'

I phoned Trevor.

'RBB?' he said. 'No idea. Slade? I don't remember a Slade. Oh, wait. Monica. No teeth?'

'Jean says she looks rough.'

'See if she's changed her name.'

He was right. Monica Slade had previously been Monica Butterworth.

'In that case,' he said, 'I know who you're talking about. Formerly a lady of the night but she must be getting a bit old for that game now. Yes, Monica. Being toothless, you can probably guess her speciality, but for the right price she'd also ride bareback. RBB. See?'

'Bareback?'

'Without a condom. She nearly copped it one time. She had a massive bleed after a knitting needle abortion. All set for Saturday?'

'All set.'

'I'll drop Mrs Buxton off in Leamington Spa, to get a blow dry, and join you at the Horn and Trumpet for a hearty breakfast. Just remind me, have I got the ring, or have you?'

My very last patient of the day was Kyle Bibby. He was carrying a parcel wrapped in pre-loved Christmas paper.

'Thought I'd bring you something,' he said. 'Only I heard you're a condemned man. Heard you was for the chop. I'm just having a little joke with you there, Doc.'

'Who told you?'

'Can't recall. Word gets around.'

Kyle's gift was a slow cooker, and by the look of its box it too had been pre-loved, but not before it had fallen out of the back of a van. I told him he really shouldn't have.

'Course I should,' he said. 'Top doctor, very understanding. I like to show my appreciation. And now you're a dead man walking, eh? You going away somewhere, afterwards?'

The uncharitable thought crossed my mind that if Kyle knew I was getting married he probably knew where I lived as well. Was he casing our joint for a break-in? It seemed a bit far-fetched and ambitious for a man who gets up late and rarely ventures further than the Brook Glen offie, but what if he was sounding me out for someone else, some more energetic member of the Bibby-Dearlove clan? Or what if he genuinely, out of the goodness of his heart, wanted to give me a knocked off slow cooker?

'We haven't decided,' I lied. 'We might just stay home and have days out.'

'Good idea,' he said. 'You wouldn't catch me going abroad. The things you hear.'

Friday morning was when I really missed Rob. Chloe was at the Chummery and I was alone, pacing around the flat, checking and double-checking I had everything. Passports and tickets for Sunday, Chloe's ring, silver bracelets for Dee and the flower-yoblets, Order of Service with my bits highlighted, wedding shoes with labels removed, Diocalm.

Mam phoned.

'What it is, your Da's just gone for a haircut and then he'll pick up your Nan and Aunty June. We should be with you about 3 o'clock. Now are you sure he shouldn't wear a dickie bow tonight?'

'Quite sure. He should wear something that cat hair won't ruin, and so should you. And have a good lunch. If Vinnie's got a good dinner lined up, it'll be a first.'

As soon as the Talbot convoy arrived at the Horn and Trumpet, I felt better. I had stuff to take care of. Nan was tired and needed a nap. Aunty June was walking with a stick, still waiting for a new knee, and needed ibuprofen. Mam was all of a flutter about everything and needed tea and biscuits. Only Da was an island of calm, examining the old livestock photos on the corridor walls, identifying breeds of sheep.

'Clun Forest. That's a Beulah Speckled. And that's a Shetland. A Katmoget, if I'm not mistaken.'

Until Mam blew her top and told him he was getting on her pippin. Chloe phoned to tell me Vinnie was getting on hers. My future mother-in-law had bought not one wedding hat but three, and she couldn't decide which one to wear.

'Like I care,' says Chloe. 'Like anyone's going to be looking at her.'

'Any reassuring smells coming from the kitchen?'

'No. The steaks won't go on till we're ready to eat. There is one thing I forgot to tell you.'

I steeled myself.

'Dee'll be here in time for dinner.'

'That should be fun. Bags I don't sit next to her. Let your Dad have her. Didn't he spirit her away to see his etchings last time she came over?'

'Did he? I didn't know Daddy had any etchings.'

It was actually his espalier'd fruit trees Laurence had shown off to Dee, but then Chloe was called away for another hat conference and it probably wasn't worth explaining anyway.

The lane leading to the Chummery is narrow and overgrown. Da, driving from the back seat, noted that you wouldn't want to meet anyone coming at speed the other way. But, as I told him, the only hazard I'd ever encountered along there was Charlie Swift and he was safely banged up in HMP Coldingley.

Mam said, 'Are we meant to know about that?'

'Yes. But I wouldn't bring it up unless they do.'

As I turned into the gateway Mam grabbed my hand.

'Look at that house,' she said. 'And the tent's up. Marquee. I mustn't call it a tent. Now Ed, I've got our slippers in my bag. We'll play it by ear, but if they've got lovely carpets, we don't want to be traipsing dirt in.'

I turned off the engine.

Mam said, 'Why are we sitting here? Are we too early?'

'No. Listen. Do not bring your carpet slippers. Leave them in the car. Do not twitter, do not curtsey, do not apologise for existing. He's a doctor, she's a doctor's wife, and they only live in this house because she inherited it.'

'Right,' says Mam.

'Well,' says Da, 'let's get this over with, shall we? My belly feels like my throat's cut.'

The front hall of the Chummery had been decorated with cream roses, Vinnie and Laurence were charming, even the cat looked as though he'd been brushed. We went into the drawing room for drinks. By eight o'clock the champagne had flowed, the peanut bowls were empty and Dee still hadn't arrived.

Chloe said, 'She is on her way.'

And I said, 'Dee's a lousy timekeeper and we have a big day tomorrow. I think we should start dinner without her.'

Vinnie leapt up and Mam made as if to follow her.

'Oh yes, do come with,' says Vinnie. 'Chloe tells me you're a marvellous cook. And I expect you'd like to find le petit coin.'

Mam looked at me for help. I mouthed 'bog'.

We'd just finished the very good, shop bought, prawn cocktails when we heard the crunch of Dee's car on the gravel.

'Fucking Friday traffic,' were her first words. 'Hello Laurence. How are your plums?' were her second.

Laurence, who I thought had seemed a bit lacklustre earlier in the evening, perked up.

'Just in time,' he said. 'How do you like your steak?'

'Still pulsing,' says Dee.

'Atta girl!' says Laurence, pouring her a glass of red.

Chloe took word down to Mrs Pickering. Five medium rare, two bloody. The steaks all arrived suspiciously quickly and uniformly grey. I caught a little glance pass between Mam and Da, the kind of shorthand people use after many years together. The steaks were inedible. It was noticeable that this gave conversation a boost. Everyone talked, anything to avoid chewing on another piece of tyre rubber.

Eventually Chloe said, 'Mummy, what *has* Mrs Pickering done? My steak is inedible.'

Vinnie sighed. 'Yes, mine's a tad gristly. Of course, Mrs P's more a cleaner than a cook. Perhaps it's all been too much for her. But nil desperandum. There are heaps of broccoli and peas.'

At that moment Henry arrived. Chloe narrowed her eyes at him.

She said, 'I'm not speaking to you.'

'Oh dear,' says Henry, 'How shall I cope? Well, I just dropped by to tell you the hog roast people will be here at 7am latest.'

Da perked up.

'Gloucester Old Spot?'

'Ah,' says Henry. 'Dan's father. Always pleased to meet a livestock man. No, it's a British Saddleback. Be glad to chat to

241

you about sheep, though. Thinking of trying a small flock myself.'

'What's your grazing like?'

'Wettish.'

'Ryelands would be a good bet. They mature fast and they're good around children. Not too flighty.'

Henry said he looked forward to more sheep talk the next day. Da glowed. Maybe it was the Bulgarian red. Maybe it was finding a pal he could converse with at the reception.

Henry peered down at our plates.

'No-one eating their steaks, Vinnie?'

'I'm afraid Mrs Pickering has rather let us down. Would you like to take them for your dogs?'

Mam waited till we were off the Chummery property before she started.

'My giddy aunt,' she said, 'that was an evening to remember. And that poor old lady in the kitchen, getting the blame.'

Da joined in.

'I'd say that was chuck steak.'

'No doubt about it. That was a braising cut. I mean, if they're that short of a bob, we could have brought them some good Welsh steaks, eh Ed?'

'We could.'

'And the state of the downstairs toilet. I'm not being funny, Dan, but the floor round that pedestal hadn't seen a mop in years.'

'So, the rose-tinted glasses are finally off.'

'How do you mean?'

'You've been talking about Chloe's folks as if they were something special. Royalty, practically.'

'No I haven't.'

242

'You thought Da should wear a bow tie tonight.'

'I did not.'

She shot a quick look in the back of the car, expecting a reaction from Da, but he wasn't listening. He was looking out into the twilight, dreaming of spit-roasted British Saddleback and maybe a spot of sheep talk with Henry.

Chapter 25

Our wedding day dawned. The weather was perfect. Trevor arrived in time for a late breakfast. In honour of the day and in the interests of not interrupting the service with a wheezing fit, he hadn't had a cigarette all week. He was wearing a nicotine patch and chewing gum, so as not to inflict his short fuse on Mrs Buxton.

Our drive to the church took us past the Chummery. Trevor pulled into the driveway.

I said, 'Don't stop. I'm not supposed to see the bride.'

'You won't. I bet she's bathing in asses' milk. I just wanted to have a look at this hog they're cooking.'

He was impressed. So was I.

'That is some pig,' he said. 'Well, he won't be called Clarence no more.'

The Reverend Spedlow was bustling about in his cassock, heading back to the rectory to get his reading glasses.

He said, 'I do hope the bride will be punctual. I'm opening the fête in Aston Cobnash at 3 o'clock.'

Trevor went inside to look around.

'Very nice,' he said. 'A pretty little country church. And quite a few early birds in their seats. Are you alright, lad? You look a bit queasy.'

I was far more nervous than I'd expected, and Friday night's sherry trifle was still sitting uneasily beneath the Horn and Trumpet's English fry. Mam, Da, Nan and Aunty June arrived.

'Guess what?' says Mam. 'Your brother is on his way. He was at Strensham services when I spoke to him, getting off at Junction 5.'

Da said he'd have been better getting off at 4a and taking the M42. Nan asked whose wedding we were going to. Aunty June needed a toilet. I went behind a gravestone where Mildred Cheese, beloved wife of William was resting in peace and relieved myself of my breakfast.

There was a spate of arrivals. Trevor and I went inside, to take up our positions. He gave me a tube of Polos to freshen my mouth.

He said, 'What's with the bowls team?'

A side pew on the bride's side of the church was occupied by seven men in petrol blue blazers and striped ties. I had no idea who they were. Apart from the Parkers and Mrs Buxton I had no idea who anyone was because the guest list was weighted heavily in favour of the Swifts and Orde-Sykeses.

At ten past twelve I was aware of a flurry of activity outside. Reverend Spud-u-Like strode out to meet the bridal party and Trevor whispered, 'Time to load you into the starting gate.'

Another five minutes passed. Then Vinnie came in looking sour. Something was up. I went over to her.

'This damned vicar,' she muttered. 'He said Chlo needed to put on a cardigan before she comes into church. A cardigan! Imagine! The man has no idea.'

'I did warn Chloe about choosing a backless dress. So, what's the solution?'

'Flo's had to lend her a pashmina, which looks completely wrong. Chlo is furious. Quelle cauchemar!'

Trevor said I absolutely should not go outside and get embroiled.

'Steady the Buffs,' he said. 'When she gets here, just tell her she looks beautiful.'

Then the rector came back, gave a nod to the organist and put on his Dearly Beloved face. I turned to watch Chloe come towards me on her father's arm. There was a little ripple of laughter, possibly at Poppy, who was wearing wellies with her ivory silk dress, possibly at Dee whose dress, also a backless number, was swamped by a man's jacket, loaned by the limo driver. And behind this odd procession I saw the shiny dome of my brother's head, bobbing and weaving, the late arrival looking for a place to sit.

Chloe was close to tears. I whispered that even the Reverend Spud-u-Like hadn't prevented her from looking fabulous and she gave me a watery smile. The first hymn was *Tell Out My Soul*. That was when I realised Mam must have been consulted. Chloe wouldn't have had a clue about my favourite hymns. And as soon as the singing started, I twigged who the bowls team men were. A Welsh choir or part of it at least, had been imported, to boost the feeble warbling of our friends and family. Chloe squeezed my arm. I'd have liked to kiss her, there and then, but we hadn't got to that part of the service yet.

246

No-one knew any just impediment and the only bit of the vows I fluffed was Chloe's full name, because I got Emily Jane the wrong way around. She had it easier. I'm just plain Daniel.

Henry, amazingly not stripped of the honour, read from Ecclesiastes: For everything there is a season. Mam read 1 Corinthians 13 and as soon as the rector had pronounced us man and wife, the blazers leapt to their feet and sang *Calon Lan*. Then it was my turn to cry.

We went into the vestry to sign the registers and Chloe grabbed Mam.

'He never guessed,' she said. 'It was so brilliant. Did you see his face?'

My mother and my wife had conspired to delight me. That seemed like a very good omen indeed. The singers were from a village over Pandy way.

'Tregaron Cross Male Voice Reserves,' says Da, with a twinkle. 'We bussed them up here, top secret mission and no expense spared.'

'Are they coming to the reception?'

'They've brought packed lunches, but they will if you ask them.'

What other memories do I have of that day? I remember that as soon as the registers were signed, Chloe took off the borrowed shawl and gave the rector a very insolent look. I remember that our little flower girls went off script and dumped the rose petals in three heaps instead of strewing them delicately, as fairies might. Also, that Lily asked me whether I was allowed to mount Chloe, now we were married.

I said, 'Mount her? She's not a horse.'

Lily said, 'You know. To get babies. When Lord Topnotch does it, it takes ages.'

Lord Topnotch is one of Henry's prize boars.

I remember that the roast pork was great, although I was so busy circulating, I only got a couple of bites. Also, that the recurring theme of Trevor's speech was the embarrassing stories about me that he knew but had absolutely no intention of telling.

'Of the occasion he accidentally turned out the operating theatre lights as the surgeon was about to open up, I shall say not a word. Nor would wild horses drag from me the story of Dan mistaking a patient's wife for his mother.'

On and on he went. Trevor had called Rob, to gather material on me, and everyone loved him.

I remember Moira, in a borrowed Red Cross wheelchair, telling me she'd had a lovely day. Bob Parker Senior hitting on my Nan. Dee getting very drunk and dancing wildly with Chloe's cousin, Justin. Whether she realised Justin doesn't play for the Hetero First XI, I don't know. In Dee's case it probably didn't matter, and it was certainly preferable to Chloe's thwarted plan to pair her off with Charlie. The very idea of Dee becoming a member of the Swift family was too horrible to contemplate.

As for my own brother, he said a grand total of three words to me - 'all right then?' and left to drive back to Cardiff.

Mam said, 'You know what he's like. Adam's not one for socialising. He came, that's the main thing. And he needed to be getting back.'

She was right. He'd come, more to please her than me, I was sure, and he was no loss to the party, unlike Charlie Swift. I knew Chloe was genuinely bereft by his absence. She'd sent him a comfort parcel so he wouldn't feel forgotten. I could imagine the chocolate bars would be appreciated. I wasn't so sure the Calvin Klein aftershave was such a good idea.

It was only when I started introducing Mam to the Tit Droop crowd that I realised the Vincents hadn't turned up. Had Helen felt mortified by the memory of how she'd tried to seduce me? Had she jibbed at the prospect of seeing me with my beautiful bride? Or had they just had a more tempting invitation?

Pam said, 'We thought it best not to say anything. Trevor said no point in putting a dampener on your day.'

'Why? What's happened?'

'Cliff had a massive stroke, Friday lunchtime.'

'Is he dead?'

'No. Still in the danger zone though. He was at the Yardley Travelodge, enjoying a bit of room service with some girl. She panicked, apparently, and didn't do anything about it for an hour. Just sat there with Lover Boy gurgling and groaning, texting her friends, asking them what she should do. Cliff's lucky he didn't go paws up. Well, I suppose he's lucky.'

'Poor Helen.'

'Poor Helen if he survives. Bad enough living with the randy bastard when he was fit and well. Imagine if he's going to be hanging around for years, needing his bottom wiped. I'm speaking as a woman, Dan, not as a physician trained to preserve life.'

Helen's world had been turned upside down.

I'd wondered whether Trevor and Laurence would reconnect, both being St Bart's men, but neither of them seemed inclined. It had been a long time, 45 years or so, and they'd never been friends. Their paths had been very different.

Laurence, now officially my father-in-law, took me to one side to discuss my future.

'You won't stay with this Birmingham outfit, one imagines.'

'It's Black Country, actually. But no. It's been a good experience for me and they'd like me to stay on, but I don't think I will. I'll start looking around once I'm registered.'

'Friend of mine has a nice private practice in Solihull. He couldn't make it today. Prior commitment to a client's daughter's wedding in Qatar. But you might have a word with him. No harm in cultivating contacts.'

I said I would. There was no sense in appearing ungrateful, but a private practice where patients are called 'clients' wasn't at all what I had in mind. I wanted to work in another Lindens, another Tit Droop, with another Trevor and a Pam Parker and a Mary or a Moira running the front desk. I was also thinking - and this might have been brought on by the emotion of the day and the amount of champagne I'd consumed - that I'd like it to be in Wales. I even pictured myself in a choir someday, wearing a blazer like the Tregaron Cross Reserves.

John Bevan said he'd known my Grandad Talbot. Glyn Meredith said he'd been at school with Mam, only a few years above her. Glyn and John had both spent their whole lives no further than ten miles from where they were born. When I was 18, I'd been raring to leave Wales and see the world. As it turned out I'd only gone as far as Birmingham and now, here I was, thinking about going back.

Chapter 26

We were only away on our honeymoon for ten days, but a lot had happened while we were gone. Moira had died. She'd succumbed to an overwhelming Klebsiella infection and gone quickly and peacefully. I'd missed her funeral. Her death wasn't unexpected, but I still felt strangely miffed. Couldn't she have waited till I got back? Why Dan? Were you her attending physician? No. Had there been some great affection between us? Not at all. In fact, when I first joined the practice, she'd been quite stern with me, though it turned out that was just her funny way and she'd eventually quite approved of me.

Mary had come straight back to work, the day after the funeral. She told me the wedding was the last time Moira had left the house, and how much she'd enjoyed watching people dancing.

'Nice bit of pork too,' she said. 'Nice bit of crackling.'

'Does your mother understand what's happened to Moira?'

'No, so that's a blessing. In recent years she used to get us mixed up anyway.'

'And how are you?'

251

'I'm all right. Rattling around on my ownsome, though. A loaf of bread lasts me a week now. Trevor says I should put in for a retirement bungalow, but I don't know as I want to. All those old people doddering around. Everybody knowing your business. And I've got two sideboards. They wouldn't fit in a bungalow. No, I reckon I'll just carry on carrying on.'

'Well I'm glad you're back at work. That temp we had was useless. Is Helen still off?'

'No, she's in. And I'll tell you something. Since her hubby took a bad turn, she's here all hours. Anything sooner than go home or visit him at the hospital.'

Helen was in her office. It was our first encounter since the fevered wine bar tussle and I was feeling awkward about seeing her, but I had to ask her how Cliff was doing. She was business-like.

'Right hemiplegia. Aphasic too, although that seems to be resolving. And very angry. Like, off the chart.'

'I'm so sorry. What's the prognosis?'

'Too early to say. Once he starts rehab, we'll have a better idea.'

'Shouldn't you take some time off?'

'What, to sit on one of those bum-numbing hospital chairs, telling him everything's going to be okay? Hell no. Why should I? Cliff's not the only one who's angry. He was having one of his lunch hour quickies when it happened. I suppose you heard?'

'Yes. And that he didn't get early treatment.'

'I don't blame the girl. She's only a kid. Nineteen or twenty. She must have wondered what the hell was happening. I hear your wedding was lovely.'

'It was. It seems a long time ago. Is Miles behaving himself?'

'Seems to be. He hasn't been to see his Dad yet. He's scared, I think. I'm not pushing him to visit while Cliff's in Raging Bull mode. He's getting pretty good at throwing left-handed. Anyway, great to have you back, Dan. Trevor's been enjoying himself but it's not nice for patients, having to listen to his coughing and wheezing.'

'I realise you've got a lot to think about, but I've got the date for my Clinical Skills test and it's sooner than I'd expected.'

'Okay.'

'And I'll be needing my Workplace Assessment at some point.'

'Don't worry. I'm on it. It'll be a glowing report.'

'Glowing' was nice, although I wasn't sure if it was what I deserved. I'd have settled for 'shows all-round competence.'

I had a full Monday morning list and only two no-shows. My last patient was Dave Stackhouse. I'd met Dave before, doing a house call to see his wife about her angina, but I'd never seen him as a patient. There was very little in his file. Trevor had treated him for a couple of chest infections and noted that he was firmly resistant to the idea of giving up smoking, but I already knew that. Smoking was Dave and Ruby's chief pleasure in life.

Dave said he had an ulster.

'An ulster?'

'Under me tongue. Ruby's been putting that Bonjelly kiddie stuff on it, but it's not helping.'

I took a look and didn't like what I saw. There was certainly a lesion at the base of his tongue, but it wasn't an ulcer.

I said, 'Dave, I'm going to refer you to Sandwell, for a biopsy.'

253

'Oh yes?' he said. 'That'll be sometime never. My sister had to wait months for a new hip.'

'You won't wait months for this. They'll see you within two weeks. If you don't hear from them, let me know.'

'I will,' he said. 'Only two weeks? Are you sure? That's as good as going private.'

So, Dave Stackhouse went home feeling very pleased. Either he hadn't heard of urgent cancer referrals or it still didn't occur to him that his 'ulster' might be something serious. Sometimes ignorance is bliss.

I'd arranged to meet Vaz that evening, to see if he had any tips for the CSA. He'd taken his three times before he passed. Being shy, it was his social skills that had let him down. Poor eye contact, failure to make those little noises that show a patient you're listening to them. Pam and Trevor had done some practice sessions with him and eventually he got the hang of it.

We met in a Starbucks in Wolverhampton, after work. He came bounding in. Trousers too short, jacket too tight, as usual. He's put on weight since Teresa's been feeding him.

He said, 'Your wedding was very beautiful. But one thing I didn't understand. Why did Trevor tell stories about your mistakes? You're a good doctor. Why didn't he praise you with good stories?'

'It's a tradition.'

'I'm glad we don't have this tradition. Now I have something very exciting to tell you. Teresa is already having a baby.'

So much for the rhythm method of contraception.

I said, 'That's wonderful news. Congratulations. But does that affect your plans to go to India?'

'Only that we will go sooner, in November. My parents are very happy.'

'Will it be their first grandchild?'

'It will be seventh.'

Vaz said the best tip he'd been given about the CSA was not to keep looking at the clock. In the test you only have ten minutes per case and when he was at the Lindens he regularly gave patients twice that.

He said, 'Dr Pam told me I must listen carefully to the patient for one minute minimum. Also, I should look at the clock only once, to make sure I had time to explain treatment to patient. This is not easy, Dan. After ten minutes they sound a buzzer, bzzzz, and you must finish and leave the room. This buzzer made me very upset.'

'Were there any cases that flummoxed you?'

'What is flummoxed?'

'Baffled you. Puzzled you. Or maybe something where you couldn't remember the diagnosis protocol, or a difficult situation where you didn't know what to say?'

'Oh yes. Then I said, "We will conduct blood tests and see what they reveal". Dan, the clinic would like to tell us, is our baby a boy or a girl, but I think better not to know. What do you think?'

I wasn't something I'd thought about. If Chloe was pregnant, I imagine she'd want to know the sex, for shopping purposes. Now Vaz had put it to me, I decided I preferred surprises.

Chloe also took a different view of Vaz and Teresa's lovely news.

'Bummer,' she said. 'So that's their India trip ruined.'

'No, they're still going ahead. Just a bit sooner, that's all.'

255

'She could have a termination.'

'What? Chloe, they're Catholics. And why would they have a termination? They don't look on this baby as an inconvenience. They look upon it as a blessing. They're very happy.'

'Okay, keep your hair on.'

'Is that what you'd have done, if you'd found out you were pregnant before the wedding?'

She said she refused to get into that discussion. She said I was giving her my Holy Joe look. Later she said, 'How far gone is she?'

'Four months.'

'She'll be what, six, seven months when they go to India? What about her wedding dress? Can it be let out? Mummy has someone who does alterations.'

'Teresa doesn't strike me as the kind of woman to worry much about a dress.'

'Really?' says Chloe. 'How extraordinary. People can be so funny.'

'Yes,' I said. 'Can't they just?'

The CSA test centre was in Croydon. I got a train down there after Monday afternoon surgery. Trevor was driving into the Tit Droop car park just as I was driving out.

'My advice,' he said, 'get to your hotel, have a bite to eat, watch a bit of telly. No revising. You don't need it. It's your clinical skills they're testing, lad, not brain surgery. And by the way, you're a good doctor.'

The Clinical Skills Assessment takes around three hours. You have thirteen scenarios to deal with, ten minutes per case, and you can take a break after case number 7, for a quick cup of coffee and a pee. When I walked into my first test, there were two women in the room, which threw me for a second. Then I understood. They were playing mother and daughter.

The case history was set up on an iPad and there seemed quite a lot to take in. Mrs Smith was a 62-year-old female. She'd had surgical repair of a hiatus hernia, was being treated with mebeverine for irritable bowel, and had a family history of ischaemic heart disease. Then I remembered Pam Parker's advice to Vaz. First, listen to the patient.

This was easier said than done because the daughter kept interrupting. Mrs Smith had pain in her right hip and groin, of six months duration.

'Not six months, Mum,' says the daughter. 'More like a year, and nobody's doing anything about it.'

I got it. This was a double challenge. To reach a diagnosis and deal diplomatically with a concerned but interfering relative.

Pulse, blood pressure and temperature were all ticked as normal. No swelling, no pain reported in any other joints. Internal rotation of the right hip caused pain, but there was no crepitus and no neurosensory deficit. When was the pain at its worst? First thing in the morning. She had trouble putting her tights on. Was it affecting how she walked?

'Yes. I'm like Hopalong Cassidy,' says Mrs Smith. And the daughter said, 'Why hasn't she been sent for an X-ray? Or an MRI. That's what I'd like to know.'

I looked at the timer. Three minutes left. Should I spend time explaining why an X-ray wouldn't be very useful and an MRI, which arguably might, involved a waiting list? No, I needed to press on. I diagnosed osteo-arthritis and prescribed physiotherapy, for exercises to improve the strength of Mrs

257

Smith's glutes and keep her mobile, and ibuprofen for pain relief.

The daughter said, 'We don't take anything like that. She has turmeric and Devil's Claw tea. We prefer all natural, don't we, Mum?'

Thanks to Freda Jarrold, I knew a bit about Devil's Claw tea. It was something she'd been giving Ron, for his bone pain.

I said, 'Mrs Smith, if you find these alternative remedies help you, by all means take them, but with a history of IBS you should be very careful with the Devil's Claw tea. It might make it worse.'

And as the words left my mouth, the buzzer went. One down, twelve to go.

My second patient was Mrs Brown, a 69-year-old retired shop worker with a recent history of hypertension. She'd been taking amlodipine 10mg once a day and her last blood pressure reading was 150/90. I introduced myself, asked her how I could help.

She said she'd had a funny turn over the weekend. Could she describe it?

'I just felt a bit wuzzy-headed. I don't think it's anything to bother you with but it's my husband. He worries about me.'

How long had the funny turn lasted?

'Not long. About half an hour.'

'And did you or your husband notice anything else? Any weakness in your limbs? Blurred vision? Were you able to speak while it was happening?'

'Ken said I was slurring my words, but I don't think I was. He's a bit deaf, my Ken. I know what you're getting at. You're thinking I had a stroke. But my mother took a stroke and it was nothing like that.'

I looked back at the iPad notes. Pulse regular, temperature normal, blood pressure slightly raised, no carotid bruits, no limb weakness or visual field deficit. They give you a whiteboard to write on, so they can see your reasoning. I did the ABCD2 assessment. Age, blood pressure, clinical signs, duration of episode. Mrs Brown was over 60, she had persistent hypertension, her speech had been affected (according to Mr Brown) and the event had lasted half an hour, maybe longer, given her tendency to downplay things.

I only had two minutes left.

I said, 'Mrs Brown, you haven't had a stroke but you're certainly at risk of one. I think you had what we call a TIA, or a mini stroke.'

She said she'd heard of that.

'I'm going to refer you to a special clinic. They might do a brain scan, to make sure there's been no damage, and they'll definitely want to get your blood pressure under better control.'

'Well,' she said, 'it all seems like a lot of fuss over nothing.'

'And in the meanwhile, I'd like you to take soluble aspirin, one a day. Are you okay with aspirin?'

I felt the time running out. What if she couldn't tolerate aspirin? Should I explain about taking it with a proton pump inhibitor? Or mention clopidogrel as an alternative? Bzzz. My ten minutes was up.

And as I closed the door behind me, I realised I hadn't warned her not to drive. But there was no time for fretting about things left unsaid because you were ushered straight from one consultation to the next, which in my case was to a room where the 'patient' was a young woman in a nurse's uniform and there were no case notes on the iPad. It was going to be a professional ethics situation.

Nurse Angie played it nervous and hesitant. She said, 'I know I haven't worked here long. I don't want to get anybody into trouble.'

Reassure her, Dan, but don't make any promises about confidentiality you can't keep.

She said, 'It's hard to know what to do for the best.'

I said something like, 'Sometimes just airing a problem with another person makes things clearer. Take your time.'

Only not too much time, dear, because I only have ten minutes.

Nurse Angie was concerned about the conduct of one of the doctors in 'our' practice.

'It's about Dr Maxwell,' she said. 'Me and my boyfriend were in Pizza Mama's last Saturday and Dr Maxwell was in there, only he didn't see me, and the girl he was with is one of our patients. See, I know her because I've done her depot contraception injections. Anyway, they were laughing and carrying on, you know what I mean? And it doesn't seem right.'

This was one I hadn't prepared for. Was the girl a regular patient of Dr Maxwell or was she just a patient of the practice who might happened to have met him in other circumstances? Was that even relevant? What if Nurse Angie fancied Dr Maxwell herself? What if she was a jealous bunny-boiler, intent on ruining a man's career? The only thing I could think was, 'keep an open mind, Dan.' Also, 'pass this one along.'

I suggested setting up a meeting with the practice manager, to discuss the options, going forward, and didn't have much else to say but there were still four minutes on the clock. Nurse Angie saw my predicament and threw me a lifeline. What if she

260

got labelled a snitch, what if Dr Maxwell found out she was the one who'd reported him and got her sacked?

I did a Trevor Buxton impersonation, sat back in my chair, rumpled my hair, told her she'd been right to bring the matter to our attention and that I understood her fears because I'd been there myself. It was the truth, though the examiners wouldn't know it. When I'd suspected Bruce Macdonald was engaging in some ethically dubious business with elderly patients, I hadn't been sure what to do or who to turn to. Whether it was the right kind of thing to mention in an exam was another matter, but I'd gone and done it and somewhere in the building I was being observed and adjudicated. Appropriately empathetic? Indiscreet? Phoney? Too late to worry. It was time for assessment number 4.

There was no patient waiting for me in the next room. Just a telephone with an angry man on the other end. I'd known a phone consultation was possible and I'd dreaded getting one. I like to be face to face with a patient, even if it is an actor. I read the notes.

The patient was Tyler Crawford, aged 7, who suffered from eczema. He'd been seen at a Dermatology out-patients clinic and prescribed E45 cream, with a hydrocortisone preparation to use short-term in the event of a flare-up. Which he had had, so his mother had brought him to the surgery earlier in the week and been given a prescription for Dioderm 1%.

'What I'd like to know,' said the phone voice, 'is why my son isn't being sent to a specialist.'

'He was seen by a dermatologist, three months ago.'

'No, I'm talking about a proper specialist for kiddies. Like Dr Wu.'

'I don't know Dr Wu. Is he a dermatologist?'

'For kiddies. My girlfriend works for him and he'd be more than happy to see Tyler only my ex won't agree to it. I mean, Tyler's my son. I've got my rights.'

So, this wasn't really about Tyler's eczema. It was about his mum and dad and the dad's new girlfriend who happened to work for a paediatric dermatologist. I tried deflecting. The notes I'd been given indicated that Tyler's condition wasn't severe. The treatment he was getting seemed sensible and this Dr Wu would probably agree. But Mr Crawford wasn't having that.

'Don't you tell me it's not severe. He's my boy and I'll be the judge of it. Sometimes he scratches his arms till he bleeds. You might fob his mother off but not me. It makes you wonder why they gave her custody when she can't be arsed to do the right thing by him.'

Whoever was playing the part of Mr Crawford was enjoying himself, but I had less than two minutes left. I told him I could see it was a difficult situation and how would it be if I wrote to Dr Wu or, better still, to some other paediatric dermatologist with no provocative connection to the girlfriend. I could ask for a written opinion on the treatment Tyler was getting, and copy both parents in.

'I suppose so,' he said. 'Pity not to use Dr Wu though, just because my ex don't like it that I've moved on. I mean, all I want is the best for my boy. Know what I mean?'

Mr Crawford had had the last word.

I had no problem with the woman who wanted her bunions fixed because I knew the pros and cons from the Barbara Humphries case. I spotted the signs of an ectopic pregnancy, having seen it recently on an emergency call-out and I handled a presentation of acute glaucoma confidently thanks to my experience with Elsie Turney. I was more than halfway through the test and feeling pretty good. I went to grab a quick coffee.

Chapter 27

There was a woman, heavily pregnant, struggling with the coffee machine. She asked me if I'd done the home visit test yet.

'Home visit?'

'You'll see,' she said.

'When's the baby due?'

'Yesterday.'

She was with a practice in Stevenage.

There was a guy there too, eating a Curly Wurly. He kept looking at me. His face was vaguely familiar.

He said, 'Birmingham, right?'

'Yes. Dan Talbot. I started in 2001.'

'George Fitzgerald. 2003.'

I was two years older than most of the candidates, due to my stupid detour into ENT.

'You're the same year as my wife. Chloe Swift?'

He stopped, mid-Curly Wurly.

He said, 'You're married to Chloe Swift?'

I didn't care for the way he said it, like *you're married to Chloe Swift?* Like, you won the Beautiful Wife Lottery, are you sure there's not been some mistake?

'Wow,' he said. 'Married. Tell her Fitzie said hello.'

It was time to resume. I still had six cases to get through.

I got a grumpy 58-year-old smoker with a persistent cough and basal crackles in both lungs. Pulse, temperature and blood pressure all normal, no weight loss, no pain, no blood in his sputum, no history of cancer.

He said, 'Don't tell me to stop smoking. Just give me something for the cough.'

He'd smoked a pack and a half a day for forty years. I told him he could buy a cough medicine over the counter but, much as he didn't want to hear it, what he really needed to do was give up the cigarettes.

'Come to the clinic. It's in the evenings, it's free, everyone there is in the same boat and we have a lot of success.'

'Naah,' he said. 'Too airy-fairy for me.'

'Airy-fairy?'

'All that talking about yourself and closing your eyes and letting everything go floppy. Not my scene.'

'Relaxation exercises do actually work.'

'If you say so. Going to the pub is what relaxes me. A pint and a smoke. So, are you going to give me anything?'

I referred him for spirometry and a chest X-ray and gave him a leaflet about the Quit Now clinic. He slid it back across the desk at me, but his ten minutes were up. I was already on my feet, on my way to see Miss Perkins, who had a frothy vaginal discharge. Eww.

'I've got thrush,' says Miss Perkins. The iPad told me a different story. A swab had revealed a Trichomonas infection. Her obs were all normal.

I explained the microbiology findings to her.

265

'No, I don't think so,' she said. 'It's thrush. I've had it before.'

I persisted, told her the Trichomonas test was very specific and very accurate, talked to her about the importance of informing her sex partner and them both attending a GUM clinic.

'What, tell him he needs to go to the clap clinic?' she said. 'Fuck that. We've only been going out for a few weeks.'

I said, 'Well let me put it this way. If you think he won't like that suggestion, how do you think he'll like finding out you knew you had an infection and didn't warn him? I'm giving you a course of antibiotics. Finish the whole prescription, don't drink alcohol while you're taking them, and don't have unprotected sex.'

I started to write a prescription.

She said, 'I hate taking pills. The other doctor gave me pessaries.'

'That was for a fungal infection. What I'm prescribing is an antibiotic.'

I had 30 seconds left and for the life of me I couldn't remember the dose for metronidazole. Not enough time to look it up in my Formulary. I guessed at 400mg.

'Still,' she said, 'it's all the same stuff, isn't it?'

The theme of my day seemed to be the argumentative, know-it-all patients. I was starting to feel rattled.

I got the home visit next. It was very well set up. Curtains closed, dirty dishes piled on the floor, and a young, unshaven male slumped on a sofa. He told me to fuck off.

The only information on the iPad was that Ryan was 24 years old and his sister had requested a visit because she was worried that he might be suicidal. Ryan hadn't long been living in the area, so no medical records were available. According to the sister, he'd recently split up from his long-time girlfriend and was very depressed. What could I possibly achieve in ten minutes?

I told him his sister was concerned about him.

'None of her business,' he said.

When had he last left his flat? He shrugged. Would he mind if I opened the curtains? Another shrug. He didn't seem jittery or absent. When someone's hallucinating or hearing voices you tend to sense it.

I told him I knew about his break-up, said it could feel like a bereavement and getting over it takes time. Should I list the five stages of grief? Or was it seven stages? No, he might deck me, and I wouldn't blame him. What would Trevor do? I remembered the time I'd gone with him to visit Eileen Prior, a woman who'd been depressed about her MS and depressed about her husband leaving her. 'Get your roots done, woman,' Trevor had said.

I asked Ryan if he'd do a couple of things for me. Shave, wash the dishes, take the garbage out. That was three things. He didn't say he wouldn't. One minute to go.

'Will you come to the surgery and see me at the end of the week?'

I don't know where they find those role-players but some of them are damned good. Ryan looked so lonely and defeated, I scribbled the Samaritans phone number on a prescription form and gave it to him.

'Friday,' I said. 'I'll expect to see you on Friday.'

Mr Whitehouse was a 75-year-old, retired accountant who had only agreed to come to the appointment to appease his wife. She said he was getting very forgetful. He said that was utter nonsense, as he was about to demonstrate. He started to list Chancellors of the Exchequer, 1900 to the present day, in chronological order. I had to stop him when he got to Bonar Law, time being of the essence.

'But here I am,' he said, 'as instructed. The things we poor men do for a quiet life.'

He was very chatty so there was no way I had enough time to give him the MMSE test. But this scenario was something I'd prepared for. I used the 6CIT. What year were we in? 2013. What month? August. I gave him an address to memorise: Bill Black, 24 Church Road, Manchester.

What time was it, roughly? Half past eleven. Could he count backwards from 20? He could and he did. And recite the months of the year in reverse order? He made just one mistake, flipping July and June. A lapse of concentration? And finally, could he tell me the address I'd asked him to memorise?

'You mean my address?'

'No. The address I asked you to commit to memory. For a Mr Black?'

He laughed.

He said, 'You must have forgotten to ask me, Doctor. Now who's the one who's got memory problems!'

I said, 'It can happen. Now while you're here, I'm going to get the nurse to take some bloods. Just to make sure you don't have an infection lurking.'

'Really?' he said. 'Well if you insist. At least I can tell my good lady I scored full marks on your little brain quiz.'

All I had time to say was, 'When you come back for the blood results, why don't you bring your wife with you? It'd be good to hear her side of things.'

'Good idea,' he said. 'Let her think we're taking her seriously, eh?'

268

Eleven consults down, two to go.

Louise was six weeks pregnant and in a panic. She'd been in contact with her niece who hadn't been well and now turned out to have chickenpox. She was terrified that her baby was at risk.

Had Louise had chickenpox herself as a child? She didn't know. Was there anyone in the family she could ask? Her Mum, maybe? No, she wasn't speaking to her Mum.

'I need to go for a scan,' she kept saying. 'I need to find out if the baby's damaged.'

I said, 'You know, you're more than likely immune. Very few children escape getting chickenpox. But we can do a blood test to check and if it turns out you're not immune, there's an injection we can give you.'

'But what about the baby?'

I was shakier ground there, but I was pretty sure the main risk to a baby was in the final weeks of pregnancy, not from birth defects but from being born with an infection. Whichever way you looked at it, Louise was worrying unnecessarily, and she definitely didn't need an urgent scan.'

'One step at a time,' I said. 'Let's take some blood and see what that tells us.'

She didn't look happy and I still had three minutes left on the clock to rectify that. I asked her how she was feeling, how the pregnancy was going, apart from the chickenpox worry, was she working, where was she planning to go for the birth? Shit, maybe I should have asked her all that at the start of the consultation, shown more general interest in her instead of diving straight in. But she'd wanted me to dive in. She was too anxious for small talk. Had I gone about it the best way or not? The fact that she was an actor, not really a worried woman

269

expecting her first baby, was immaterial. Everything I said and did was being observed. That was the point.

I was flagging, drained, hoping for something nice and straightforward for my final consultation. A simple case of tonsillitis, or threadworm. The kind of stuff I saw all the time at Tit Droop. I got Brandon, a 22-year-old IT worker whose brother, aged 26, had died suddenly at the gym, doing bench presses. The cause of death was hypertrophic cardiomyopathy. Brandon handed me a letter. It was from the Medical Genetics department of his local hospital, inviting him to genetic screening.

The iPad told me that his obs were all normal and he had no history of breathlessness or chest pain, no finger clubbing, carotid bruits or abnormal heart sounds. The hospital letter very handily helped me by mentioning that hypertrophic cardiomyopathy is an autosomal dominant condition. The question was, could I draw Brandon a family tree, to explain how the condition was inherited. And then, what advice could I give him?

Did Brandon and his brother have the same parents? Yes. Were they still living? Yes, both, and in good health. But the laws of Mendelian genetics suggested that one of them had the cardiomyopathy gene. They just didn't know it. What if they didn't want to know? What if, actually, unbeknownst to anyone except the mother, one of the sons had a different, secret father? That's the kind of can of worms you can prise open with genetic screening.

I looked at the date on the letter. July 10th.

'When did your brother die?'

'May.'

Then I knew exactly what to say. Brandon and his folks were still reeling from a sudden death. It was far too soon to start poking around in the family gene tree.

I said, 'My advice is, put the letter away for now. It's an offer you can take up any time, but it's not something to go into lightly. You might think of doing it before you decide whether to have children yourself?'

He looked at me as if I was crazy. He was 22. Fathering kids wasn't on his agenda.

He said, 'So have I got it? This heart thing?'

'You have a 50 per cent chance. And if turns out you do have it, there are treatments. But you've just lost your brother....

The buzzer went.

'.... You should give yourself time to get over that.'

When I told Chloe about the Brandon case, she completely disagreed with me. She thought I should have recommended screening ASAP.

She said, 'What if he needs a cardio-defibrillator implant?'

'What if he does? What if he doesn't? People ask their GP for advice all the time, then ignore it. It's up to Brandon, who isn't real anyway. He was a hypothetical patient, may I remind you. Incidentally, I saw the bloke vaping outside the test centre as I was leaving, whereas Brandon was a non-smoker.'

Still, I began going over the day's cases, thinking about that I could have done better, which was almost everything. Was I going to have to retake my CSA and go through the whole ordeal again?

I said, 'Someone called George Fitzgerald asked to be remembered to you.'

'Fitzie? You saw Fitzie? He's gone into general practice?'

271

'Apparently. How well did you know him?'

She flushed.

'That well, eh? I guessed as much from the look he gave me.'

'It was yonks ago.'

'Of course.'

'Long before you. Anyway, you had girlfriends before me.'

'Yes.'

Not many, to be honest. I was a bit shy about asking girls out and if Chloe hadn't made the first move, I'd never have dared ask her.

'Fitzie. In general practice? That's amazeballs. Where's he working?'

'I didn't ask.'

'He was hugely wealthy. His family own half of somewhere in Ireland. How did he look?'

'Apart from the cystic acne, the missing incisor and the male pattern baldness, quite a dish, I'd say.'

Chapter 28

My 10 o'clock was Betty Cheever. I knew Betty from the Patient Participation Panel. A nice woman, but one who was inclined to ramble on and branch off into irrelevant topics. I didn't ever want my patients to feel I'd rushed them, but I did have ten other patients to see that morning.

Betty was limping. She had pain in her left heel and couldn't put weight on it. It sounded very much like plantar fasciitis. She'd already tried icepacks and rest.

She said, 'Cheryl says I need to see a thisiopherapist.'

Cheryl was her daughter and was possibly right. However, Cheryl wasn't necessarily au fait with current physiotherapy waiting lists.

I said, 'If it's what I think it is, you need to do some stretching exercises. I can show you, if you like. No need to wait around to see a physio.'

She agreed, a bit begrudgingly, I thought. Perhaps she was worried what Cheryl would say. I demonstrated how to do wall pushes, to stretch the Achilles tendon, then looked for something to use as a resistance band. A scarf would have been perfect, but the weather was too warm for scarves. Then I remembered Trevor's discarded tie. Beige, knitted, tossed into a drawer the day Glenys Allsop had said it was roughly the colour of her faeces.

I started showing Betty how to loop the tie round her toes and pull on it, to stretch the tendon.

She said, 'I don't know that I can manage that, Doctor. My leg's paining me as well. It's throbbing.'

I got her to roll up her trouser legs. Was her left calf swollen? Possibly. It was hard to be sure. She's not a slim woman. Was her calf warm? Definitely. I got her to her feet so I could look at the back of her calves. Any redness? Yes, clear as day. Betty had signs of a deep vein thrombosis.

Had she been sitting a lot? She was just back from a coach tour of North Wales, she said. Lovely hotels, bed, breakfast and evening meals included, and the coach had even had a toilet and a telly. I did a Trevor Buxton and asked her where they'd been. It bought me a bit of thinking time. If I sent her blood for a D-Dimer test, would we get the result by evening? Would I be better off sending her straight to hospital for an angiograph and let them do the D-dimer? Should I get another opinion, or should I grow a pair and make my own decision, for crying out loud?

Capel Curig, Llyn Ogwen, Llanberis, Caernarfon, Betty was intent on giving me the full itinerary of her coach tour, with café prices in all locations, for a pot of tea and a scone. I only stopped her in her tracks by telling her I was sending her to A&E.

She said, 'But Cheryl says I just need to see a thisiopherapist.'

274

I said, 'Betty, all due respect to your daughter but you have signs of a blood clot in your lower leg and it's important to get it checked. I'm going to give you a letter. I want you to go straight from here to Sandwell.'

'Well that's a nuisance,' she said. 'Could I go tomorrow? I've got a perm booked for this afternoon.'

You don't want to over-dramatize things, especially when there's a Cheryl waiting in the wings to tell you you were wrong, but it seemed to me that a potential pulmonary thrombosis trumped a hair appointment whichever way you looked at it. Betty went off with the letter.

I said, 'Let me know what they say.'

'What?' she said. 'You mean, phone you?'

'Yes.'

'Am I allowed?'

'Of course.'

She liked that.

'I will,' she said. 'Where my Cheryl goes, you never see the same doctor twice. And if you leave a message, they never call you back.'

She sat in the waiting room while Mary tracked down Cheryl and asked her to run her Mum to the hospital. They were leaving when I went to call Bill Mutch in for his appointment. I was prepared for a browbeating from Betty's daughter. I almost ducked back into my office for a second because this Cheryl sounded like the kind of relative who thinks she knows best. But she didn't say anything. Just gave me a lingering look.

Jean Boddy was coming out of the kitchen with a Cuppa Soup.

She said, 'Is that a question mark I see over your head?'

'A faint one. I've just sent a patient to A&E and now I'm having second thoughts.'

'Tell me.'

'Mrs Cheever. She's 68, presented with plantar fasciitis but then I discovered her calf was swollen and tender. And warm.'

'Any pitting?'

'No, but the superficial veins were slightly swollen.'

'Heart rate?'

'120.'

'You did the right thing, Dan.'

'You think?'

'Definitely.'

'She was annoyed about missing a hair appointment.'

'Well, important to look your best, I suppose, in case you end the day in a mortuary viewing room.'

Afternoon surgery had finished and the front door was locked but Mary doesn't put the answering machine on until she's ready to leave.

'I've got a Cheryl Cheever on the phone,' she said. 'She'd like a word with the trainee doctor.'

Uh-oh. Betty's daughter was going to give me her expert opinion after all.

'Dr Talbot,' she said, 'I just had to phone and thank you. The hospital said it was a good thing you sent Mum over there this morning because she'd got a great big blood clot in her leg. They said if that had floated up to her lungs, it could have killed her.'

'Are they keeping her in?'

'No, I've got to pick her up later. They gave her an injection, as soon as they saw her leg, then they sent her for a scan and now she's just waiting for another scan. They're giving her pills as well. Anti-something.'

'Anti-coagulants.'

'They said she'll be on them for months.'

'It sounds as though everything is under control. Tell her to come and see me in a week or two. Tell her I'm sorry she missed her hair appointment.'

Cheryl was effusive with her thanks.

She said, 'And to think, you're not even qualified yet.'

Which turned out not quite to be the case because when I got home Chloe had opened my post and then zipped down to the supermarket for Chicken Kievs and a bottle of wine that cost well north of my usual £15 ceiling. I had passed my CSA.

Chloe had already alerted the Chummery.

'You mean your parents knew before I did?'

'Just Mummy. Daddy's at a Bart's reunion dinner.'

'What did she say?'

'She said "jolly well done" of course.'

'In what language?'

Chloe doesn't understand why I find Vinnie's Franglais so funny. She says her mother speaks better French than anyone else in the village but Bishop's Wapshott only has 1,300 residents so she may be right.

I phoned home. Da answered. Mam was still at work.

'She's got a slow one,' he said, 'and you know what she's like. Always likes to see it through. Won't leave till it's in the cradle.'

'Only I passed my MRCGP.'

'That's a mouthful. Well done. And what does that buy you?'

'No more exams. I'm a fully qualified GP.'

'You going to set up shop on your own?'

277

'Not unless there's a big stash of Talbot money you haven't told me about. No, I'm going to look for a permanent job. Anyway, tell Mam.'

'Tell her yourself. She's just walked in the door.'

'Tell me what?' says Mam.

'You sound tired.'

'I'm getting too old for this lark. I've been rubbing a girl's back for hours. Poor dab. She was only seventeen and all on her own. She'd got her sister down for a birthing partner, but she never turned up.'

'Where was the father?'

'Where indeed. So what have you got to tell me?'

'I passed my CSA.'

'I knew you would. I said to your Da, at the wedding, how you'd come on a tidy bit, matured like, you know? Well we're very proud of you. I'm just saying, Ed…'

She insists on relaying everything back and forth to Da. If only someone would invent a phone you could put on loudspeaker.

'So now what?' she said. 'Will you move?'

'To be decided. I can stay put if I want to. I've been offered it.'

'We liked Trevor. And the chubby one.'

'Pam. She's a part-timer and Trevor's on his way out. He's too ill to work full-time. Helen's the boss now and she's not really my style. Anyway, I'm not in a hurry.'

Mam phoned back twice that evening. Once between the chicken and chocolate mousse, to say there was a practice in Usk advertising for a salaried doctor, and then again when we were otherwise engaged. She left a message to say there were also vacancies in Pontypridd and Cardiff.

278

'Not that I'm being pushy, mind, and I know you have Chloe to consider, but it'd be lovely to have you living closer. I'm just saying.'

Chloe said, 'She's right, you do have me to consider. I have a career too.'

It was a conversation that was overdue. While we were both still training there had been little point. We had to do what we had to do. But a big wide door had now swung open. We could go anywhere, even overseas, as long as we could both find work. Now the question was, who got to decide where or when? Did our careers carry equal weight?

I said, 'You've been on at me to leave Tipton since the day I started there.'

'Sure, leave Bitch Face's practice. But that doesn't mean you can drag me off anywhere you please.'

'Are you telling me you want to stay in this area? You haven't seemed very happy at the Arden.'

She said she hadn't been but now she was really getting into it.

'Okay. So how do you see the next few years going? Like, how are we going to manage things when we start a family?'

'Haven't thought about it.'

'I think you should. Could you be a part-time cardio?'

'Only if I kept really, really up to date. But why part-time? That's what creches are for.'

I didn't want an argument. We'd had a lovely evening. I've just never seen the point of having children and then only being with them first thing in the morning and last thing at night.

She said, 'If we both worked somewhere near the Chummery, Mummy could be our childminder. What? Don't look at me like that.'

But even dear Chloe recognised how riddled with comedy that idea was.

'She could strap it to her golf bag, I suppose. Like a papoose.'

'And once it had learned to walk it could caddy for her. What was she like when you were kids?'

'Same as she is now. Flo and I longed to go to school because we'd heard they gave you hot food at lunchtime. We had babysitters, various girls from the village. Not Norland trained, more like Rough and Tumble of Family Life trained. Mummy didn't see the point of qualifications. She used to advertise on a card in the post office window.'

'Then I think we've established that Granny Swift wouldn't be a child-minding option.'

'You want to go for one of those Welsh jobs.'

'Not particularly. Although Mam would be ace at looking after our children. If we have any.'

Chloe said she couldn't live in Wales because people talked funny.

'You understand Mam and Da well enough. You understood Nan and Aunty June.'

'No, but other people. They speak Welsh.'

'Not to nice, polite English girls, they don't. And they are entitled. In Turkey you didn't complain about people speaking Turkish.'

'That's completely different.'

'How so?'

'Turkey is Turkey. Wales is part of England. Kind of.'

I took Eeyore hostage and threatened to disembowel him if she didn't repeat after me, 'The Principality of Wales is but one part of the United Kingdom. I acknowledge that it has its own history and language and I do solemnly swear to undertake a programme of re-education on this topic to the satisfaction of Daniel Talbot, MRCGP.'

'Anyway,' she said, 'About a job for you. Daddy has a friend with a private general practice in Solihull…'

'I know. He told me.'

'Solihull would be convenient.'

'It would. But I'm not planning on going into private practice.'

'Are you a Communist or something?'

'Don't you think you should have asked me that before you married me?'

Chapter 29

Helen went through the motions of congratulating me, but it was all a bit lukewarm.

She said, 'So now I suppose you'll abandon us.'

'Obviously, I'll give you fair notice.'

'Please consider staying,' she said. 'Talk to Kasper about what you'd need. We can put together a tempting package.'

I promised I'd think about it.

Cliff was being moved to rehab. She said he'd gone from angry to depressed.

'And how are you?'

'I'm still stuck on angry. It's not just his own life he's banjaxed. It affects me too. Selfish, randy bastard.'

I said, 'But Helen, he could have had a stroke anywhere. He might have been at home, or behind the wheel. That could have been a disaster.'

'He wasn't though, was he? He was in a fucking Travelodge with a bimbo.'

Pam Parker's husband had been to visit Cliff. I hadn't realised they were friends.

Pam said, 'They're not. Bob went to save me from committing an act of utter hypocrisy. He's a dear, my husband. He didn't stay long, mind.'

'Helen's in a mess.'

'No wonder. Cliff's probably not going to walk again, plus double incontinence. It's hard enough to care for somebody when you love them, Dan. What must it be like when you despise them?'

'The thing that really seems to bug her is that it happened in a Travelodge.'

'That's Helen for you. A budget hotel. The ultimate humiliation. So where to next, Dr Talbot? I presume you won't be with us for much longer?'

'Probably not. I do like it here, mainly, but I've had a few issues with Helen.'

'You mean her mood swings? I rather enjoy them. It's how I imagine it feels surfing big Atlantic rollers. But I see from your face you didn't mean her moods. Oh Dan, has she been ferreting in your boxers?'

'She didn't get quite that far. Forget it. I shouldn't have said anything.'

'If it's any consolation, you're not the first and I doubt you'll be the last. If you stay on, before you know it, we'll have some new trainee for her to pat down. But don't stay. We all love you, but you should move on.'

Which was almost exactly what Trevor said.

He also said, 'You don't want to end up like me.'

'Actually, I do want to end up like you. You've got patients you know really well, patients who trust you and don't want you to retire. When I'm your age I'd like to be you, but without the COPD.'

'That's very flattering. The tide's against you though, lad. Family medicine's not like it was when I started out. The customers and the paper-shufflers all demand too much these days. But you're going to make a cracking GP, wherever you end up. Did you see the letter about the Hastilow child?'

That name again.

'Maisie?'

'The six-year-old with genital warts in her mouth, God help us. Pam referred her to paediatrics.'

'What's the latest?'

'Social services paid a visit. The mother said there'd been a change of guard in the step-father department so social services went away. Then last week mother and child turned up in A&E. The wee lass had a third-degree perineal tear and half her rectum hanging out.'

I felt sick.

'They've repaired her?'

'They'll have done their best, I'm sure. She's got a temporary colostomy until she's healed, so we might get involved in the after-care.'

'What about healing inside her head?'

'What indeed. She'll get sessions with a child psychologist. Will they help? Your guess is as good as mine. Can't give her her childhood back, can they?'

'Will she be taken into care?'

'Depends. They certainly won't let her home if the perpetrator's still on the scene. He's probably scarpered, but it seems the mother has a taste for men who violate little girls.'

'It's so sad.'

'It is. Furthermore, someday Maisie'll have kids, if the step-daddy hasn't completely buggered up her plumbing. Literally. And then, what will pass for normal in that household?'

It was the end of afternoon surgery. Mary said a parcel had come for me. She brought out a box.

'What is it?'

'Do I have X-ray eyes?'

'Who delivered it?'

'A courier.'

As soon as I started to open it, everyone appeared.

Nurse Linda said, 'Been online shopping between patients, Dan?'

It was a very nice Italian sweater. Pale blue, lambswool. There was a card. *From Cheryl, thank you for saving Mum's life.* xx

Harold said, 'Very nice. All I've ever been given is a book voucher. Did you perform CPR?'

I said, 'I didn't save her life. All I did was send her to Sandwell with a suspected DVT.'

'And you were right?'

'As it turned out. But I can't keep this. Can I?'

Helen snatched the note.

She said, 'Kiss kiss? I think Dan has a lady admirer. Oh Lord, why couldn't she just send you something we could all share. A box of Belgian chocolates would have been about right.'

'So what do I do?'

'Phone her. Say it's against practice rules. Tell him, Kaz.'

Kasper said, 'It's against practice rules.'

'As a matter of interest, is she actually a patient here?'

No-one could recall a patient called Cheryl Cheever but then Mary chimed in and said someone of that name had just registered and made an appointment for 4.45 on Friday.

Linda said, 'And we all know what that means.'

'She's grabbed Kyle Bibby's favourite slot.'

285

'She means to catch you when you're tired, your resistance is low and everyone clearing off for the weekend. One by one the lights go out at Tipton Road West, until all that's left is Dr Dan, Cheryl Cheever and a 40-watt desk lamp.'

'I'd better have Linda or Chris in with me.'

Helen said, 'No, you won't. You'll finish at lunchtime and Trevor will take your afternoon list. He'll sort her. Pity about the sweater though.'

And that was exactly how things were handled. Trevor came in to have a gentle, fatherly chat with Cheryl. The sweater, which she told him to stick where the sun doesn't shine, disappeared into Helen's bag, and I had an afternoon off. I went into Birmingham and bought a motoring map of Great Britain. There were plenty of openings for a newly registered GP, the trouble was some of them were in places I'd never heard of.

It could have been an exciting time. In theory we could go anywhere. But just as I'd start picturing myself in some lovely little town in North Yorkshire or Somerset, I'd remember it wasn't only me, it was us, and Chloe's career had to be factored in. I pared down my search. The West Midlands, which was her preference or Wales, which was mine, and wherever we went, it had to be within commuting distance of a hospital with a cardiology department.

There were jobs going in Redditch and Worcester and Coventry. Also in Rhyl and Prestatyn and Llandudno, all on the North Wales coast. I'd never been to any of them, but I found myself dreaming of sea air and long walks on the beach.

Chloe looked over my shoulder and said, 'We are not moving to Wales.'

Sunday afternoon we were pulling out of Morrison's car park when her phone rang.

She kept saying, 'What? When? Say that again. What? How?'

'It's Flo,' she said, 'I think she's blubbing and I can't understand what she's saying. You speak to her.'

She handed me her phone and Flo apparently handed hers to her husband because I found myself talking to Henry. I put us on speaker.

'Nothing desperate,' he said. 'Vinnie's had a bit of a prang, on the road between Gorst Leigh and Wapshott Underwood. We've spoken to Laurence and he says it sounds like she's cracked a couple of ribs.'

'Chloe said Flo sounded very upset.'

'Touch of shock. Lily was in the car with Vinnie, but she's quite unharmed. Rather thrilled by it all actually and begging for a repeat. The child's made of rubber.'

Vinnie's car had skidded on mud and landed upside down in a ditch.

'Has she gone to hospital?'

'That's the thing. Vinnie declines to go and Flo rather feels she ought.'

Chloe took over.

'Henry,' she said, 'tell Mummy she's to go to hospital immediately. Tell Flo to blow her nose and take her there. In fact, why haven't you called for an ambulance?'

'Well,' he said, 'Vinnie rather forbad it. We were directly behind her when it happened...'

Then Vinnie herself came on.

'Darling, don't fuss,' she said. 'I'm perfectly alright. Daddy says he'll strap me up when he gets home.'

287

'Strapping you up is not the answer. We don't do that anymore because it stops you breathing properly. Daddy's terribly out of date. Where is he anyway?'

'He's the other side of Kenilworth, shooting clays. But he'll be home this evening. We have some dire soirée to attend.'

'What soirée?'

'Drinks with those people who bought The Paddocks. He's in the security industry, apparently, and worth a mint.'

'Mummy, please go to the hospital.'

'Compromise? I'll go in the morning. It's Sunday afternoon. Casualty will be full of sprained ankles and one could be waiting around for aeons. It's such a faff. Now Lily wishes to speak to you.'

Lily reported that Granny had turned her car completely upside down and said the F word.

She said, 'Daisy and Poppy wish it had happened to them. They're hugely jealous.'

And in the background we heard, 'Oh no we're not.'

Henry was organising a tow-truck to haul Vinnie's car out of the ditch where it had come to rest. All evening Chloe agonised over whether she should have driven to the Chummery to check on her mother.

I said, 'There's no point in going now. Your Dad'll be home and they were going out to see what the new neighbours have done to their house.'

'Covered everything in gold leaf, probably.'

'And laser beam security sensors everywhere.'

'Honestly, why is Flo so utterly hopeless? Why didn't she bundle Mummy into her car and take her to A&E?'

'I wouldn't like to try bundling your mother anywhere she didn't want to go. Try to switch off. Relax. You can resume nagging in the morning, if necessary.'

Chapter 30

By Monday morning Vinnie was feeling well enough to go to a Ladies' Golf Team lunch. Her car was a write-off, so her chum Pippa gave her a lift.

'See?' she said, when we spoke to her that evening, 'what a colossal waste of time it would have been to go to the hospital. Laurence has put me in a compression wrap and I'm tip-top.'

Chloe said, 'I told you not to use a compression wrap. You're just asking for pneumonia.'

'Excuse me,' says Vinnie, 'but Daddy has been a doctor a great deal longer than you. I think he may be allowed to decide what's best. The Paddocks, by the by, is a fright. They've covered all those good oak floors with fluffy pink carpet. I mean, everywhere. Even the littlest room. Imagine what it's going to smell like after the menfolk have missed their aim and sprinkled around the pedestal.'

On Wednesday morning she had a slight pain under her left ribcage and was feeling too nauseated to go to the driving range. A tummy bug, she said. Chloe took yet another day off work to go and see her. I was with Glenys Allsop when my phone buzzed. Glenys was doing fantastically well with her new liver, but her marriage was in trouble. The post-transplant Glenys was full of beans and Pete couldn't handle it.

What exactly was he struggling with? Going on weekend mini-breaks, signing up for Italian classes, having more sex. Pete preferred to stay home and keep on top of the gardening, and he didn't want to go to Italy. They'd always gone to a bungalow in Minehead and had a pleasant time, so why fix what wasn't broken. He'd called her a raving nympho.

I found her the number for Relate.

'Counselling?' she said. 'Pete'll never agree to that. He doesn't believe in it.'

My phone buzzed again.

I said, 'That doesn't stop you from going. Make an appointment. It can't hurt to talk to someone.'

'I suppose so,' she said. 'Or I could just bugger off to Italy and find myself a man.'

I'd missed three calls from Chloe. No messages. I called her. Her phone was busy and I had five patients still to see. For the next hour we kept missing each other. It was lunchtime when I finally got her.

'She's dead, Dan,' she said. 'Mummy's fucking dead.'

Trevor said I should leave immediately. I said I'd finish surgery first. Vinnie would still be dead. It wasn't like there was anything I could do.

'On the contrary,' says Trevor, 'there's a lot you can do and number one is give that girl of yours a strong shoulder to lean on. Go. I'll cover for you here. What was it? A thrombosis?'

'Sounds like a ruptured spleen.'

'Didn't they scan her, after her accident?'

291

'She refused to go to the hospital. She'd been out socialising. Sunday night, all day Monday, she was fine.'

'A slow bleed. It can happen. And two doctors in the family. I hope there won't be any finger pointing.'

Fat chance. War had already broken out at The Chummery. Chloe blamed her father for not being more attentive. Laurence blamed Flo and Henry for not taking control after Vinnie's accident. Flo blamed Laurence and Chloe for not dashing to the scene immediately.

The story, as I pieced it together, was that the nausea and pain had worsened so that by the time Chloe arrived, Vinnie was desperate. She was too weak to stand up and her pulse was fast and thready. Laurence had already left for London. Flo was doing meals-on wheels. Chloe had called for an ambulance. A bedside ultrasound had revealed Vinnie's peritoneum was flooded with blood and her spleen was mashed. They'd given her oxygen and started a transfusion while they waited for a theatre to become available, but she'd plunged into haemorrhagic shock and arrested. Chloe, the cardiologist daughter, had had to stand back and watch a team of strangers trying to resuscitate her mother. They'd got her pulse back twice, then it had disappeared for good.

At the Chummery everyone appeared to be sleep-walking, apart from Henry, who sat on a kitchen chair making phone calls. I asked if anyone had broken the news to Vinnie's parents. Chloe had been over to their nursing home and told them. Grandpa Orde-Sykes had wept, Granny Orde-Sykes had said, 'How sad. But of course she was terribly old.'

Not realising your child has died is possibly the only upside to dementia.

Laurence seemed genuinely astonished by what had happened.

'She was A1 this morning,' he kept saying.

And Chloe kept saying, 'No she wasn't, Daddy. She was feeling rotten.'

Flo cried a lot, but she fed the cat and warmed up some cans of tomato soup for the humans. Lily watched television, Daisy and Poppy played at funerals. People started arriving, women mainly, well-heeled, lean and fit, golfers. Everyone spoke in whispers. Was there anything they could do? No, but thank you anyway.

I called Mam. She said, 'I hardly know what to say. Only what a good job the little one wasn't hurt. Was she in her kiddie seat?'

I suspected not. Vinnie had her own ideas about child safety.

The house emptied. Flo took her children home. Chloe went up to bed. Laurence, Henry and I sat in the twilight exchanging platitudes. Our lives hang by a thread. We know not the hour. Sixty-seven was no age at all.

I said, 'Will you have the funeral at St Botolph's?'

'Good God, no,' says Laurence. 'Vinnie couldn't stand the padre. She thought him the most jumped-up little twerp.'

Eventually all I could see of Henry was the glow of his small cigar. Then Chloe appeared, still dressed.

'Charlie,' she said. 'Has anyone told Charlie?'

'Ah,' said Henry. 'I'm afraid that one slipped my mind.'

We didn't sleep much. I was wondering when I could decently go back to work. Chloe was convinced that her brother would be released from prison the very moment the

293

governor heard of his tragic loss. I hadn't the heart to warn her the penal system probably didn't work like that.

Henry wasn't around the next morning because one of his boars, Lord Tailcoat, had a hot date on a farm near Warwick, so it fell to me to phone HMP Coldingley and ask them to tell Charlie his mother had died. They said the chaplain would break the news to him and he'd be able to make a phone call. Also, that he could apply for temporary release to attend the funeral but we should understand that Coldingley was a Category C facility. If Charlie was allowed out, he'd be handcuffed to a prison officer. I kept that information to myself for a while.

Trevor told me to take the rest of the week off. He said Helen would completely understand. There wasn't much for me to do though, apart from hug Chloe whenever a wave of grief hit her. Peace had broken out between her and Flo and they were busy planning their father's future. I'd never known Chloe to agree with anything Flo said, but on one point they were unanimous: Laurence could not live alone at The Chummery.

I said, 'I don't see why not. He's fit, he's busy and Flo's just down the road if he gets sick.'

They said he didn't know how to cook and had no idea what it took to run such a big house.

I said, 'What about Mrs Pickering? She can still do the cleaning. And how often does he eat dinner at home anyway? Even Laurence can boil an egg.'

They said I didn't understand. Which was true.

By the time Laurence returned from the undertaker's Flo and Chlo had hatched a plan to save him from starvation and

294

grubby sheets. From Monday to Friday he was to go to Flo's for dinner. Having the grandchildren around him would stop him feeling sad and lonely. Chloe and I were to take over at the weekends.'

I said, 'What do you mean, take over?'

'We'll come here. Look after him. Do nice things to keep him occupied.'

'What, every weekend?'

Chloe said, 'It's only fair. Weekends are hectic for Flo. The yoblets have riding lessons and ballet classes.'

I told them they were being ridiculous. Then Laurence came home and told them the same.

'Utter piffle,' he said. 'I shall stay up in Town from Monday to Thursday and on weekends I'll be busy in the garden.'

Flo said, 'What if you have a fall?'

'What if I do?' he said. 'I had a fall last year, tripped over a damned rake handle. Vinnie was in the house, had no idea. I don't think she even noticed the bruise on my cheek. Now, I've picked out a coffin, oak veneer, quite plain and with the slightest scratch on the lid, on the outside of the lid I should add, so they gave me a discount.'

Chloe said he shouldn't have put himself through an ordeal like that. He should have asked the funeral people to come to the house.

'Nonsense,' he said. 'I was in town anyway. In fact, it was very interesting to go around the showroom. I think I might go back and pick out a box for myself. They were telling me that one can prepay these days and make substantial savings. There's the risk the firm might go belly-up, I suppose, but they seem pretty solid. Established 1928.'

He went off to answer yet another phone call.

Flo wasn't happy about the word 'veneer' appearing in the coffin spec. I wasn't thrilled about having my weekends commandeered to babysit a man who clearly didn't need it.

I said, 'Laurence is doing fine. I think you ought to back off. Give him time to get used to his new circumstances.'

Flo and Chloe both glared at me. I decided I might as well get the Charlie situation out in the open while they were feeling affronted. As soon as Laurence came back into the room I said, 'I've spoken to Coldingley. If Charlie comes to the funeral, and it's discretionary so he may not be allowed to, he'll be handcuffed.'

Flo said it was too beastly. Chloe said Laurence should speak to one of his lawyer friends. Laurence said, all things considered, mightn't it be better if Charlie didn't come.

Chloe said, 'But Mummy would be devastated.'

And Laurence said, 'Technically speaking, Mummy won't be there.'

Another fitful night. Chloe agreed, reluctantly, that I should go back to work until the funeral. She had something bigger on her mind. What if her father decided to live in London full-time? What if he sold The Chummery? I wondered whether it was his to sell.

Chloe sat up in bed. She said, 'What do you mean?'

'I was always under the impression it belonged to your mother. Hasn't it been in her family for three generations? Did she leave a Will?"

'I don't know. I'd better ask Daddy.'

It was 2 a.m.

'Do not disturb your father. He took a pill. Let him sleep.'

'But what if she didn't leave a Will?'

'I don't know. He'll probably get the house anyway, or maybe it passes to you and Flo and Slow.'

'They don't need it. Slow's got his shag-pad and Flo's got the Grange. The Packwoods are filthy rich.'

'And we'll be buying a four-bed detached in Rhyl, so we won't need it.'

'Not funny. Is Mummy really dead? I keep thinking it's a dream.'

'Me too. I'm really sorry.'

'We'll have to see all those rellies again, so soon after our wedding. The Suffolk crowd might not come.'

'Will people come back here afterwards? For tea and sandwiches?'

'Is that usual?'

'I'd say so. If people have travelled a long way. Although maybe Flo's place would be better?'

'Why?'

'It's warmer. Their Aga seems to work. What about hymns?'

'No hymns. Mummy wasn't terribly pi.'

'What then? A few words about how marvellous she was and then off she goes, through the curtains? People certainly won't want to drive all the way from Suffolk for that.'

'She was marvellous. I didn't realise until now.'

Vinnie, who had been a perpetual source of irritation to Chloe, was transformed in death. The best mother ever.

Chloe clung to me like a limpet all night.

'Don't die, Dan,' she kept saying. 'Please don't die.'

Chapter 31

I don't like sneaking around behind Chloe's back but sometimes things are best kept on a need to know footing. She was at The Chummery, presiding over the funeral arrangements and watching like a hawk for Laurence to break down with grief. It was getting on his nerves and I'd certainly had enough of the whispering and tiptoeing. I pleaded the urgent need to take Friday afternoon surgery and headed back to Tipton. This left me with a free weekend. It seemed like the ideal opportunity for something I'd been itching to do. I drove to the North Wales coast.

By half past ten I was having a second breakfast in Rhyl, where there was a vacancy for a salaried GP to join a multidisciplinary team in a purpose- built health centre serving a varied demographic. By lunch time I was in Conwy, where there was an exciting opportunity to join a practice with 100 percent QOF ratings. Eight sessions a week, flexible hours and six weeks annual leave.

Chloe called me, for no particular reason.

She said, 'You're in the car.'

'Just out for a change of scene.'

'You should have come here and kept me company. I'm bored.'

'No, you're not. You're busy organising a funeral and you've got Flo. You don't need me.'

'She says we have to pick an outfit for Mummy to wear and then take the rest of her clothes to a charity shop. It's so heartless, so ghoulish.'

'What does Laurence say?'

'Don't know. He's out. Some friends dragged him off to play golf. He's being so brave. Where are you driving to?'

'Just pootling,' I lied. I was actually looking out at the beach and the ruins of a Victorian pier. 'Sort of north west. Exploring.'

'Uh-oh, the yoblets have arrived. I suppose I'd better go and be an aunty. Do you think children should go to funerals?'

'It depends on the child, I imagine. Flo and Henry's three are pretty robust.'

'That's what Flo says. She says they're used to the piggywigs going for the chop. I love you.'

'I love you too.'

'Say the Gary thing.'

'Dw i'n dy garu di.'

I felt ridiculously excited driving home, as though I was on the verge of some new adventure. Nothing could have been further from the truth. I was married to a woman who'd refused even to discuss moving to Wales and that was before her mother died. That was before she and Flo had decided their father was in such a delicate psychological state he must never be left alone. They even hovered outside the bathroom door if they judged he'd been in there too long.

By Monday morning I'd come to my senses and I knew I had to be patient while Chloe came to hers. Get the funeral over and done with and the sorting of Vinnie's clothes and Laurence's return to work. Let time prove to her that there was no need to plan our future around our parents' needs. Not yet, at any rate.

Dave Stackhouse's biopsy results were in. He had a Stage 2 squamous cell carcinoma on the underside of his tongue, lymph nodes clear, no evidence of metastases. Recommended treatment: surgical removal of the tumour and a margin, followed by radiotherapy. Reconstructive surgery at a later date, if required.

I phoned, to see if he wanted a chat. I got Ruby.

She said, 'It's cancer. The hospital told him.'

'Does he have a date for the operation?'

'He's thinking about it.'

'Thinking about it?'

'Whether to have the operation.'

'Can I talk to him?'

'He's out.'

'He should have the surgery. We've caught the cancer early. His prospects are very good.'

'They said he'd have to give up the smokes, though.'

'Will you tell him I called? Tell him I'd like to see him?'

'Yeah,' she said. 'I'll tell him.'

Trevor called me. He was in the Black Bear.

'Come and join me for a swift one,' he said. 'You can have a glass of that fancy water. There's something going on here I wouldn't want you to miss. Lounge bar, as per.'

The Bear was busy for a Monday lunchtime. There seemed to be a party going on. Trevor slid over so I could sit beside him.

'Recognise anybody?' he said.

'Is that Harry Darkin?'

'The very same. Anyone else?'

'No.'

'Hold on. You'll see her when that fat lump shifts himself. There. See? In the blue hat?'

It was Connie Riley. She had flowers pinned to her coat lapel.

'Is it someone's wedding?'

'I'd say so. See the aforementioned fat lump, elegantly attired in trainers and an anorak? That's Connie's son, Derek.'

'You don't think Connie and Harry have…?'

'I'd bet my shirt on it. Why so surprised? Wasn't it you who told me Harry was courting her? If I remember rightly, he'd told her he still had lead in his pencil.'

'You haven't spoken to them?'

'I was waiting for you to get here. Let's go over and say hello.'

Connie turned quite pink when she saw us.

She said, 'I know what you must be thinking.'

Trevor said, 'I'm thinking what a lovely couple you make.'

She said, 'Derek thinks it's too soon. But it's been a year nearly, since I lost my Jimmy.'

'None of Derek's business,' says Trevor. 'You grab a bit of happiness while you can. So is Harry moving in with you or are you moving in with him?'

She took us to one side.

'I have to watch what I say because you never know who's listening. We're keeping both bungalows, for the time being. Till we see how things work out. He does snore so.'

We congratulated Harry. He said he'd worn down Connie's resistance with tea dances and Tesco reward points.

As I said to Trevor, it was quite a turn around. The last time I'd spoken to Connie she'd been avoiding Harry, scuttling past his gate, hoping he wasn't on the lookout for her. Now she'd gone and married him.

Trevor said, 'The enduring mystery of a woman's mind. Here, you don't think Harry's put her in the pudding club, do you?'

He seemed settled for the afternoon.

'No racing to watch?'

'There's always racing to watch. As a matter of fact, I've got twenty quid invested in the 3.30 at Sedgefield. But Mrs Buxton's sister is visiting so I think I'll sit here and watch it. How are things in the house of mourning?'

'Strange. Chloe and her sister insist on being there, even though there's nothing much to do till the funeral. Laurence is out and about. He played golf on Saturday and Sunday, and he's gone to London today to see a couple of patients. And then there's the Charlie question. He might be brought out on licence for the day.'

'So? Oh, you mean he'll be handcuffed.'

'Chloe's upset about it. Flo thinks an hour of public humiliation might do him more good than eighteen months inside. Laurence doesn't seem to care one way or the other.'

'Hmm. I'm with Flo on this one. She's the one married to the pig farmer?'

'Yes. Older sister.'

'I was thinking, that house of theirs would make a good surgery. You could set up on your own, like my old man did. Nice area too. A better class of patient. I'll bet you don't get many Kyle Bibbys to the pound around there.

'No thank you. I don't want to live with my father-in-law, and I don't want to work alone. I like knowing there are wiser heads than mine in the building. And I quite like having a few Kyles on my books.'

'Me too. Life's rich tapestry, etc.'

I worked a couple of out-of-hours sifts to make up for the ones I'd missed. Things were quiet, apart from two calls about feverish infants. I hate those conversations. Some parents, first-timers especially, panic easily. It helps if they've got a granny on site, an old hand who's seen it all before, but often there isn't anyone. And I can't go out to assess every hot and cranky baby. I need to be calm and systematic, even if the parent is yelling at me.

Is the child conscious? Is he responding to normal stimuli? Does he have a rash? The sound of a patient grizzling in the background is encouraging. When they're too ill even to cry, like the second call I took on Tuesday night, that's a red flag. I went out to Kayden Wragg, three months old, hot, silent and refusing to feed.

The houses had no numbers that I could see. I was doing my third drive-by when I stopped a woman on foot and asked her if she knew a family called Wragg, or any house with a young baby.

She said, 'Might be over there. The one with the bathtub in the front garden. They've got a bab.'

Mr Wragg seemed surprised to see me. I had to wait on the step while two dogs were caged. Mastiffs, he said. Soft as tripe once you got to know them. People with frightening dogs always say that.

The house was over-heated, the television was loud and there were two children asleep on the sofa. Kayden was in a bouncing chair, awake but flat. He showed no interest in the strange man talking to him. When I stripped off his top to check for a rash it was like handling a doll. His temperature was 38 degrees and his breathing seemed slightly laboured. His nostrils flared but there were no crackles in his chest, the anterior fontanelle looked normal and he didn't have a rash.

I asked for the television to be turned off. They muted the sound. I asked for his favourite toy, which seemed to throw them. They said he mainly liked watching telly, but eventually a fluffy rabbit was found. It was late, I was tired, I was on the floor, doing rabbit voices, while two enormous hounds paced around and eyed me from their cage and Kayden's parents watched a silent screen. Kayden himself seemed indifferent to my bunny impersonation. Was it because he was sick and listless, or was it because I'm a bit rubbish with babies?

Did they have Calpol in the house? Yes, they had Calpol. Were they satisfied with my diagnosis that their baby had a slight infection, probably a cold, and there was no need for him to go to hospital? Yeah, they were satisfied. I told them to give him water if he wouldn't take milk.

The mother said, 'water?'

'Boiled and cooled.'

'You mean water from the tap?'

'Yes.'

'He won't like that,' she said. 'He likes Pepsi.'

I was just parking back at the call centre when Neil, the nurse practitioner phoned me.

He said, 'Your name's mud. Baby Wragg's parents aren't happy.'

'Now what?'

'Sounds like status epilepticus. They reckon you only stayed five minutes.'

'I stayed a lot longer than five minutes.'

'I know you did. Don't worry. They're a pair of complainers.'

'I'm just outside. Should I turn around and go back?'

'No, there's an ambulance on its way to them. Come on up. I'll put the kettle on.'

Then I started agonising. Should I have hung around for longer? I couldn't think of a good reason. Feverish babies sometimes have seizures, usually with no harm done and it was purely by chance that he'd started fitting just after I left. The parents hadn't seemed very interested in me or the baby. They'd barely spoken to me. I'd undressed Kayden and then dressed him again without them lifting a finger. Were they annoyed because I'd asked them to mute the television?

'Don't tell me you made them turn the telly down?' says Neil. 'You high-handed bastard.'

'I don't understand these people. They showed no interest in the baby while I was there. They treated me like I was some big nuisance who'd barged into their house. I mean, why did they even call us?'

'Oh,' says Neil, 'that's easy. They called us because we're here. In the olden days they might have thought twice about

305

dragging their GP from his bed, but we're on tap. Open all unsocial hours. We're a bit like a pizza delivery service, really.'

Everyone said the same thing. Babies are almost always better by morning, and I'd done due diligence, gone out to the call, examined the little fellow. Still, the Kayden thing bugged me for days. His parents weren't satisfied with the service they'd received.

'We're not here to win popularity contests,' was Pam Parker's advice. 'Let it go. When's your mother-in-law's funeral?'

'Monday. I'll be back for Tuesday morning surgery.'

'Take your time. It's probably not my place to say it, but much as we love you, we can manage without you. If you ask me, talking about retiring was the worst thing Trevor ever did. Sitting at home, watching the racing, dodging his sisters-in-law, it's not good for him. He bucks up when he gets behind that desk. If we prop him up and give him an oxygen cylinder, I reckon he's got years of doctoring left in him.'

Chloe and Flo had pulled together to make the funeral arrangements. It was to take place at Oakley Wood crematorium. They'd chosen the smaller chapel. It was hard to guess how many people would attend - Vinnie had had a lot of acquaintances but few close friends - and Flo thought better to have standing room only rather than be left with half the seats unoccupied. A brief, secular ceremony led by some officiant who hadn't known her, a eulogy delivered by Henry, who could be relied on not to break down, the Lord's Prayer, as a nod to those who like that kind of thing, and the final Committal, during which poignant time a recording of Always

306

Look on the Bright Side of Life would be played. Then back to Packwood Grange for soup and sandwiches.

On Sunday evening we heard that Charlie would be allowed to attend. His friend Pig had delivered a dark suit and tie to Coldingley.

Laurence said, 'Well that's a relief. One feared he might appear in an orange boiler suit.'

Laurence likes watching TV documentaries about American prisons.

Mam called me.

She said, 'Tell Chloe I'm thinking of her. I know what it's like to lose your mother. Even when you didn't get on with her.'

I said, 'Mam, will you do something for me? Write down what hymns you want at your funeral.'

'Why, has Vinnie left them stumped?'

'They're not having any hymns. It was a toss-up between Vera Lynn, Bette Midler and Eric Idle.'

Chloe had commandeered what little hot water there was to take a bath. Her phone kept chirruping. Unless authorised, never look at the messages on your wife's phone.

Chapter 32

Here's what I promised myself. I wouldn't say anything until the funeral was over and we were back home, hopefully by Monday evening. I would then ask her, calmly and without pre-judgment, what the hell she was doing exchanging text messages with her old boyfriend, George Fitzgerald. Several times she asked me if I was okay. She said I seemed subdued.

I said, 'Funerals affect me that way.'

'Really?' she said. 'Gosh, but it's not like it's your mother's.'

She and I rode with Laurence and Granny and Grandpa Orde-Sykes. Flo and her family were in the second car. As the hearse stopped outside the chapel entrance a white van pulled in behind us. Fortress Custody and Escort Services. Charlie had arrived.

Granny O-S said, 'Is that a laundry van?'

'It's Slow,' says Chloe. 'It's Charlie. Granny, I did tell you he might be coming.'

'I'm sure you didn't. Does Lavinia know he's coming?'

That started poor Grandpa O-S weeping again.

'You stupid old woman,' he said. 'Lavinia's dead. This is her funeral. Can't you get that into your thick skull.'

Chloe tried to calm him, said it wasn't Granny's fault if she couldn't remember things, but he didn't want to be calmed.

He said, 'No-one knows what I have to endure. The woman is completely doolally. We're here to bury our darling girl and that barmy old bat doesn't even realise it. It's not fair, Chloe.'

Charlie had put on weight. The shirt his friend Pig had taken for him was far too tight. His hair needed washing. The two guards were very discreet but there was no hiding that he was handcuffed. Flo and Chloe walked over to speak to him. He couldn't look them in the eye. When they slid Vinnie's coffin out of the hearse, he sobbed like a child. I felt sorry for the poor chump.

Lily said, 'Is Granny really inside that box or is it pretend?'

Poppy said, 'I told you, runt. It's not pretend.'

'Can we see?'

'No. It's not allowed.'

'Why?'

'It just isn't.'

'But what if they brought the wrong box?'

'Don't ask silly questions. The box has her name on it, and anyway it's not a box, it's a coffin.'

Daisy was very quiet. She clung to Henry's leg, even when he had to get up to deliver the eulogy. He had to drag her along with him, which raised a laugh and broke the tension. It was like Charlie wasn't the only one who was manacled.

Henry did what he could with the material he'd been given. A thumbnail sketch of Vinnie's life. Born 1950, the beloved daughter of John and Anne Orde-Sykes. Attended the Royal Warwick Girls' Academy and the Ecole Vieux Glion in Switzerland. Worked as a receptionist at a private clinic on

Wimpole Street where she met young Dr Laurence Swift. They married in 1972. The devoted mother of Flora, Chloe and Charles - Charlie's sobs grew louder at that point - and treasured grandmother to Poppy, Daisy and Lily. A scratch golfer and in her eleventh year as captain of the Royal Leamington Spa Ladies' Golf Team. She would be greatly missed.

None of the things that I'll remember her for made it into the authorised version. Her mangled French, her damp beds and stingy, inedible catering. And the way she'd wrestled with her snobbish tendencies and overcome them to make me feel genuinely welcome as her son-in-law.

Andrea Bocelli started reminding us it was Time to Say Goodbye and the celebrant warned us that the coffin was about to disappear from view. Lily asked me where it had gone. I wasn't sure how much to tell a four-year-old but Poppy jumped in.

She said, 'She's gone to get burned up now. Remember, I told you Lils?'

Lily nodded, climbed onto my lap and buried her head on my shoulder.

I didn't see Charlie leave. He was taken away straight after the ceremony. Chloe was furious because she hadn't been allowed to kiss him. 'Bloody jobsworths' she called them.

A lot of the mourners whispered their condolences and melted away. Perhaps they'd heard Poppy telling me we'd be getting mousetrap sandwiches and cat sick soup. Some of those who did come back to Packwood Grange had an agenda Primmie Bowen wondered whether anyone had spoken for

Vinnie's recently purchased fairway wood, as she'd love to have it as a memento. Sarah Maxwell-Murray suggested that the laser range finder Vinnie had won in the summer tombola might be re-donated for the golf club's Christmas prize draw. She called it 'recycling.'

Granny Orde-Sykes bustled about and from time to time asked if anyone had seen Vinnie. Grandpa was parked in the corner of the living room with a glass of sherry.

'You're a doctor,' he said. 'Can't you put me out of my misery? Give me a nice big shot of morphine. Horse breaks a leg, you shoot it. Dog's in pain, you give him an injection. Bury your daughter, they give you a small glass of Bristol Cream.'

It was my first ever request for euthanasia. I'd often thought about how I'd reply, but now it had happened I was lost for sensible words. Time heals? When you're in your nineties you don't have a lot of that. There's still so much to live for? Such as what? Long days spent with a demented wife.

I said I was sorry I couldn't help him, and I meant it.

He said, 'Take me to Beachy Head, I'll do the bally job myself. Might get Flora's chap to do it. Packwood. He'd drive me. He seems a decent sort.'

Chloe was under the impression we were staying another night at The Chummery. I'd told Helen I'd be back at Tit Droop for Tuesday morning's surgery.

She said, 'Well I'm staying. Tonight of all nights, Daddy can't be alone.'

Henry offered a tour of the pig arks for anyone who was interested. A middle-aged woman, blonde, buxom, said she'd

311

love to see them. I heard Laurence say, 'Make it quick then, Jen. One ought to be making a move.'

Henry led us outside. His Lady Dahlia had a litter of nine, now three weeks old and running around, very interested in humans.

The blonde said, 'You're Chloe's husband. We haven't been introduced. I'm Jennifer, Laurence's secretary.'

Obviously, he had a secretary. A man with his kind of practice, it went without saying. I'd imagined him with a stream of well-spoken girls in velvet hairbands. Girls who could type a bit and always needed Friday afternoons off. Jennifer told me she'd worked for him for seventeen years. And yet I had never heard her name.

I asked her how she thought Laurence was coping.

'He'll be fine once we get back to London. His diary's full. Don't worry, he won't have time to mope.'

'He's going to London tonight?'

'Of course. There's no reason for him to stay up here.'

Was it mean of me to enjoy telling Chloe?

'Going back to London?' she said. 'Who says?'

'Jennifer.'

'But he's still in shock.'

'He has a backlog of patients to see. Jennifer thinks it's the best thing for him and as a matter of fact, I agree with her.'

'Dan,' she said, 'she's a secretary. She makes tea, buys stamps, tidies the mags in his waiting room. She does not know what's best for Daddy.'

'Okay. Here's what's going to happen. Your father and Jen are going to drive back to London. I'm going to drive home. If you still choose to stay at The Chummery, all alone, that's up to you, but I can't think of a single reason for you to do it.'

She said I was being horrid and insensitive. And I hadn't even started asking questions about the messages on her phone.

Mam called to ask how things had gone.

'All according to plan. Charlie was there, sandwiched between two custody blokes. You had to feel sorry for him, really. Laurence is back at work tomorrow and so am I. Flo's made a start on sorting Vinnie's clothes. Chloe's the only one who doesn't seem ready to move on.'

'It was her Mum. She'll be feeling it.'

I said, 'Mam, she and Vinnie did nothing but bicker. Chloe's a daddy's girl.'

'Put her on. I'll have a word.'

'She's not here. As far as I know she's sitting alone in that draughty house trying to prove some point that escapes me. How's Nan?'

'About the same. Now she says her Golden Jubilee tea towel has gone missing and the finger of suspicion points to that poor woman next door.'

'It'd be funny if she was right, though, if Mrs Baines actually is a kleptomaniac.'

'You mean a klepto who only steals floor cloths and tea towels?'

'Chloe's grandad's struggling. He's heartbroken about Vinnie but his wife can't remember anything for more than a minute. She kept saying "save some of that soup for Vinnie. She'll be here directly." It's so sad. He asked me to give him an injection and put him out of his misery.'

'Poor old chap. And I'm sure he won't be the last to beg you. What it is, Dan, doctors used to do it, on the QT. They reckoned even the old King was given a helping hand. George V, that would have been. But they daren't do it nowadays.

313

We've got Harold Shipman to thank for that. Your Da says we should get DNR tattooed on our chests. What do you think?'

'Sounds a bit extreme. Why don't you just write one of those Living Wills.

'It's on my list. When I retire and I'm a lady of leisure.'

'You're finishing next month, right?'

'No, I'm staying on till January. We're short-staffed. So, what's happening about your job?'

'Stalemate. I fancy a change, somewhere by the sea. Chloe's idea is Warwickshire, and that was before all this happened. Now she's got it into her head that Laurence needs looking after, there'll be no budging her.'

I was ironing shirts to get me through the week when Chloe phoned. She said she thought I might have called her to make sure she was alright.

I said, 'Why wouldn't you be?'

'Because I'm lonely. And this house is spooky. Everything creaks and rattles.'

'Everything has always creaked and rattled. It's because none of the doors and windows fit properly. But if you're not happy there, come home.'

'I can't. I've drunk some wine. Quite a lot, actually.'

'Then go to bed.'

'Do you miss me?'

'Yes. Lots.'

'You don't sound like you miss me. You sound cross.'

'I'm tired, Chloe. It's been a long day. Go to bed. In the morning, tell Flo you're leaving, close up the house and go to work. I'll see you tomorrow evening.'

'Let me say goodnight to Eeyore.'

'Chloe!'

'Pleeeease. Bring him to the phone.'

I actually fetched the stupid animal from the bedroom. I can't believe I did that. Why didn't I pretend to do it? Or just tell her to grow up? A 28-year-old cardiologist mewing down the phone to a stuffed donkey. It seemed to comfort her though. The next time she called me she was in bed.

'Can I speak to Eeyore again?'

'No, he's asleep and I'm not waking him.'

'Aww. What shall I do if Mummy's ghost appears to me?'

'Ask her where she's hidden the key to the log store. Mrs Pickering can't find it.'

'You know how you sometimes say prayers? Will you say one for Daddy?'

'If you think he needs it.'

'I do. I think he's just being terribly brave.'

'Consider it done. Goodnight, Chloe. I have to be up by seven and so do you.'

Chapter 33

Trevor had caught a cold and it had gone to his chest. His breathing was very laboured. Pam Parker was nagging him to go home.

She said, 'Give in to it, you silly old bugger. We can't let patients see you like that. You'll give the place a worse name than it's already got.'

He said it wasn't a good day to be at home because they had the plumbers in, installing a new walk-in sit-in shower.

'So what?' says Pam. 'They won't be working in your snug. Make yourself a hot toddy. Turn the telly on. Put your feet up. Have you got oxygen at home?'

'Not allowed. Mrs Buxton's worried I'll light a cigarette and blow us both up.'

'She does have a point.'

He said, 'I could take your morning clinic. Give you a break.'

'Trevor,' she said, 'I don't need a break from work. I need a break from the madhouse I live in. Anyway, you can't. It's my Lady Bits morning. I'm doing cervical smears.'

Vaz was keen to see me. He and Teresa were back from India with a stack of wedding photographs. We met at our usual

316

Starbucks. He was one very happy dude. The trip had gone without a hitch, Teresa loved his family and they'd loved her. Now all they had to do was prepare for their baby's arrival in January.

He said, 'I talk too much. How are you? You are very quiet today.'

I told him about Vinnie.

'You're sad for Chloe,' he said. 'Now I understand.'

I didn't mention all the other things that were on my mind, like finding a job somewhere Chloe and I could agree on, like convincing her that her father didn't need nannying, like finding out why she was in touch with an ex-boyfriend.

Chloe was home ahead of me. She'd already opened a bottle.

'What happened to not drinking mid-week?'

'I'm going through a difficult time.'

'Okay. Let's talk about it.'

'No point. You won't understand.'

'Try me.'

'I wasn't ready for Mummy to die. And she needn't have. It's all my fault. I should have insisted she go to the hospital.'

'You did try to persuade her. So did Flo. She might have listened to your father, but he thought he was doing the right thing and there's absolutely no point in picking over this. It's not going to bring her back and you have to get on with life. We have to.'

'I am. I've been to work today.'

'Good. That's a start. We need to talk about our future, too. Where are we going to settle? It's time for me to move on from Tipton and we need to make some decisions.'

She said I couldn't possibly expect her to think about that. It was far too soon. She said I was bullying her.

I was tired, I was hungry. The fridge was empty. Chloe's dirty laundry was strewn across the bedroom floor. I'd really had it.

I said, 'Is that why you feel the need to send text messages to George Fitzgerald? Because your husband's a bully?'

All the air seemed to go out of the room.

'You've been spying on me.'

'It didn't seem like spying, at the time. Your phone kept buzzing and you were in the bath. I wouldn't mind if you looked at my phone. I don't have any secrets from you.'

Which, apart from two close calls with Helen Vincent, was the truth.

'You had no right.'

'Yes, I see that now. And of course, I really wish I hadn't. But I did. So how did he find you? I presume it was after I saw him at the exam centre?'

Silence.

'He's got some nerve. I told him we were married.'

'I needed someone to talk to.'

'You had me to talk to. Wait, what? You mean *you* contacted *him*?'

'He's an old friend.'

'He's an old lover, Chloe.'

She said I was being ridiculous. I was fairly sure I wasn't. She went to bed with Eeyore. I ate cold baked beans from the can and slept on the sofa, or rather I tried to. I was angry with Chloe. I was angry with myself for marrying a spoilt child. I was even angry with poor Vaz for being so damned settled and contented.

A freeze set in at home. We hardly spoke. At work I was ratty with patients who didn't listen to my advice and downright furious when Betty Cheever's nympho daughter, Cheryl, slipped under the radar on the pretext of accompanying her mother to a Warfarin check-up. I'm afraid I shouted at Mary.

She said, 'If Mrs Cheever wanted her daughter to accompany her, what was I supposed to do?'

'Send them to Helen, or Jean or Harold. Anyone but me.

'All the lists were full. And any road, what was the harm? She couldn't hardly flash her bozzies at you with her mother sitting there.'

It wasn't her bozzies Cheryl had tried flashing, but I didn't want to go into the icky details of that with Mary. I shouldn't have shouted at her. I went out at lunchtime and bought her a box of chocolates. She said there was no need. She asked me if I was alright because it was very out of character for me to lose my temper and did I know I was wearing odd socks.

Trevor appeared while I was doing letters.

I said, 'You're supposed to be at home with a nebuliser.'

'I know. But I can't seem to stay away from this place,' he said. 'What's up, lad?'

Word had reached him. Dan's out of sorts. I told him pretty much everything.

He said, 'Is Fitzgerald the one that she...? Last year?'

'No, that was Jamil. Bloody Jamil. I was forgetting about him. What is it with Chloe? Or is it me? Have I made a big mistake?'

Trevor didn't say I hadn't.

He said, 'Let's talk about something else for a minute. How's the job hunt going?'

'It isn't. Everything's on hold. I've seen a couple of places I quite fancy but they're in Wales and Chloe has other ideas, particularly since Vinnie died. She's convinced her father needs looking after.'

'That'll soon get tiresome, for all of you. You could put your foot down. Go after a job you'd really like and if you get it, tell her to make her mind up. I'm sure the girl loves you, Dan. Give her a week or two of playing the doting daughter and I reckon she'll come to her senses.'

'And if she doesn't?'

'If she doesn't, then perhaps you did make a mistake. It can happen. Unfinished business with an old flame, you know? And if that's the case, you'll have to face it and move on. But it hasn't come to that yet. So, I hear Cheryl Cheever made another attempt on your integrity? I thought I'd warned her off.'

'It was embarrassing.'

'She give you a flash of her knickers?'

'I'm not sure she was wearing any.'

'That's something they don't prepare you for in medical school. Not in my day, at any rate. Let me know how it goes, lad. And if you need to bend an ear, you know where to find me. What joys are lined up for you this afternoon?'

'Legend Busby. Kyle Bibby. Kevin Hodge.'

'Stinky Hodge! You'd better see if you can get that window to open.'

'Not a chance. It's been painted shut.'

'Here, you'd better have this tube of Polos, then.'

Things always seem better after a chat with Trevor, even when they're actually still the same. By the middle of the afternoon I was seriously thinking I might tell Helen I'd stay on at Tit Droop. It would be one question answered, one thing

320

settled while I dealt with the Chloe problem. But when I went to make a quick cup of tea, Helen happened to be in the kitchen and happened to let her hand linger far too long on my back. It was definitely time to move on.

Kevin Hodge usually makes an appointment just to make sure we're not going to stop his diazepam prescription. He's in and out quickly, which is a blessing because he has bad body odour of unknown origin, most likely soap-dodging. But I was out of luck. He wanted to see me about a boil and it was in his armpit.

I popped in a Polo and examined him. How long had he had the boil? About a week. I prescribed frequent warm compresses. Often that's enough to make it open and drain spontaneously. And if it didn't?

I said, 'If it's no better in a week, make an appointment, to see the nurse and get it lanced, and ask for a prescription for antibiotics. Any doctor'll do. It doesn't have to be me.'

Jean Boddy loaned me her tea tree oil spray, but the memory of Kevin Hodge lingered in my room all afternoon. Even Kyle Bibby mentioned it.

'Bit of a whiff in here today, Doc,' he said. 'No offence.'

'None taken. I think it's the drains.'

'Could be a dead rat. We've had them on Cherry Tree, round the bins and that. See, if a rat's feeling a bit humpty, he crawls away somewhere quiet, to die. Then you're left with the pong. You need to get the council in.'

Legend Busby was my last patient of the day, with his Mum, Karen Checkitts. If she hadn't been with him, I wouldn't have recognised him. He'd grown and filled out. Suddenly he was a real young man.

Karen said, 'Tell the doctor why we're here, Ledge.'

He blushed. 'Got scouted,' he said.

'And?' says his Mum.

'Going to Derby County on trial.'

'And? Tell the doctor the other thing.'

'Wolverhampton Wanderers are interested in me as well.'

Legend was possibly on the brink of a football career.

I said, 'That's the best news I've heard all day. Congratulations. And the last time I saw you, you were proper poorly.'

Karen said, 'That's why we're here really. He needs a medical and a letter. Just to say he's alright to train.'

I told her to make a double appointment for the following week.

She said, 'The scout said he's got the makings of an outstanding midfield player. He said he's got excellent ball control.'

I said, 'Ledge, do you remember Nurse Chris who took your blood last time? She's on duty today. Look in on her before you leave and tell her about Wolves. She's a big fan. I think she's a season ticket holder.'

He gave me a shy grin. It'd really be something if football worked out for him. A story to tell the kids one day. Legend Busby, the sickly boy who'd seemed unlikely to live up to his name. I was his doctor, once upon a time.

I made a call to Prospect Recruitment before I left work that evening. Chloe came in late and went straight to bed. I didn't ask her where she'd been. She was talking on her phone when I went into the bedroom.

322

I said, 'I'm not sleeping on the sofa again. I've had backache all day.'

'Whatever,' she said.

I clung to the edge of the mattress and she clung to hers. The stupid donkey probably got the best night's sleep. On Wednesday morning I said, 'Don't you think this is rather silly?'

She shrugged.

'Don't you think we should talk?'

'There's nothing to talk about.'

She left without eating breakfast.

I worked an out-of-hours on Thursday evening and when I got home her wheelie weekend case was by the door.

I said, 'Are you leaving me again?'

She said she'd be going straight to The Chummery after work on Friday and she didn't know when she'd be back. I could have told her that I was going away myself, driving to North Wales to meet David Parry, senior partner of a friendly, forward-looking, paper-light, 4000 patient practice. But she didn't ask.

I'd just checked into my B&B when my phone rang. I didn't recognise the number. It was Henry.

'Ah, Dan,' he said. 'Bit of a situation here.'

My stomach lurched.

'Is it Chloe? Is she hurt?'

'No, no. Just, erm, emotional. Very.'

'What's happened?'

'It's with regard to Laurence and his, erm, secretary.'

I could hear female voices in the background.

'Is Chloe there? Can I speak to her?'

323

'Not sure that's possible. As I mentioned, she's very, erm, emotional. Actually, I'll put Flo on. She can explain.'

The first thing Flo said was, 'What's going on with you two?' She didn't wait for an answer. She said, 'I told Chlo not to come down this weekend. There was absolutely no point. As she has now discovered.'

'Henry mentioned Jennifer.'

'Yes. She's here. Well, at the Chummery, actually. With Daddy, of course.'

'Laurence is at The Chummery with his secretary? The operative word being 'with'?'

'You sound surprised.'

'It seems a bit soon.'

'Why? Everyone knows it's been going on for years, so why pretend?'

'Chloe didn't know.'

'So one gathers. And to think I've always been considered the dimwit of the family.'

'Did your mother know?'

'It was a perfectly good arrangement.'

'Poor Chloe. What a shock.'

'The thing is, Dan, she can stay with us tonight, but I really can't have her drooping about the place all weekend. We're terribly busy. Henry has weaners to transport and it's Poppy's birthday party tomorrow afternoon. You know how impatient Chloe can be around small people. She should go home.'

'I agree.'

'But she says you're being horrid to her and don't want her there.'

I said, 'Flo, when have you ever known me be horrid to your sister? To anyone? I do think Laurence is being a bit tactless. I mean, couldn't he have waited a couple of months? But tel

Chloe she can go home tomorrow without fear because I won't be there. I'm away for the weekend.'

'Oh,' says Flo. 'I don't think she knows that. May I tell her where you'll be?'

'No need,' I said. 'It won't mean anything to her.'

My landlady was very attentive to me. Did I need any more towels? How many rashers could I manage? Taking a little holiday, was I? The zoo was very interesting. Alligators and all sorts. Take the Rhos exit off the Expressway and you can't miss it.

'Just looking round,' I said. My wife and I are considering a move to the area.'

My wife and I. How hollow that sounded.

I'd arranged to meet David Parry at his surgery. I walked down the hill. The sky was grey, the sea was brown and a queue was forming outside a methadone clinic. The surgery was in an old house, Victorian. The sign was in Welsh. MEDDYGFA PARRY & HUGHES. There was a small parking space at the side with an immaculate Peugeot and a bike with a double baby trailer. I smelled coffee.

David Parry was about fifty, greying, halfmoon specs, a very nice checked shirt and tweed jacket. He clearly belonged to the Peugeot. Iestyn Hughes was in jeans and hadn't had time to comb his hair.

I got a very warm welcome, a good first impression, nothing like the day I'd been interviewed at The Lindens. Mary glowering at me through the locked door, Trevor caught flustered and unprepared and Helen arriving late and annoyed. But this was different. I wasn't a trainee any longer.

325

I said, 'I should tell you from the kick-off, I don't have much Welsh. Nothing like enough to do a consultation.'

'Welsh?' says Parry. 'Oh, you mean the surgery sign. Don't worry, I'm the same. If I ever knew any Welsh, I've forgotten it. My parents didn't believe in it. No, the sign is Iestyn's touch. He's an enthusiast. Bringing his children up tri. Lingual, that is. Tri-lingual.'

Iestyn said, 'My wife's Polish.'

They showed me round. Monday to Friday they had a nurse and a receptionist. The out-of-hours service was based in Bangor and it would be up to me whether I signed up for it. Neither of them had. David was the only full-timer. Iestyn job-shared with his wife, Aggie, who was expecting again. They already had three-year-old twins.

David said, 'Hence the vacancy. Aggie's keen to carry on working but it's not easy with children, as my wife would tell you. Even when they get older, there's always something.'

His wife had her own practice, in Llandudno. They lived in Deganwy.

'Which is probably where you'll want to be,' he said. 'Deganwy or Rhos, both good places. Come over tonight and see for yourself. Come for a bite. Is your wife with you?'

I mentioned there'd been a recent death in the family.

It was all very casual, as though the job was mine if I wanted it and our meeting was just a formality. They were like a double act, David quite deprecating about the town, a seaside resort long past its best, he said, and Iestyn giving it a positive spin.

'Colwyn Bay's what I call a real town,' he said. 'Not one of those fancy places full of second-homers.'

They had a lot of seniors on their list, some local born and bred, some retired Midlanders.

'Brummies mainly,' says Parry. 'It'll be home from home for you. I'll be honest, Dan, there is another side to the town. We've become a bit of a dumping ground. All those old hotels, you see. Gone out of business. They're perfect for bail hostels and the like. So, we do have our share of ex-cons and sex offenders. But nothing you won't have come across in your training, I'm sure. Nothing you won't know how to handle.'

There he went again, talking as though it was a done deal.

When I set off to have dinner with the Parrys, I was veering towards turning the position down. I was a married man and I had no business applying for a job behind Chloe's back, even if her back seemed currently to be turned on me. Of course, even one glass of wine can mess with a person's mind. Or was it lovely, comfortable Miriam Parry, dishing out moussaka in her lovely, comfortable kitchen, who worked some kind of magic on me?

She said, 'I hope you come. I reckon you and Aggie would make the perfect balance between David and Iestyn. David's very conservative. Well look at him. Saturday night and he's still wearing a tie. Iestyn, on the other hand, is very beans and sandals. Aggie's normal. Normal for Polish. Tell us about your wife.'

'She's a cardiologist, registered last year.'

'Perfect,' says David. 'Glan Clwyd would be the place for her. It's just outside Rhyl. They have an excellent cardio centre. Renowned.'

A teenage son drifted in. Joe. He shook my hand, queried what was in the moussaka, took what was left of the pre-dinner cashews and drifted out again.'

'Morbid fear of aubergines,' explained Miriam. 'Have you come across it?'

Their daughter, Becca, was away, in her second year at Manchester, doing dentistry.

David said, 'So whatever else falls apart, we'll at least grow old with good teeth.'

Deganwy and dinner with the Parrys changed my mood. I didn't care that Colwyn Bay was full of hostels and pensioners on walking frames. I liked challenges. I liked old people. I wanted the job. I wanted a house with a view over the Conway estuary and a garden almost as big as the Chummery's. I also wanted a wife who looked at me the way Miriam Parry looked at David. On Sunday morning I drove back to reality.

Chapter 34

I called Mam from the Stafford Roadchef.

I said, 'I've been offered a job in Wales, but you won't like it.'

'What do you mean?'

'Colwyn Bay.'

'I see. In Wales, but even further away from us than you are at the moment. Was it something we said?'

'It's nice up there.'

'I'm sure it is. It's nice down here too. But Dan, what I'd like doesn't come into it. It'd be lovely to have you nearby, but me and your Da are fine. We're still in our prime. And if a time comes when we're not, your brother's not far away.'

'I haven't decided about the job. I've told them I'll think about it.'

'What does Chloe say?'

'She doesn't know about it yet.'

'Well that's putting the cart before the horse. You can't take a job without her agreeing to it. You're a team now, boy. So long as you both shall live, remember? Or is there something else you want to tell me?'

I said, 'I don't know, Mam. I really don't know.'

I told her about Chloe getting in touch with George Fitzgerald. I told her about Laurence bringing Jennifer to The Chummery, and Vinnie not dead even a month.

She said, 'I'm not saying I like the sound of any of it. Their ways aren't our ways. Mind you, I don't know who your Da might have lined up if I go first. But I will say this. Chloe's been through a lot lately. Give her a fair chance. Go home, see if you can patch things up. I won't ask what you're doing for Christmas.'

'I think you just did. I've no idea. Have you invited Adam?'

'Not much point. It was hard enough getting him to your wedding. You know you're welcome, you and Chloe, but I don't want atmosphere, Dan. So I'll say no more.'

The lights were on. Chloe was home. I felt nervous. Not how you should feel going home to your wife. She was wearing a furry onesie and drinking hot chocolate. Message clear: I'm feeling delicate. Be nice to me.

She said, 'I thought you'd left me.'

'No you didn't. My bathrobe's still here. My Alanis Morissette albums are still here.'

'Where were you?'

'I'll tell you in a minute. Depending on how you answer this question. What's going on with you and George Fitzgerald?'

'Nothing's going on. I only got in touch with him to tell him about Mummy.'

'He knew your mother?'

'Of course. We were an item for quite a long time.'

'I'll bet Vinnie liked him.'

'She liked you too. But there's nothing going on. We just messaged a few times.'

'With lots of flirty emojis.'

'They weren't flirty. They were just smileys, to cheer me up.'

'Cheering you up is my job.'

'Please don't go on about Fitzie. Something terrible has happened. Daddy's sleeping with that Jen woman. That secretary.'

'I know. Flo told me it's been going on for years.'

'I don't believe that for one minute. She got her claws into him while he's vulnerable.'

'Flo said everyone knew. Even Vinnie. And your father has never struck me as a pushover. So Jen's moved in?'

'Weekends. Daddy stays at her place in the week. It's unbearable, Dan. Mummy's only been dead for five minutes. And this Jen person, she's fired Mrs Pickering.'

'About time somebody did. She was useless.'

'Where were you when I needed you?'

'I was scoping out a possible job.'

'What, all weekend?'

'It was in Colwyn Bay. I wanted time to meet the partners and look around. They've offered me the job, but I haven't given them an answer. I needed to find out where you and I stand. When you left here on Friday, I wasn't even sure you wanted to stay married to me.'

She said she did, she did, she absolutely did.

'Tell me about the job.'

'Explain about George Fitzgerald, first. Tell me the truth. Have you still got a thing for him?'

'No!'

'Why did you split up?'

'Because he was a bit gormless. And pretty useless in bed. Tell me about the job.'

'Really? Useless in what sense?'

'In the wham bam sense. Tell me about the job, Dan.'

'It's a small practice, in a small town.'

'But in Wales.'

'Yes. It's on the coast. There's a sea view from the upstairs rooms of the surgery, well, almost a view. There's one full-timer, David Parry, and a couple who job-share but she's expecting. Iestyn and Aggie.'

'Is it temporary then? Like, maternity cover?'

'No, it's permanent, salaried, eight sessions a week, out-of-hours is optional.'

'Compared to Trevor's place, how grotty is it?'

'Does it matter? It'd be me working there, not you.'

'So it is grotty. I knew it.'

'The town has seen better days. But the area's great. Sea, mountains. It's fabulous.'

'Say it the Welsh way.'

'Fabluss. We could buy twice as much house as we can afford round here. Plus, there's a major cardiac centre about twelve miles away.'

'What major cardiac centre?'

'Glan Clwyd.'

'Never heard of it.'

She said she could tell I wanted to take the job. I didn't push it. We pottered around for a while, getting ready for Monday morning. When we sat down to watch *Poirot's Last Case* we were joined by Eeyore.

She said, 'If you go to Clogwyn Thingummy, can I please come with you?'

332

'It's called Colwyn Bay. And yes, I'd like you to come with me. That's why I married you.'

She put her head on my shoulder.

'By the way,' she said, 'Fitzie failed his CSA. Second time he's taken it. Like I said, he never was terribly bright.'

'And not great in the sack either?'

'True.'

Later, much later, she said, 'Dan, where actually is Clogwyn Bay?'

Also by Laurie Graham

DR DAN'S CASEBOOK
THE FUTURE HOMEMAKERS OF AMERICA
THE EARLY BIRDS
PERFECT MERINGUES
ANYONE FOR SECONDS?
THE DRESS CIRCLE
THE TEN O'CLOCK HORSES
DOG DAYS, GLENN MILLER NIGHTS
THE UNFORTUNATES
MR STARLIGHT
AT SEA
LIFE ACCORDING TO LUBKA
THE IMPORTANCE OF BEING KENNEDY
GONE WITH THE WINDSORS
A HUMBLE COMPANION
THE LIAR'S DAUGHTER
THE GRAND DUCHESS OF NOWHERE
THE NIGHT IN QUESTION

For news of the next Dr Dan book and other projects, go to
Laurie's website, http://lauriegraham.com and join her mailing list.

Printed in Great Britain
by Amazon

57339469R00201